TALES
from the
DREAM
ZONE

Short Stories edited by
Polly Alice McCann

FLYING KETCHUP PRESS ®
KANSAS CITY, MISSOURI

ACKNOWLEDGMENTS

Appreciative acknowledgment of thanks to editorial help by Dr. Alice Hixson and Christa Miller, as well as design intern Raegan Moran. Very special thanks to the International Association for the Study of Dreams for their work in sharing working knowledge of the dream studies field as well as connecting and inspiring dreamers.

Flying Ketchup Press ® is a trademarked small press seeking submissions through Submittable.com to discover and develop new voices in poetry, and short story. Our dream is to salvage lost treasure troves of written and illustrated work– to create worlds of wonder and delight; to share stories. Maybe yours.

Find us at www.flyingketchuppress.com

All inquiries should be addressed to:
Flying Ketchup Press
11608 N. Charlotte Street, Kansas City, MO 64115.

Editor: McCann, Polly Alice
Illustrator: McCann, Polly Alice

ISBN-13: 978-1-970151-12-1

EPub ISBN- 13: 978-1-970151-25-1

Library of Congress 2020912677

DEDICATION

To those who dare us to follow our dreams.

*O*nce I found a collection of short stories in an old red cloth binding- forgotten on a shelf. It was during a dark time in my life when I didn't have much hope. Each story was better than the last. Afterwards, I decided that life was full of possibilities and magic and love. I decided I could become a writer, an artist, an adventurer. Anything was possible. That's what I hope one of these short stories might do for you. Short stories are to entertain and satisfy. They are meant to make readers think and wonder about the character's decisions, reactions and world view. Short stories are great morning, evening and night, and any time in between– and often they become a lifelong friend traveling with you along life's journey.

Polly Alice McCann

Table of Contents

A. A. Rubin lurks in the shadows, for it is there that magic can still be found. You may have thought you saw him in the back of the bar or going into the subway station, but when you looked back, he was gone. His work has appeared recently in journals, including Kyanite Press, Pif Magazine, and Constellate Literary Journal. His story "The Substance in The Shadow" has been named a Fiction War finalist, and his story "White Collar Blues" was nominated for the Carve Magazine/Mild Horse Press online short fiction award. Mr. Rubin holds a BA in Writing/Literature from Columbia University and an MA in Teaching of English from Teachers College Columbia University. He can be reached on twitter and facebook @thesurrealari.

The Light of My Afterlife
A. A. Rubin

*L*ara longed for the days when the room had been lit by candles. She missed the soft, warm glow and the interesting patterns the wax formed as it fell—but most of all, she missed the way the shadows shifted on the walls as they danced with the flickering flames. That had been proper lighting for haunting—you could move with those shadows fluttering in the corners of the room, and at the edge of people's vision. It was nothing like the bright, clinical fluorescent lights that illuminated the hospital room at present. That light was intense and constant. It burned coldly and did not flicker. What few shadows there were hidden under the bed and behind the myriad of machines connected to the patient. A young woman about the same age as Lara had been when . . . well, she didn't really like to talk about it.

The patient was hardly worth haunting. She hadn't opened her eyes in weeks. Even if she did, Lara doubted she had the strength to turn her head to see the shadows behind the medical equipment, much less get up and look under the bed, which, while not glamorous or romantic, still, at least, was a traditional spot for haunting.

The physician, on the other hand, was a prime target. He was tall, handsome, and good-natured, Lara had observed over the past few months. She longed for him to notice her, feeling that candle-light-heat warming the place where her heart used to be.

Truth be told, Lara had been trying to get physicians to notice her for half of her life and all of her death. She had been a sickly child confined to the hospice run by the Sisters of Mary convent for most of her adolescence. This prevented her from attending the requisite balls and soirees in which she might attract a handsome husband. The only men whom she saw, not counting the old priests, were the physicians who occasionally stopped by the ward to check on the patients. In those days, her disease was considered incurable, so most of her care was left to kindly old nuns. The nuns were kind, but they didn't have access to the medicines that the physicians gave her to ease her pain.

One day, near the end of her mortal life, a physician was walking between the rows of beds flanked by two nuns. That day, she had been in agony. The pestilence had progressed to the point where she didn't even have the energy to scream or to shake; actions that were sure to attract the attention of the approaching surgeon. As he passed, all that Lara could muster was a faint whisper.

"Save me," she said, but not loudly enough for the sisters or the healer to hear. They must have thought she was sleeping. She was a hopeless case, anyway. Better not to disturb her slumber. "Save me," she repeated, over and over again, long after the trio had passed her by.

Save me. Save me, save me.

That night, long after the candles had burned out in their sconces, Lara died with those same words on her lips. She found, contrary to what the Sisters of Mary preached, she had not ascended to the pearly gates, nor descended into the pits of flame and brimstone. Instead, she remained stuck in this room, even in her incorporeal form, an undead soul still in search of salvation.

Over the years, the hospice was torn down and rebuilt as a hospital. Lara's essence remained confined there. She often wondered if the new innovations would have been able to cure her illness had she lived in a different time. But these musing where only curiosities to fill the time she spent waiting to accomplish the one thing she needed to do to be released from this purgatory and, finally, rest in peace. She knew with a certainty that it was the thing she had never experienced in her mortal life. The key to her salvation was finally getting the physician to notice her.

The doctor entered on his appointed rounds. Lara hid under the bed where the shadows were. When you were a ghost, that's where you had to go to be seen. In the light, ghosts would be completely invisible to the living. She supposed that's why the last person to see her had called her a shade. The doctor never looked under the bed; he kept his eyes fixed on the patient and her monitors.

Lara tried to shake the bed by pushing up on the bottom of the mattress. Her hand went right through the springs and cushioning. She forced herself up through the bed and even the patient, but as soon as the harsh, bright light hit her, she disappeared again from view. The doctor gave no indication that he saw her before he left the room.

Everything came back to that modern electric lighting. Lara needed to get rid of it somehow. She had heard of spirits who, with enough focus and concentration, could affect the physical world. She decided that she was still stuck in a candlelight mindset. Her thinking was like the flames of her beloved candles. It danced and fluttered, blown hither and thither, like the flickering flame in the wind. She needed to focus. Perhaps, if she focused all her attention always on a single task, she might be able to accomplish something.

Lara floated up to observe the light carefully. There was a wire there connecting the lamp to the ceiling. She grabbed at it, but, as expected, her hand passed right through the casing. She did not have time to be disappointed

because the lighting in the room flickered. This was a positive development. She passed her hand through the wire again and again. The light flickered, buzzing with the same electric hum that the fluorescent bulbs made when they were dying and needed to be replaced.

When the nurse came in to check on the patient, Lara tried the trick again. The lights faded, and the nurse paused, briefly, in the middle of changing the IV before going back to her task. Lara repeated the trick three more times and was sure she saw the lights dim, but after that initial glance, the nurse went about her business.

Lara, though buoyed by her initial success, knew she had to try harder. Left, again, in solitude, Lara took to examining the wire. Why was it that she could affect the lights particularly and not anything else?

Lara lengthened herself until she was as thin as the wire itself. True, she usually stayed in the shape she had been when she died, but that was mostly out of convenience. Her non-corporeal self wasn't bound by the same physics to which it had been when she was alive. Slipping through the rubber casing of the wire slowly, making sure not to come out the other side, she spiraled herself around the inside of the wall, like a paper-thin snake– coiling herself around the copper line at the cable's heart but without touching it. From this vantage point, she could see everything.

The wire casing and copper thread looked, to Lara, much the same as anything else in the room: hazy and unsubstantial. Just as ghosts look ephemeral to the living, the reflections of the waking world appear in the same manner to those unable to rest in peace. They are dull and colorless, mere shadows of the thing they represent. The electrical current, on the other hand, burned with the intensity of 1,000 candles.

She reached out tentatively to touch it. It crackled and buzzed, clearly affected by her touch. She reached out again, with more certainty this time, and left the misshapen form she still thought of as her hand in the middle of the wire. The electricity pooled up against her hand, unable to pass. Like her, she surmised, the current was incorporeal; they were both sustained solely by energy. That must have been why she could affect it.

Outside of the wire, the fluorescent light flickered and went out. Without its energy source to sustain it, it faded from existence and died. Not that there was anyone around to see it. The patient still slept, and the physician had completed his appointed rounds.

Lara decided to see how far her new powers went. She raced up the rubber tube winding her way through the length of the copper coil. She zipped and zagged through the wire, following the current around the circuitry running between the fixture, the wall, and the equipment that kept the patient alive.

She learned the flow of the current and how she could affect it. At the end of the night, the overhead lighting, the monitors connected to the patient, and the hospital bed were all under her control. Her thoughts refracted with prismatic possibilities. Candles or no candles, she was ready for a proper haunting.

The next day, when the physician returned for his regular rounds, Lara was prepared. When he entered the room, she dimmed the lights down to a faint phosphorescence, then let them return to their original intensity. The doctor glanced up briefly but continued his examination of the patient. Lara caused the pulse monitor to flash sporadically. Then as the physician bent over the bed to test the patient's pulse manually, she managed to force the bed to lower slowly then snapped it back up quickly. Its side rail struck the doctor under the chin. He stumbled backward into the IV tower, which skittered haphazardly into the wall.

Within minutes, the room was teeming with activity. Nurses and orderlies rushed in, attending first to the doctor, then to the patient. The lights continued to flicker and dim. It was a shame she couldn't dance in the effect as was proper for a spirit, but she couldn't figure out how to keep it going without being physically inside the circuitry. As a specter, she could see through the rubber casing, but she knew that the still-living humans could not. Still, observing the chaos she caused was nearly enough—for now.

Amidst the confusion, two humongous orderlies entered the room with a stretcher. They slid a plastic board under the patient. Lara shook the bed, but the muscular men soon had the patient onto the stretcher. She would have been removed immediately, but the orderlies had to wait for portable versions of the machines that were keeping the patient alive to arrive before transporting her elsewhere.

They never got the chance.

Lara knew she could not leave the room– proven many times over during her ghostly existence. She dreaded losing the patient—and with her, the physician—right at the moment, she figured if she didn't come up with something quick, she would have to start all over again.

She gathered all of the charge she could—all of the power from all the outlets in the room; all of the electricity her ghost-form could handle—and hurled it back through the main outlet into the hospital-wide electrical system. The bolt flashed through the circuits overloading the safety systems and shorted the fuses in a wild, prismatic flash.

The hospital went dark. People fumbled for electric lanterns and flashlights and made frantic calls to the maintenance crews. Lara left the wire, to return to the shadows. While they weren't candlelight, they were about as good as she was going to get. She danced and fluttered.

No one noticed her between

the chaos and general hubbub. The chaos she had caused.

The power outage did not last long. It only took 5 minutes for the crew to get the backup generators running. All around the hospital, lights flickered back on, computers booted back up, and medical equipment hummed back to life.

Lara's ephemeral form faded as the light drove out the darkness. Still, as she hovered near the ceiling, she thought she saw a spectral shape resembling the patient rise up into the ether– though it was difficult to see under the oppressive glow of the fluorescent bulbs.

The physician and the nurses, who had by now recovered their wits, were frantically working on the patient's body, engaged in an activity Lara didn't really understand.

As she watched the scene from above, Lara heard an unearthly voice—a voice she knew in her spectral soul could not be heard by the living—faintly whisper, Save me, save me, save me. 👁

Light of My Afterlife

Angelique Fawns is a journalist who began her career writing about naked cave dwellers in Tenerife and parasailing in Australia. With a full-time job creating commercials for Global TV in Toronto; and living on a farm with her husband, daughter, cows, horses, fainting goats and an attack llama; finding time to write is a challenge. Thank goodness for the local pub! She grabs her laptop and escapes there to type stories on weekends and after hours. You can find her fiction in *Ellery Queen Mystery Magazine, The Gateway Review: A Journal of Magical Realism,* and *World Writer's Collective.* Other samples of her work are at http://www.fawns.ca & give her a shout @Raingirl51

The Versa Vice

Angelique Fawns

Was she in love with Indira? She was stunning with her lithe brown limbs, thick dark hair, eyes the colour of chocolate. Sherri thought she might be getting some reciprocal vibes from her. It was tough enough making friends, but trying to find that one special friend? Sherri hadn't come out to her parents–or even herself, for that matter–until the final year of high school. Now here she was in her first year at university in Toronto. Her main regret, she had never been kissed. By a boy or a girl.

Perhaps tonight her luck would change?

Indira, a classmate in her English Lit lectures, chatted with her about assignments and upcoming exams. Frequently those elegant hands would grab Sherri's arm or pat her on the knee.

It took her breath away. Girls like Indira never paid attention to Sherri; this was her high school fantasy come true. The popular girl wanted to be her friend! Maybe even more?

Yesterday with a lilting laugh and suggestive wink, her gorgeous companion suggested dinner. So far, the date had been going smashingly. They shared a vegan flatbread at Boston Pizza, conversing about their classes. They were deep in the world of Joseph Conrad and his genius characterization when they were finished eating. Indira footed the bill then offered to drive Sherri back to the dorm. When she parked, Sherri leaned toward Indira with eyes closed, her lips pursed.

"Uhhh, Sherri, I think you've got the wrong idea. This isn't a date. I just needed help with my English Lit essay," Indira said, leaning away with a frown.

Was it possible to roll out the car door and disappear into another dimension? Maybe Indira wasn't into girls, or just wasn't into Sherri, This was the most embarrassing moment of her life.

Was there another world where an alternate Sherri was living an amazing life? One whose brown hair was slightly less limp, eyes a brighter blue, and physique more hourglass? At a minimum, she'd take better gay-dar.

"I've always had trouble with Joseph Conrad. For sure, I will get a better mark now...well worth the price of a flatbread," Indira said.

When another dimension DID NOT open up and let Sherri slip out of existence, she put a big fake smile on her face.

"Right. Well, thanks for dinner. Keep your heart out of darkness."

Tears gathered at the corner of her eyes as she sat in the parking lot.

Did she really make a Joseph Conrad joke? Sherri grabbed her purse and stumbled out of the car walking in the other direction without looking back at Indira.

She should have known someone so stunning was out of her league. It's only in movies like Kissing Jessica Stein, where the hot girl starts a torrid affair.

Of course. When Indira took out her English Lit paper and asked about "civilized versus savage imagery, "... Sherri should have known she was being used as a tutor.

Sherri let the tears roll while trudging back up to her room. All that time applying eye shadow, blush, and mascara onto her pudgy, pleasant face. She thought she looked halfway decent when she left the dorm, but now she was going to look like a Jackson Pollock painting. She crawled into bed. Maybe she would meet a cute girl in her dreams. Her eyes closed and she slipped into a deep sleep.

She's on the run, and they're gaining on her. The terror. Her frantic search for help reveals no one on the empty street. Up ahead, there's the dull gleam of the subway entrance lights. A side street access, serviced by rotating cages and token machines.

She charges down the stairs, almost slamming into the entrance barriers. A quick search of her pockets turns up lint, mints, but no token. She's trapped. Her two tormentors catch up with her. She recognizes them– her vicious grade two teacher, the one who used to whisper, "You are going to fail," in her ear. And her nasty high school Phys-Ed teacher who had singled her out in gym class calling her fat and unfit.

They advance on her...

She woke with a gasp. Pajamas sweat-soaked and heart pounding. She's had this dream before. After that nightmare, going back to sleep was unlikely. Sherri got dressed and went to find an early breakfast.

Avoiding the chilly September weather, she padded through the underground tunnels that connected all the buildings. There on the wall in the Student Center covered in post-its and flyers, one announcement read, "Back-to-the-Books Bash! Phi Delta Theta Mixer for ALL university freshmen. BYOB!"

Did she need to deliberately add more humiliating moments to her life this week? Who would she go with? Her eyes drifted down the board to another posting:

Looking for subjects for a psychology experiment. Twenty dollars per participant. One hour. Friday, September 22. 7:00pm. Psychology Lab B.

That was tonight! She ripped the posting off the wall and went in search of a chocolate chip muffin. High octane carbs would help fuel her for a day of classes. Luckily, there was no English Lit on Fridays. The day passed slowly. After a week of scribbling notes during lectures in theaters full of other first-year students, she needed a break. Sherri wandered around until she found the campus pub. As long as she brought either a book or a laptop, she could justify sitting at a table and not feel out of place.

There was an empty booth at the back. Sherri sat so she could people watch, then propped her laptop up in front of her. Foursomes were playing Euchre, study groups sat and talked, and couples flirted.

Indira. She was there holding court at the bar with three handsome guys hanging off her every word. Beautiful lips flashing and eyes glowing. She obviously loved the attention. That answered the gay question. Her laughter rung out over the bar. Sherri was too humiliated to go up and chat with her, and luckily her corner was dark enough to keep incognito.

One vodka and tonic later, Sherri went back to her room. She did not go to the fraternity mixer. Being a hamster in the experiment sounded better, actually. She quickly changed into clean yoga pants, a cotton sweater, coaxed her hair into a messy bun, and headed over to the Science building.

Psychology Lab B wasn't hard to find. There was the musty smell of body odour in the hallway– an industrial, dingy grey made worse by a few of the fluorescent tube lights flickering in the room. Quite a few people were waiting. Surprisingly, a lot of students were willing to spend their Friday night earning twenty dollars instead of partying.

Her stomach sank when a familiar musical voice reached her ears. Indira was chatting with a nice looking fellow at the other side of the room. She flicked back her thick hair, caught Sherri's eye, and walked towards her.

"Sherri! How are you? Thanks for your help last night with my Conrad paper. I thought you spent most of your time studying. Glad to see you out and about, " she looked down her nose.

"Sure, Indira. Whenever you need help, let me know." Could she be anymore of a doormat? It was time to find a quick exit; she didn't need twenty bucks that

badly. Her stomach shuttered. Time to high tail it out of here. Wait. Her escape route suddenly blocked by a thin, tall man in a lab coat. Unkempt with grey hair, he sported a hipster beard, and his lab coat blended in with the tired grey as the walls.

"I'm Professor Ratcliff. We are conducting a study on the susceptibility of individuals for deep hypnosis. There are twenty of you registered here today, so we are going to do this in two groups of ten," he said, pacing in front of them. Consulting a clipboard, he read off the first ten names on his list.

Sherri heard her name called but not Indira's. She would stay if she didn't have to actually sit with the narcissistic mean girl.

"Would you all follow me into the lab," Ratcliff ordered leading them forward.

The room featured a big round table set up with audio stations. The lighting was dim, with no exterior windows. The musty smell of sweaty bodies became stronger. Two assistants fluttered around, helping everyone find a seat. They put headphones on each student and attached two probes to their temples. A soothing male voice came through her personal headphones with a British accent.

"This experiment will only last around half an hour, so get comfortable and focus on what I am saying. The sensors attached above your ears are going to be monitoring your brain waves. You won't even notice them working. So please take a deep breath, close your eyes."

Sherri closed her eyes, took a deep breath, and let the melodious voice wash over her.

"Let's start by taking notice of how our bodies are feeling today. Starting with the top of our heads and working down to our feet, assess how each body part is feeling. Imagine a warm ray of sunshine flowing into the top of your head and start to travel down through your body. Bringing warmth, bringing comfort, and making you feel very sleepy…"

With a start, Sherri jerked up from her chair when she felt a set of hands on her shoulders. She hadn't even noticed that she'd fallen asleep.

"You missed your cue to come out of the hypnosis," the assistant said. "I bet we are going to find you are highly susceptible."

Sherri stood up and followed the rest of the group to collect her cash on the way out the door. Should she go to the pub and do more people watching. No, she didn't want to bump into Indira there, so instead went back to her dorm room to turn in for the night.

Monday morning, a text came in from an unknown number.

"Please return to the Psych Lab B Monday evening (tonight) at 6:00 pm. We have some follow up from Friday's experiment. Please text C to confirm. You will receive another $20 payment."

"C," Sherry texted back. Why were they being called back? During classes that day, she found it very hard to concentrate.

She stood outside the door of Psych Lab B at exactly 6:00 pm, but instead of throngs of milling students, this time, she was the only one. Then she heard some footsteps hurrying down the hall. Lightfast heels tapping.

It was Indira, her cheeks flushed as she stopped beside Sherri. Of course, little miss perfect was also going to be here. It was just her luck. Why did she have to be so gorgeous? Sherri's stomach roiled and clenched.

"Hi! Are we the only ones here?

I wonder what this is about?" Indira asked, on hand on her taunt hip.

How could Indira act like that awkward moment in her Mini Cooper never happened? It was like she had no empathy whatsoever. She was trying to think of something witty to say when the Professor opened the door with a manic look on his face.

"I'm so glad the both of you made it! Come on in! We have lots and lots of work to do. So much work..." he said, his whole body agitating vertically.

The girls exchanged confused looks and followed him in. The two assistants were there again. Instead of looking bored, they both looked smiled behind thick glasses. Eyes bright like Christmas morning.

"What we were doing at the last experiment was searching for people susceptible to hypnosis . . . able to be deeply hypnotized. But we are also looking for something else. Something far more exciting. We are looking for students who can have potentially lucid dreams. And you two, you were off the charts! It's lucky to find one student a year who MAY be able to accomplish the higher levels

of lucid dreaming. But to find two of you in one session! And such strong markers!" Ratcliff paced back and forth in front of them.

"Umm. Lucid dreaming? What's that?" Indira said.

"Lucid dreaming is when you are aware you are dreaming and can control what is happening in your dream. We believe having control over the subconscious mind may be the key to unlocking the hidden abilities of the human brain," Ratcliff said, rubbing his hands together.

"What if I'm not interested in participating in this?" Most of Sherri's dreams were nightmares. She's not sure she wanted to spend any extra time in that creepy dreamland. Plus, how much being close to Indira could she take? She couldn't forget the embarrassment of their previous encounter.

Panic flashed over Ratcliff's face, "You will be handsomely rewarded for your time! And it won't take up much of it. No, not much of it at all! I can even see about maybe granting you extra credit for being involved. Sherri, your markers are the highest I have ever seen."

"Well, hard to turn down extra credit," Sherri said. It was nice to be recognized as good at something, even if she didn't quite understand what. Maybe she could learn to dream about rainbows and waterfalls instead of vengeful teachers?

"With two of you," Ratcliffe said, "we can take our research even further. This project has been ongoing for three years. Past participants are controlling their dreams and have full recall when they awake. However, we haven't been able to achieve interaction. Both of you demonstrate a remarkably high amount of beta-1 frequency in your brains. And the amount of activity in your parietal lobes is off-the-charts. We are hoping you two can meet in the dream state, control your interactions within the dreams, and interact with each other."

Sherri tries not to frown.

Imagine the implications," Ratcliffe continued. "Espionage, military uses…"

Military uses? Spy stuff? Sherry didn't like the implications, but Indira didn't look worried. "Cool. Money and extra credit? I'm in."

"I'm in too," she said. It could help fund the college research department, how could she quit now.

"Okay, let's get this going. I've had so many failures with other students, but with you two…" Professor Ratcliff said with a big smile cracking his wrinkled face. "Follow me! Yes, into our inner sanctum."

He led them out of the waiting area, past all the headphone stations, and into a room with two retrofitted dental office chairs. One wall was all glass with monitoring devices. Rows of desks perched on the other side. Through another set of doors, the two girls and assistants followed the scientist with a spring in his step.

"Okay, let's get you set up here! Sherri, you are here in this chair and, Indira, in the other, please," Ratcliff gestured to the scary-looking recliners. At least the air seemed fresher in here, lighter with a new coat of paint on the walls.

The two assistants set up the girls with temple probes then added extra monitors to their arms, legs, chest, back, and belly areas. Sherri whispered, "I feel like Frankenstein's wife. If they bring out anal probes, I'm jetting."

The assistant had "Chan" on a little card pinned to his shirt. "The extra probes are for recording your isometric muscle movements. We are hoping to understand and document all your emotions in the dream state. It will be interesting to see if you and Indira can actually interact with each other. With these machines, we will observe when you are corresponding in unison." He slipped the headphones onto Sherri's ears.

The other assistant, a small thin woman named Heather, hooked up Indira to the equipment. Then the doctors left the enclosed room.

The lights dimmed.

Her headphones filled with the soothing British voice, "You are feeling very sleepy. Very very sleepy. Concentrate on your breathing. Feel the breath slowly fill your body and then gently exhale. Let's think about the beach. A white sandy beach with little rocks that roll beneath your bare feet as you walk the sand...the endless sand. Look out on the water as the waves lap over the shore. It's endless, it's soothing...listen to the waves."

A white sandy beach with lapping waves sparkles in from of distant cliffs. Scrub grass grows on the dunes beside her. Soon, very far off, she sees another figure strolling on the beach.

At first, an unrecognizable silhouette, Sherri decides to close the distance between them. She runs, kicks up the dirt beneath her bare feet. She loves the roughness of the grains of sand, scraping her heels and squelching through her toes. It feels so real. Somehow she knows it's a dream. Wait. Normal rules don't apply here, right? Sherri concentrates on her legs. They move faster.

Now she's flying, almost running on top of the beach, no longer having her feet sink into the damp sand. The wind is in her hair. Freedom.

Wait. It's Indira. Sherri digs her heels into the sand, tumbles into the surf, and the cold water drenches her.

Indira jumps back with a big grin to avoid getting splashed. "It works! We are both in the same dream, Sherri. I would have said this is impossible, but look at us! Together."

Sherri pulls herself up off the ground, shaking white foam and sand out of her hair. "So. Let's have some fun."

What's that? A few feet offshore, an enormous dragon pushes up through the waves. It soars over the girls. They both duck and get drenched in the waterfall cascading off its body.

Lookout! Sherri calls.

"What was that!?" Indira yells over the splash and fiery roar.

"I made it! I imagined it," says Sherri. "Try it. Your turn!"

Indira crinkles up her nose and stares towards the horizon. A horse with a big horn sprouting out of its forehead gallops down the beach. Its body is opaque, but the ocean glimmers through it. Rather than a frothy pounding of hooves, there's just the sound of the waves. When it gets closer, it dissolves and merges with the foam.

"Wow. That's harder than it looks," Indira gasps hugging her knees to stop the dizziness.

Finally, something Sherri does that outshines this girl who is perfect at everything. Nothing seems to bother her. The sky gets darker, blurry, and then fades away.

"You are now going to wake up, feeling refreshed and ready to go on with your day," a melodious voice instructs them from the air.

Sherri opened her eyes and had to blink a few times before the blurry lab became clear. A smile tickled her lips like a cat who just lapped up a bowl of cream.

So this is what power feels like.

Indira also woke up, panicking, and trying to rip her headphones off but gets tangled in some cords. Heather rushed in to help her.

"It worked! OMG, I think it worked. At first, it didn't seem like you were interacting at all with each other, but then your movements were totally coordinated. I wish we could have kept you under longer! But slowly to start, we mustn't exhaust you."

"What was going on with you a the end, Sherri? Chan asked. "I thought for a moment you were in trouble, and I wanted to pull the plug and bring you out immediately, but Dr. Ratcliffe said to keep you under. That you were producing endorphins of pleasure not of stress. I've never seen a student pick this up so quickly." As they walked out of the pod, Dr. Ratcliff beamed and was practically dancing on the spot.

Sherri smiled at him but said nothing. She needed to do some careful thinking about this. Where Indira looked flustered, Sherri was calm.

"Well, I think we have

something here. We actually have something. Just when I thought the funding was drying up. Chan, you take Sherri and record everything she can remember about her time in the lucid state, and Heather, you do the same with Indira".

After their debriefings, Indira invited Sherri to go to the pub.

"You have to tell me about those Wonder Woman moves of yours! Indira said. "How did you run so fast? And your dragon kicked my unicorn's butt. You are pretty great, Sherri, an English Lit genius and now a superstar Lucid Dreamer," Indira pushed a stray strand of Sherri's hair behind her ear.

Was she flirting? Or did she not know how her touch put Sherri's system into red alert?

"Sorry, maybe next time. I'm crazily exhausted after all that lucid dreaming stuff. Time for some normal sleep," Sherri said, heading quickly down the hall.

She might be a dragon-conjuring wonder woman in her dream state, but now she was just fat Sherri. The Sherri, who'd never even been kissed. She slipped on her fuzzy pajamas and curled under the sheets.

That night Sherri had another dream:

She's running. Running for her life as the blood courses through her and panic fuels every step. Her teachers are after her again. Then she stops. She turns to wait.

They materialize out of the darkness, flickering like characters from the Mad Max remake.

"Stop. I command you," a great booming noise comes out instead of her usual soft voice. She sounds like the wizard from "The Wizard from Oz."

They stop. Expressions of confusion replacing their usual teachers-from-hell countenances.

"Why are you chasing me?" she asks.

Her grade two teacher's face contorts into an ugly snarl. "Because you are stupid. And you are going to fail fail fail. You will never be smart enough for grade three."

Sherry shorts. "I passed grade three a long time ago. I'm not stupid. Go away and don't come back."

Then she looks up at the sky, and her enormous dragon drops down with a yowl and snatches up the elementary school teacher. Sherri can hear the screaming as the bony old woman is carried away into the night.

The Phys-Ed teacher steps forward like a Pokémon gearing up for his battle turn, "You can never make the team. You are too slow. Too fat."

Sherri doesn't even bother arguing with him. She looks down at the ground, and a big hole of water opens up beneath the sneering man. He drops with a splash, and a hoard of ravenous fish with sharp teeth attack him. Sherri watches him thrash until he's dragged under, leaving only a bloody pool. Then the pool disappears, and the street lamps come back on. It is an ordinary street in a regular neighbourhood with nothing frightening about it at all.

Waking up, Sherri was a new woman. No stomach issues. More powerful. More capable. And she had an idea... a delightfully devilish idea. It rolled around in her subconscious, growing like a well-watered seed, slowly taking root.

At the next scheduled lucid dreaming session, Sherri walked with an extra lilt in her step. She met Indira in the hall,

"Hi! Enjoying the experiment?"

Sherri let her eyes roam over Indira's lithe curves.

"I always knew I was meant to do something big. This is groundbreaking research, and you are going to help me be as good at it as you are, aren't you Sherri?" purred Indira as they waited outside the lab door.

"Maybe I can teach you my techniques later. So, you are in what dorm?" asked Sherri, she needed to know where Indira lived for her plan to work.

"I am in the co-ed dorm, edge of campus."

"What room number?" Sherri asked, giving Indira's firm bicep a light squeeze.

"Three-O-Two. Of course, I have one of the few single rooms given to first-year students," Indira said, flexing a little under Sherri's grasp.

"The co-ed building, 302. Got it," Sherri grinned.

The door opened, and Professor Ratcliff ushered them in. If possible, he seemed to radiate with even more energy than the last time.

"I can't wait to hear what you dream next. The Beta activity! The monitors! I've never seen anything like it! Sherri, are you sure you haven't done this before?" Not waiting for an answer he asked, "Yes, what will you dream next?" He jittered with excitement.

The girls went straight to their chairs to be strapped in by Chen and Heather. The room dimmed, and the girls are hypnotized back to the dream world on the beach.

The familiar feel of sand is between Sherri's toes, and she can feel the cool ocean breeze. She sees Indira further down the beach again. She runs right at her, picking up as much speed as she can

The faster she goes, the higher the waves crash aggressively onshore. A chilly wind whips Indira's thick black hair around her face.

Indira smiles when she sees Sherri getting closer, but then her expression turns to concern.

"Slow down, Sherri, you're running too fast. You're going to..."

CRASH. Sherri pummels into Indira. She doesn't slow down even a fraction. The collision between their bodies creates a searing pain.

Sherri woke up with a gasp and the worst headache ever. She kept her eyes closed for a minute as she waited for the intensity of the throbbing to subside. When she did open them, she felt long hair tickling the sides of her face. Running her hands down her waist, she doesn't find soft fat flesh. Instead, there was a flat belly. Her hands slid up to her chest and felt two large lovely mounds. Much bigger and firmer than her old ones.

A big smile crossed her face. She could get used to this perfect body. Now she knows, she didn't love Indira. She wanted to BE Indira.

She's done with Professor Ratcliff's experiment.

"Can someone please come unstrap me? I have places to go." It's not going to be hard to get that first kiss now, she smirked.

From the chair beside her came a loud terrified scream. ◉

the *Versa Vice*

Ashley Memory draws her inspiration from the ancient Uwharries of Randolph County, North Carolina, where she lives with her sculptor husband, Johnpaul Harris. When she's not musing on a metaphor, she's brewing raspberry jam or poking around an abandoned cemetery imagining the lives of the people sleeping underneath her feet. Such adventures feed her imagination and fuel her writing. Her poetry and prose have recently appeared in Ginger Collect, Okay Donkey, The Disappointed Housewife and Coffin Bell. New poems are forthcoming in Turnpike, The Phoenix and The Red Clay Review. Her work has been nominated for a Pushcart Prize, she's a two-time recipient of the Doris Betts Fiction Prize. For more, check out her fruit-inspired blog, Cherries and Chekhov, at https://ashley-memory.com/.

Sunday Afternoon Cocktails

Ashley Memory

"Elliot, really! You shouldn't have to work on a Sunday!" cried Christina. She'd just swirled into her new cashmere poncho when her husband told her he needed to go to the office for a meeting with his new clients. Her hands trembled, and she gave up tying her scarf.

"You know how much I hate going somewhere without you."

She actually hated parties even more.

"Come on, Chrissy. It's just a simple little cocktail party! My co-workers shouldn't have to wait for me before they dive into your world-famous spinach dip."

Elliot gently bundled her new scarf, silk, in a peacock eye pattern around her neck, then shooed her to the door. He loaded the steaming dish into the back seat.

"I'll be there within the hour," he called, climbing into his car.

His cavalier demeanor probably covered his own nervousness. This was his first big assignment at Lockwood and Young Associates—the most prestigious architectural firm in Raleigh. And she reasoned the invitation to a party at the home of the senior partner was a very good sign for an ambitious architect, not yet thirty.

"Don't forget the address!" Elliot yelled through his window. In the wake of gravel dust, Christina thought she heard him say twelve-oh-four Brandywine. Or did he say Ballentine? Yes, it had been Ballentine. She was certain.

The house at 1204 Ballentine sat in a newly gentrified section of the city where people restored old buildings to their own whims. Chartreuse siding covered the exterior. Pink gingerbread on the porch resembled eyelashes as though the house were a giant Venus flytrap, and the people behind the lace-paneled windows, flies. Christina stayed in the car for five, then ten minutes, trying to quell a wave of fear that only grew stronger the longer she sat there.

Christina hated parties. It had to be since childhood when her extraverted parents had dragged her downstairs to show off a new ballet step or act out a song title in a game of their drunken charades.

Wait, hadn't it only been last night she had a dream she was at a party with Elliot but he'd disappeared, abandoning her to strangers. The guests had quickly devoured her spinach dip then turned to her. Christina remembered waking up just as an elderly woman with oversized blue glasses extended a claw. Why had she remembered this just now?

She shivered. The car dash read a quarter past two, and Elliot would arrive in forty-five minutes. She could endure anything for that long. Couldn't she? The sight of a couple walking up the sidewalk triggered a surge of hope. Maybe they would be nice people she could sit with

before Elliot arrived. She hurried out of the car and caught up with them on the steps.

The woman, in her fifties, wore a white fur stole dripping in crystals.

"These are the most marvelous parties in the world. Deirdre Livengood," she said, introducing herself. "And my husband, Hoyt."

"It's my first time," she answered. "My husband Elliot's meeting me here later."

"You're a babe in the woods, about to be devoured by wolves," Hoyt, in tweeds and a matching cap, flashed a malevolent smile.

"Hoyt, please don't scare the poor girl. She looks like Mata Hari in front of the firing squad."

"Aren't you clever, my dear." Hoyt opened the door and inclined his head in her direction. "Be a brave girl now."

Inside, Christina bristled at the scent of tangerines and cloves. Just like her dream! Loud laughter and faint piano chords laced through the cacophony of conversation. Terrified, she turned to leave but found herself pushed through the entryway by the Livengoods. They alternated between announcing "Elliot's wife.... first time.... Elliot's wife.... first time...." to everyone in the way. There was no spare chair, no safe little nook to be found anywhere. Christina felt the prickle of the rash she knew would soon cover her neck and creep up her face.

She stood in front of a young woman with a Maltese on her lap, hoping for an amiable expression. Instead, the woman rolled her eyes.

"I'm as bored as a Presbyterian waiting for the second coming," she said, inhaling an e-cigarette offered by a man with a chin-strap beard.

Christina held her hand to the Maltese, but the dog stiffened and growled.

"Elliot said to ask for Mark," she said, looking around the room for someone who could be his new boss. But there wasn't anyone.

"Mark isn't here yet," said a woman with an English accent wearing a crocheted tunic. She swooped in and took Christina's scarf and the plate from her hands. "Most indelicate of him. He's so late he'd miss his own funeral– Oh dear, that's so dreadfully cliché."

"Notoriously late!" said a bald man in a leather vest with a crookneck cane. "In fact, Mark is still looking for the moon when the sun comes up."

Restrained laughter trickled through the room. Another coughed. Someone else called out: "On a scale of ten, what would you rate that Mark?"

"Eight point five!" said a young man in a T-shirt that read Intentionally Left Blank. He leaned over to Christina: "I've never heard of anyone getting a ten, so you'll probably never hear a nine, either."

"Seven!" yelled a voice from the kitchen.

"Three," said Mademoiselle Maltese solemnly.

Christina stood still near the entryway, afraid to move until fingernails raked across her arm.

She gasped.

"You didn't have to bring anything." An Arctic-haired woman peered at her through cobalt blue-framed glasses. "We never ask that of new people." She offered Christina a slice of tangerine.

Christina shook her head, knowing that taking food meant she might never leave.

"Have one," she insisted.

"I'm being chased by a legion

of demons," erupted a young man. Breathless and sweating, he thrust a glass of sangria into her hands.

"One demon," answered his pursuer, a taller fellow in knee boots. He lashed at the younger man with a riding crop. "But I'm the worst kind! Call me Grendel."

Christina winced as Grendel advanced, steeling herself against the tangle she expected.

He swerved, missing her by an inch, but the glass crashed to the floor, spilling wine and fruit onto the wood. Christina's face burnt scarlet.

"Well done!" said a man with the crookneck cane. He moved to Christina's side. "My dear, it's like reliving the Exxon Valdez disaster!" This time everyone in the room laughed. Her face, still scarlet, stung with embarrassment. "Does Elliot's poor little wife have a name of her own?" Crookneck asked.

They were teasing her! New bravery, fueled by anger, coursed through her body. If this was a nightmare, She knew that only the dreamer had the power to change the dream.

"Christina." The sudden strength of her voice surprised her. "My name is Christina."

"What kind of husband would deliver you alone to people like us?" asked Deirdre.

"A husband like Nero. Elliot is as bad as Nero," said a man with the chin-strap beard.

"No," said Mademoiselle Maltese. "Elliot is as uxorious as Henry the Eighth."

The room exploded with laughter. Crookneck bowed. Chin-strap kissed the woman's hand and then the paw of the Maltese. "You two are as scintillating as a glass of Perrier."

"My husband isn't perfect," she said. "But he wouldn't have sent me here if he knew how cruel you all are." She turned a circle, facing them all, one at a time. "You ought to be ashamed of yourselves."

Now Deidre glided over. "You thought we were serious? Oh Christina, heavens, no!"

Grendel threw down his riding crop, and Mademoiselle Maltese sighed heavily.

"My dear Christina," Crookneck spoke. "You are guilty of nothing more than accidentally crashing the November meeting of the Rhetorical Device Society. Last month we covered oxymorons. For this month, our theme is hyperbole. Every single utterance you heard this afternoon was, in fact... well simply an exaggeration."

Christina threw a hand to her mouth. The confusion over the address! "I'm supposed to be at 1204 Brandywine!"

"Ballentine and Brandywine. Is that a spoonerism?" asked Mademoiselle Maltese. "I thought we were doing spoonerisms on the tenth of March!"

"The menth of tarch," said Hoyt. He whispered to Christina, A spoonerism is—

"I know perfectly well what a spoonerism is." Christina's indignation trounced her mortification. "It's when corresponding consonants or vowels are accidentally transposed. It is named," and here she paused, prolonging her victory, "after ordained minister William Archibald Spooner. For your information, I happen to be a research librarian."

The phantom piano fell silent. Mademoiselle Maltese swooned, and the dog scampered after a rogue sausage ball that fell from the plate of Grendel.

"Now I want my purse and my scarf. You can keep the dip. No, wait a minute...." Christina grabbed the dish from the hands of the Arctic-haired woman, who had just shoveled it with a cracker. "On second thought, no, you can't. It's far too good for people like you."

On her exit, Christina pivoted beautifully, and as she did, her scarf swirled around her neck in a perfect arabesque of turquoise and black. As she sashayed out of the house, she held the spinach dip high in the air, like a sacred offering to a god on a plane far above them all.

Once in the car, she saw Elliot had left her several increasingly frantic messages.

"Where have you been?" he demanded when he picked up the call. "I've been worried sick."

"I'm fine. I've, well, let's just say I've taken a little detour."

"Look, if you want to go on home, I'll completely understand."

She heard the faint tinkle of glasses and muffled conversation in the background "It's actually a little dull here. Frankly, I'm bored as hell."

"Nonsense!" said Christina, still riding high on a surge of victory, with an undercurrent of mischief. She was a dangerous woman, and she knew it. "I wouldn't miss your little cocktail

party for the world!" She plugged the correct address into her GPS.
"I'll be at Brandywine in ten minutes." 👁

Sunday
Afternoon

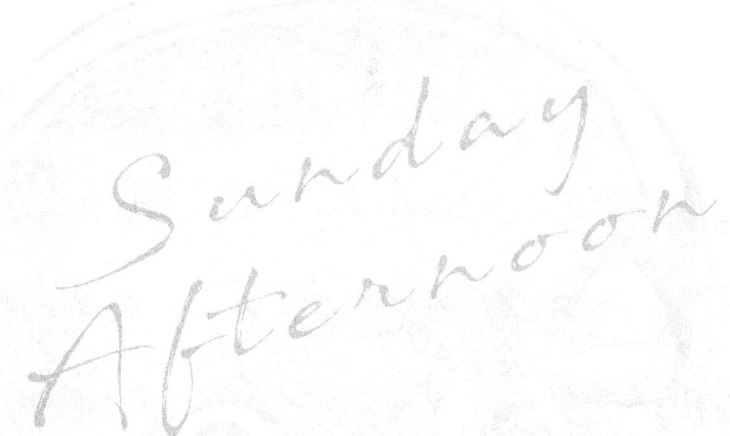

Cocktails

Briant Burt writes speculative fiction. He has published more than twenty science fiction and fantasy stories in various magazines and anthologies. His short story "The Last Indian War" won the Writers of the Future Gold Award and was anthologized in Writers of the Future Volume VIII. His debut novel, Aquarius Rising Book 1: In the Tears of God, won EPIC's 2014 eBook Award for Science Fiction. Aquarius Rising Book 2: Blood Tide won the Readers' Favorite Gold Medal for Science Fiction in 2016. Brian works as a cybersecurity engineer and lives with his wife, three sons, a mongrel puppy, and an adopted stray cat in idyllic Southwest Michigan. The cat, in particular, remains unimpressed with his literary efforts unless they come with tuna. You can find his award-winning Aquarius Rising eco-fiction trilogy on all major online bookstores and samples of his previously published short fiction on Curious Fictions.

MIST AT TWILIGHT

Brian Burt

*D*r. Tammy Bryant—Tam to her friends, Dr. B to her coworkers—carded through the security door and slipped into the Memory Center of Doster University Hospital. As always, the place assaulted her senses with its earnest but forced cheerfulness. Paintings of gardens, wood-lined lakes, and sunlit meadows spilled splashes of color across the walls. Quilts by local artisans hung here and there, hand-stitched with floral flourishes and homey words of comfort. Potted ficus and philodendron plants flanked the entrances on each side of the common area at the center of the wing. An uneasy blend of air freshener, antiseptic, and incontinence filled Tammy's nostrils. Soft jazz played over the sound system, ostensibly to soothe the residents. That was Chief Nurse Flores' excuse. In truth, she just adored jazz, repeating her personal playlists over and over, driving her staff mildly crazy in the process.

A glass display case hung beside each door along the hallway. Relatives had filled them with each room occupant's favorite curios, family photos, treasured mementos. Tammy's eyes flitted past these with a twinge of guilt, as if she were trespassing on sacred ground. The contents of those shelves struck her as intensely private, shrines to beloved elders who had wandered into the fog and been lost beyond any hope of rescue. Despite the heat, she shivered. In the secret recesses of her heart, she dreaded these visits. Shameful. She was a physician, a neuroscientist. She had been trained to handle all of this—the insubstantial phantoms who haunted the halls of the Memory Care Unit—with clinical detachment. And yet, every trip through the security doors jabbed a spike into her gut.

Coming here felt like staring into a crystal ball and seeing her own fate reflected in its depths, one that terrified her beyond belief.

"Hey, Dr. B. You here to see your fella?"

Tammy flinched at the sound of Nurse Jesse Bronson's voice as the cheery young woman stepped out of a doorway farther up the corridor. Tammy smiled, faking a composure she didn't feel. "You bet. Is he in his room?"

Jesse nodded. "Always is this time of day. In his usual place."

Tammy noticed the box in Jesse's hands; the denuded interior of the room behind her, like a carcass picked clean by scavengers; the empty display case beside the door. "Did we lose somebody?"

"Mrs. Alverson," said Jesse. "Passed in her sleep. A blessing, really... she'd been sliding downhill pretty fast over the past couple of weeks. Not a tragedy. Poor woman was a prisoner in her own body. Now she's free."

"Amen," said Tammy. "But the room won't stay empty for long. I think the waiting list is north of fifty."

"Job security, I guess," said Jesse. "Honestly, I wouldn't mind a little less demand for our services." She shifted the box in her hands. Something rattled as the residue of Mrs. Alverson's final days slid about like disarticulated bones.

"Say hi to your fella for me, Dr. B," said Jesse before she clip-clopped down the hall.

"Will do," said Tammy. As if it'll make a difference....

Tammy turned into the main hall flanking the common area, swerving to avoid a forlorn, droopy-eyed resident hunched in a locked wheelchair, wisps of silver hair sticking up like tufts of milkweed floss. Tammy forced a smile to cover her instinctive grimace and hurried on, pausing outside the entrance to Room 147. She studied the display case beside the door: a plaque commemorating career achievement in medical service, a Chicago Cubs World Series pennant, a framed photo of a distinguished gentleman with graying mustache and temples grinning beside a young woman in a blue graduation cap and gown. That picture always made her ache. She steeled herself and walked inside.

The figure in the tan recliner beside the bed bore little resemblance to the man in the photograph. Most of his hair had receded; what remained had gone snow-white. He didn't so much sit as appear to have collapsed into the cushions and been arranged there, stooped shoulders leaning awkwardly to the right. He wore faded maize and blue sweat pants and a sweatshirt with a wolverine emblazoned on its front. He didn't react when she entered the room. No surprise. His slate blue eyes—once so sharp and bright—had grown filmy, the windows of an abandoned house. He stared out at the garden, not registering the butterflies flitting between blossoms in the carefully tended flower beds, the birds preening and sipping from the ornamental stone fountain. He saw none of it. Maybe he glimpsed something else, ghostly and elusive, conjured from a distant time and place.

"Hi, Dad."

He didn't answer, didn't shift his gaze in her direction. Again, no surprise. He hadn't interacted with her in months. She sat on the end of the bed, ignoring the lumpy mattress and the creaky springs, concentrating on his face. Features slack; no sign of recognition. Unwilling to surrender yet, she tried again.

"You love that view, huh? Would you like me to take you for a stroll in the garden? It's lovely out, not too hot or cool, a perfect Spring day. Your favorite season, remember? 'When Mother Nature tries on Her new dress and dazzles us all.' I smiled every time you said that." Because Spring is when the world comes back from the brink of Winter's grave... when every flash of green offers proof that wilted things revive.

She tried to catch his attention with words, with smiles, with gestures, to no avail. She should never have gotten her hopes up. She knew better. And still, his... absence... made her want to sob and scream and curse all at the same time. Her father, her mentor, her confidant. He'd always been there, especially after the stroke stole Mom away. Now he was marooned somewhere, dim and desolate, where she couldn't reach him no matter what desperate life line she heaved into the mists, hoping he'd grab hold. With a sigh, she pulled her phone out of her jacket pocket and began to dictate.

"Subject: Frank Bryant; age: 72; Alzheimer's stage: severe. Day seventeen since nanomedic version 2.0.3 injection. No visible change in affect. No responsiveness to external stimuli. No improvement in verbal or non-verbal communication. Despite the success in animal models, this first human trial appears to be a failure."

A tremulous croak interrupted her note-taking, each word labored. "Tammy? Tammy dear? When did you get here?"

She froze. Her heart thudded against her ribs. The shrunken figure in the easy chair had straightened. For the first time in months, the slate blue eyes fixed directly on hers, forming a connection. They were clear and bright. They saw her. He saw her. He smiled. Her heart thudded harder. She couldn't speak, afraid that any ill-chosen word might shatter the spell. He spoke, haltingly but without a trace of slurring.

"Such a lovely Spring day. Can we go for a stroll in the garden before dinner?"

He reached out a bony, palsied hand. She took it. She squeezed it, barely able to believe the solidity, the weak but unmistakable way he squeezed hers back. He kept his eyes locked on her own, utterly lucid, utterly there. At that moment—professional appearances be damned—she leaned forward, hugged him, and began to cry.

***

"I'm grateful for what you've done, Tammy." Frank Bryant studied both sides of the paved path outside the Doster Memory Center with newborn eyes, as if every clump of wildflowers, every manicured bush, every decorative stone bench evoked a sense of wonder. He paused beside a rugged ninebark, brushing his fingertips against a cluster of pink-white blossoms while he struggled to catch his breath. For the first half dozen strolls through the gardens, Tammy had pushed him in his wheelchair. Now he walked under his own power—slowly, unsteadily, taking frequent breaks—and savored that taste of independence. "Grateful. Still, you didn't keep your promise."

She ignored the accusation, having no desire to revisit the old argument. Instead, she switched into research mode, gathering information.

"What do you remember from before the treatment?"

Her father's bright eyes filled with shadows. His expression clouded. Fear, frustration, or just fierce concentration as he fought to untangle jumbled memories? "Bits and pieces. Fragments from our discussions of the nanomedic prototype, preliminary results with mouse models. The cognitive tests you made me take, over and over. The retirement party... in the back room at the Doster Cafe? That awful cake shaped like a disembodied brain." He glanced at her, desperate for confirmation.

"Nurse VanderMeer made the cake herself, even frosted it with a scalpel. She said it took four tries to get it right. You said that was why she became a nurse instead of a surgeon and everybody laughed. That was three years ago."

Frank nodded, dismayed but not surprised. "Three years. A sense of time's passage is just one more thing I lost."

She squeezed his shoulder, shocked at how emaciated he had become, how the curve of his collar bone pressed against paper-thin skin. She asked the question, the big one, the one she wasn't sure she really wanted him to answer.

"What was it like? The... progression?"

He sighed. Despite the blue sky, the warm Spring sun, he shivered. "Like stumbling into a fog that thickens in every direction. You lose sight of the landmarks that anchor you to your life:

names, numbers, places, faces. You sense them there, just out of reach, but you can't grasp them; they slip through your fingers. The world grows dark, distressing, filled with traps and tripwires, each step a puzzle you can't solve. You feel yourself—the core of who you are—sliced away one sliver at a time. I called it 'the long goodbye' to my patients' caregivers. What a cruel euphemism... crueler than I imagined."

Tammy couldn't breathe. She stood there, frozen, encased in ice. A breeze tousled her father's silver hair. His gaze shifted from some distant, haunted landscape back to her. He smiled. The sunshine, its vigor restored, melted her limbs and she could move again. Some primal part of her wanted to run away.

"But you, Tammy dear, came into the fog and pulled me out. I'm me again. Frankly, I'm shocked that you got permission to include me in the trial."

Tammy forced a grin as they meandered along the path. "We had your consent form on file already. You were literally the first volunteer. And it didn't hurt that the study lead was your daughter and your personal representative.

There was grumbling about conflict of interest, sure... but everybody knew how you felt about it. Colleagues lobbied for you. And you were a perfect candidate: late stage, no other viable treatment options; none of the drugs helped, not even the experimental ones."

Frank paused, winced, then sank shakily onto a stone bench beside the path. After steadying him, Tammy sat beside him, solicitous and worried and clinical all at the same time. "Should I grab the wheelchair?"

"No. I just need to rest. And... we need to talk. Because there are drugs that would've helped me. We both know which ones."

Tammy closed her eyes. Yes, she knew. As a physician, she could get her hands on them if she really needed. Of course, her father knew that; counted on it. Scraps of the recurring conversation echoed in her head, repeated ad nauseam in the privacy of her father's Doster office when symptoms began to manifest. It's safe and painless, dear, with the right doses in the right combination. I'll just fall asleep....

"There were other options. My option. I had to try."

They sat in awkward silence for a long moment. Finally, Frank wrapped one trembling arm around her shoulders and nodded. "Of course you did. And it worked spectacularly... so far. How are the other patients doing?"

"A mixed bag. Some have shown dramatic improvement, like you; others are regaining cognitive function more gradually or in more limited ways. Almost every subject has made measurable progress."

"Any side effects? Regressions?"

"Not so far."

"Not so far," he repeated. "But it's early days. We both know that initial improvement isn't always sustained; progress doesn't always last. I've treated enough brain injuries over the years to earn my skepticism. I've seen enough Alzheimer's 'breakthroughs' trumpeted in medical journals to distrust miracles."

"This isn't a drug cranked out by Big Pharma with more marketing hype than promise. This is a paradigm shift. It could change everything!"

"It could. But revolutionary treatments take time to refine. They spawn unforeseen complications. Nobody pitches a no-hitter the first time they take the mound, Tammy."

"Thanks for the pep talk, Dad."

Frank's voice softened. "I'm not criticizing. What you've accomplished is amazing. I pray it really is the miracle we've all been looking for. But if it isn't... then, Tammy dear, I expect you to keep your promise."

"I made my own promise. I won't give up."

"And I won't give up my dignity. Not again." He struggled to rise. Dutifully, Tammy helped him to his feet, hiding the flush of anger on her cheeks, the mist in her eyes. She would do anything for her father. But not that. As she escorted him to his room inside the Memory Center, her conscience weighed a thousand pounds.

That weight doubled when Frank began to spasm and collapsed. She caught him, lowered him to the floor, and shouted for the nurse.

***

Tammy stared at her laptop with bloodshot eyes, too sleep-deprived to make sense out of the patterns on the screen, too desperate to surrender to exhaustion. Her tidy, spartan office was well lit, but the light outside her window had faded into bruised shades of dusk. Another day lost. With a groan, she rubbed her temples, took a swig of bitter, lukewarm coffee, and returned to sifting through the diagnostics uploaded from her father's implanted nanomedics. Somewhere in that ocean of data, there had to be a clue to what was causing the seizures. There had to be! So far, the answer eluded her.

She studied the map of her father's brain, jerking the mouse back and forth as she explored the convoluted landscape of his cerebral cortex. The surreal, color-coded terrain on the display would look like a psychedelic jungle to most people, but she read its features with the ease of an expert trail guide. The nanomedics had removed a decent chunk of the amyloid plaques clogging neural pathways; they'd cleared many of the neurofibrillary tangles as well. No problem there. In the worst places, where too much damage had accumulated, they used their own internal structures to bypass the blockage and route signals to intact neurons, rewiring the network to restore some level of function.

In the worst places…. There they converged, drawn by the need to bypass snarls of blockage. The nanite density was higher in these areas of her father's brain. Instead of a neuroscientist, she tried to think like an electrician. The nanites were routing electrical impulses; in crippled, high-traffic areas, they multiplexed, transmitting numerous signals at once. If Frank's mental activity spiked— if his mind raced—she cursed and ran a simulation. The results confirmed what she already knew.

Her miracle cure restored cognitive function, but at a price. In advanced Alzheimer's patients, with extensive damage, overloads could occur. She'd unleashed a lightning storm inside her father's brain; she was electrocuting him from the inside out. Her fingers trembled on the keyboard as she scrolled through the analysis, drilled down into predictions of mounting side effects and projected outcomes. Not good. The acid burn of coffee and stale pretzels fought to rise up her esophagus. How do I fix this?

Her phone chirped. When she read the text message from Nurse Bronson, she realized that time was running out.

Room 147 stat

She raced through the hospital corridors, clumsy and distracted, bumping into an abandoned meal cart and almost colliding with the night janitor, mumbling apologies as she stumbled past and carded through the security door into the Memory Center. Most residents were either in their beds or parked in front of the television in the common area. The place felt deserted, cemetery-still. She reached her father's room and pushed the door open to see Nurse Bronson leaning over her father where he lay, pale and sweaty, beneath tangled sheets. Jesse glanced up, nodded, then turned to her patient. "Try to relax, Frank. I need to step outside to bring Dr. B up to speed, won't be long." Frank Bryant shuddered, mumbled, turned his head toward his daughter. Those eyes… still bright, still lucid, but brimming with something that made Tammy flinch: pain. And flickers of fear.

Jesse steered Tammy into the hall and closed the door. The resigned look on her face drove the spike of guilt in even deeper.

"Seizures are growing in intensity and frequency. We tried benzos, phenobarbitol, but they're not cutting it. None of the meds are helping. He's been asking for you, Dr. B. Getting insistent. Thought I should get you down here."

Tammy nodded, sick and numb. "Meds are useless, at least for seizure control. Pain management is the best we can do. Prep a morphine drip."

"What dose?" asked Jesse. Tammy recognized the question behind the question; it was one that every Memory Care staffer had asked at some moment in their career when caring for a late-stage, suffering patient.

Tammy knew what answer her father would want to hear. She choked on it, the words strangled by her conscience. "Standard palliative dose. Do it by the book. I'll keep an eye on him, explain what's happening."

Jesse nodded and strode toward the nursing station to order the IV. With leaden steps, Tammy slipped back into her father's room, closing the door behind her. His pain-fogged eyes met hers. In that instant, he knew.

"You figured it out, didn't you? And it's not good news."

She approached the bed and took his hand, his skeletal fingers intertwining with hers. She struggled to keep her expression calm, to hide the guilt and panic burrowing beneath the surface. "Yeah. Guess I blew the no-hitter, Dad, just like you warned me would happen. I should've listened."

He forced a smile. "You pitched a hell of a game. You could start for the Tigers tomorrow. Tell me what's happening."

She squeezed his hand, fought to keep her voice steady, and explained everything in a way only a fellow neurologist would fully grasp. Her father—his brain ravaged by Alzheimer's—followed every word.

"So the harder I think, the clearer my mind becomes, the worse the side effects. The candle burns faster and faster."

"Yes," she said. "There must be a way to compensate for the clustering effect. There must be. I just need time to design a mitigation."

"Time we don't have."

She didn't bother to respond. There was no need. Her father's pinched, wrinkled face blurred behind a stinging veil of mist.

"No tears," he said with a voice far stronger, far gentler than it had any right to be. "You offered me a blessing. You gave me back myself, Tammy, at least for a while. You gave me a chance to say goodbye. And you kept your promise."

It took a moment for the implications of his last statement to sink in. Her downcast eyes jerked up. Her father's gaze met hers, bristle-gray brows furrowed in concentration. "I love you, dear. No regrets."

His hand clamped shut on hers, vise-like, as the seizure started, swelled, rippled through his body like storm-swept waves rolling across Lake Michigan. She tried to pull away, could not escape his death grip. He jerked and spasmed, lightning crackling inside his skull and racing along his nerves. She leaned forward to steady him with her free hand, crying out for help. The door banged open. Nurse Bronson flew into the room, an IV cart abandoned in the hall. Too late. Too late to be anything except a witness.

The spasms subsided. The fevered light behind her father's eyes winked out. His chest settled beneath the sheet. Jesse checked for pulse, checked again, then bowed her head. Tammy didn't bother. There was no point.

Frank Bryant had thought himself to death.

* * *

Frank Bryant had no use for a traditional funeral. To honor his wishes, the wake was held at Flannigan's Brew Pub, just half a mile from the Doster Hospital complex, where friends and colleagues toasted his memory with the establishment's own lovingly crafted pints of whiskey-barrel stout. Dark, foaming glasses were raised and guzzled. Increasingly tipsy patrons offered increasingly funny, crude, and maudlin testimonials to the dearly departed doctor. Tammy counted as many laughs as tears and considered that a fitting tribute to her father, exactly what he would have wanted. His spirit hovered over the festivities, loosening mourners' tongues and brushing gently against her beer-reddened cheeks, softening her grief. No regrets. Those ghostly words echoed in her head, the last she'd heard her father utter. Despite the gaping hole in her heart, they brought some comfort.

After three loud and drunken hours, the celebration of her father's life wound down. People trickled past Tammy, singly and in groups, mumbling condolences and offering everything from bear hugs to awkward handshakes before they stumbled into the parking lot. Finally—to her sorrow and relief—the crowded bar grew empty. Tammy collected her father's memorial photo and personal effects from the table pushed against the back wall, thanked the pub's owner and serving staff, then wandered outside.

Winter battled to reassert its dominance, swallowing Spring in a pearly gloom. Perfect weather for the occasion. Tammy tucked the bag containing her father's mementos under one arm and began the hike back to the hospital. The walk gave her time to think, to review the mundane tasks assigned to her as her father's executor. Going through the mental checklist distracted her from darker musings.

No burial to arrange. In keeping with the hospital's mission, and his own convictions, her father had donated his body to the medical school. He wasn't finished teaching. Tammy was his sole beneficiary, so the inheritance was straightforward, the will uncontested. She planned a bequest to the Memory Center in his name; he would appreciate the irony. The Center may be where memories go to die, Dad… but they'll remember you. Even if it's just a faded photo or a dusty plaque hidden in a corner, you'll be remembered.

She trudged up the sidewalk toward the hospital campus, exhausted and achy, dreading the next item on her checklist. Lingering vapors of that last pint of stout soured her breath, hammered at her temples. Such a long day. Such a long, draining week. Part of her wanted to delay, to drive home to her apartment, to soak in a long, hot bath and put this off a day. Another part of her—the methodical, obsessive-compulsive part—just wanted to get it over with, to cross this last task off her to-do list.

She sighed, took a shaky breath, and carded into the Memory Center.

Tammy found Nurse Bronson lingering outside her father's room, gazing at the display case beside the door. Jesse wore a somber smile. In her hands, she held a sturdy box that Tammy recognized, with a pang, as one of the personal-effects boxes… what the staff called "cardboard coffins." The nurse turned to Tammy, expecting her.

"Last visit for your fella, huh? It was a lively wake, Dr. B. He would've loved it. Felt like he was there, raising a pint."

Tammy nodded. "You tidying up for the next patient?"

"No," said the nurse. "I saved that duty for you." She held out the empty box. "Didn't feel right doing it myself. Not this time."

Tammy took the box, nodding numbly. "Thanks."

"Take all the time you need." Jesse turned and left, giving Tammy a chance to grieve and reminisce in privacy.

Tammy opened the glass door of the display case and slowly, reverently removed each souvenir, nestling them in the bottom of the box. Then she moved into the room, exploring the dresser, the table, the closet in search of hidden treasures. The photo of Mom and Dad on their wedding day, posing in front of the terraced gardens outside the Doster chapel. The baseball signed by a dozen Cubs players from a team in the nineties that barely won half their games. The hideous coffee mug shaped like an open skull after craniotomy that proclaimed, "I really AM a brain surgeon." Each object injected another needle into her heart, drawing blood but also dulling pain, some perverse form of psychic acupuncture. She left

the clothes in the dresser and the closet. She had no need of them, and the staff could reuse them for other residents. The last thing she found, in the drawer of the bedside table, was a note written in a familiar, cryptic doctor's scrawl. Still, she could decipher it easily enough.

If at first you don't succeed... keep pitching. Don't give up!

Love, Dad

She sank onto the bed, reading the note again and again. He had known. Of course he had. And still, his last message offered absolution.

Tammy carried the box to her office with the reverence of a pallbearer, of a priestess cradling a holy relic. She sure as hell intended to keep pitching until the manager dragged her off the mound. Her father's nanomedics had provided a wealth of data for analysis, especially around the terminal event, the fatal "brain storm." She planned to learn a lot from his intentional departure, enough to design fail-safes into the devices. She plopped down behind her desk, did a last quick check of emails. Amazing. Every one of the patients in her clinical trial, despite her explanation of the risks, had elected to continue their treatment. They and their caregivers had all signed the necessary waivers. They—like her father—considered every additional hour of lucidity worth the risk.

They found their way out of the fog. Why would they go back?

Several patients had written comments, filled with a passion that surprised her. They didn't consider her father's fate to be a tragedy, but a blessing; a feature, not a bug. That gave her pause. Maybe I shouldn't have fought so hard against keeping my promise, Dad. Maybe I was thinking more of me than you? She was too exhausted, too emotionally frayed to decide. She'd leave that thorny problem to medical ethicists and attorneys.

She shut down and closed her laptop. Enough for today; more than enough. As she made her way into the parking lot where the chill, damp fingers of dusk wrapped around her, where moisture saturated the air with evaporated grief, her spirits rose with an inexplicable buoyancy. A familiar voice whispered in her head.

You gave me back my dignity, Tammy dear, and my ability to choose. That's not a loss... at least not on the scorecard that matters.

She slipped behind the wheel of her Prius and pressed the button to start the car's humming electronic brain. She wouldn't quit. She'd keep fighting to improve the nanomedics, to build a better foghorn that would guide the lost ones back, to reunite them with their essential selves. And—as she lay in her lonely bed that night with only her father's ghost for company—she'd reconsider all the outcomes that might be deemed a victory. Was a lethal lightning strike inside the skull a problem to be fixed or a last-resort solution to be offered to patients devoid of hope; was it complication or compassion? She knew what her father would have said. While she pulled out of the parking lot and turned toward home, he whispered the answer over and over, refusing to give her peace.

Peace isn't usually a gift, Tammy. Most of the time, it's something you have to earn... maybe by securing it for others.

She had her epiphany, then: a tweak to the nanomedic firmware, to the list of potential side effects in the disclosure, to the waiver signed by patients or their caregivers. She imagined a mental switch the patient could flip if they felt themselves slipping back into the mists. She probed virtual pathways in the brain map to find a way to deliver that final, irrevocable treatment without prolonged pain, paroxysms, or delays.

People chose the way they wanted to live. They should be allowed to choose the way they wanted to die. Dr. Tammy Bryant realized, in that moment, that most of all she craved that freedom for herself. 👁

Mist at Twilight

Masha Kamenetskaya is a writer, editor and journalist, originally from St. Petersburg (Russia) but currently living in Budapest (Hungary). She writes both in Russian and English and co-edits a literary magazine, Panel.

In the Editing Room

Masha Kamenetskaya

*T*wo of them, a man and a woman, were wearing raincoats that night, though there was no rain. It was chilly, and they were cold. He had on a coat of a light grey color, a sophisticated hue. She wore a dusty white coat, though she never knew how to wear white properly. He wanted to leave, but she kept talking. Her face was pink and puffy, though she never shed a tear. They were looking over each other's shoulders. She saw a small group of people laughing in front of the 24/7 shop and a cat crossing the street. On the sidewalk, a woman who was looking for something, perhaps keys, in her purse. She exchanged quick glances, and the women disappeared inside a building.

"This is strange," the woman in the white coat said.

"What now?" he asked, hiding his irritation behind a comforting voice.

"The strange feeling that I have."

He sighed.

"It's like even if we move on and never meet again. Like even if we forget what this was about, we'll remain on this very spot."

"I don't understand a word of what you are saying," he informed her.

He didn't see much over her shoulder—behind her, there was a brick wall, and that was all.

TAKE 1:

Beatrice returned home. Leo, her husband, was doing dishes, and the only part of him she could see was his back. That was the only part of him she had observed lately. When, for instance, she accidentally popped into the bathroom while he was taking a shower, it was his back she saw, not anything else. When Beatrice stayed late at work and returned to a quiet, snoozing home, Leo was sleeping too—with his back turned to the bedroom door.

Only once during these days stuffed with new schools, new jobs, settling in and sorting out, did Leo greet her with his full face and eyes wide-open. She rushed in, braking sharply on the doorstep as usual, and witnessed her husband casually sitting in the kitchen, starting up the laptop.

"It's pretty shitty, you know—the kids have chickenpox," Leo said. He rose to kiss Beatrice, and she kissed him back.

"Squirrel can't have chickenpox, she already had it," Beatrice said, making herself a Marmite sandwich.

"So?" Leo said. He had a pile of books in front of him, several were open to the first page. The cover of the book that was on the top of mountain, "My Happy Days in Hell."

"You can't have chickenpox more than once in your life."

"Who says that?"

"Scientists."

"I would ask for a second opinion," Leo said doubtfully. "By the way, she says not to call her Squirrel anymore."

"We don't?"

"We don't."

"What are we supposed to call her?"

"Lily. That's what we named her once."

"Oh," Beatrice sighed. "I didn't see that coming."

"How could you see that coming?" Leo asked.

"Well, you know, sometimes I see things before they happen," she said, moisturizing her face with a wet cotton pad.

She looked at Leo with squinting eyes and, quite unexpectedly, noticed that he was already wearing pajamas. When did her husband take off his trousers?

"But still, Lily may not be able to have chickenpox, but Hedgehog can."

"She is covered with red spots!"

"I guess it's acne?" Beatrice said, looking at his bare chest.

"Hedgehog has those red bubbly spots."

"Then it is chickenpox," she said meditatively. "That's how it happens. One moment and everything is changed and is gone."

"No, no—it's all there! All over her face and his body."

"I will check the kids and call the doctor tomorrow," Beatrice said, looking at the boiling kettle as if it were her companion.

She poured tea from the teapot and added some hot water.

"You are damn tired, aren't you?" Leo said, trying to express sympathy but yawning instead.

"After that moving affair, I've even started doubting my own intuition," she said, more to a biscuit than to Leo.

"If you are less intuitive here, it would be a good enough reason for me to live happily ever after." Leo laughed his customary squeaky laugh.

"But children, they couldn't make a choice," Beatrice said, glancing at her Tarot cards lying on the windowsill.

"Are you working tomorrow?" Leo checked the alarm clock on his phone.

"The movie is a piece of shit, but there are some great folks around."

"Try to keep to night shifts because I will be swamped from eight to three—I have to stay with the faculty after classes." Leo headed to the bedroom. Before disappearing in the dark room, he said: "If you worry that the children didn't have a choice, I presume that you believe we did?"

Beatrice looked at the picture stuck to the fridge: four of them, all two years younger, smiling at camera with the North Sea in the background, the severe wind blowing through their hair.

Now, two years later, here they were: sleeping all four together in a king-size bed in a rented flat. Squirrel had a shorter haircut asleep next to Hedgehog, whose chickenpox ointment glistened in the dark. Leo, his hands under the pillow, filled the whole bed. His enormous legs occupied half of the bed, Beatrice tried to fit in next to him—barely. It seemed while one half of her body managed to sleep, her other half stayed hovering floating in the air.

TAKE 2:

It was evening in Budapest. The setting sun sketched a rim of light on the buildings and bridges. It was the same sketch as forty-something years ago, when Beatrice was taken out of the country. In less than an hour it would be dark.

At work, in the film studios, Beatrice tried to piece together film frames for a scene where a group of beefy tattooed people were not going to kill (but never did) some weedy guy. The guy already looked half dead before being shot. Beatrice didn't feel very much alive herself, Since she had run out of her store of cheese and apples, all she could do was go to the coffee machine. Its weak swill was hardly the best weapon against fatigue and hunger. As she put another 100-forint coin into the coffee machine, she could hear some mumbling coming from Editing Room Number 2. But she never saw anyone.

"Somebody, shoot me," Beatrice said to herself.

The director, who was supposed to help, who normally sat by her shoulder, all vigorous and creative, had escaped from the editing process to Lake Héviz. As if there was anything vigorous about going to the thermal baths.

When Beatrice went out for coffee for the fourth time, there was no sign of the coffee machine. In its place, a lemon tree instead.

Before Beatrice could comprehend the strangeness, she saw a man who looked familiar.

"Why would they replace this stupid tree with a coffee machine?" "I really need some coffee,"

"There used to be one," Beatrice answered, surprised.

"Not anymore! Would you like a cigarette instead?"

They went outside.

"You know, I haven't smoked for years. Since, you know, before I was married," she remarked, leaning against the wall.

"Everyone smokes in Budapest."

"When did you begin working

here?" Beatrice asked.

"Two years ago, almost."

"Enjoying it so far?"

"Well, I have a job that I like. Living the dream. What's next?"

"What do you do now?"

"I'm a set designer. And Budapest is the loveliest setting for any backdrop," he added proudly.

Suddenly, the man looked taller than she remembered, and he smelled of a nicer cologne than when they had been inside. He also seemed to have instantly put on weight, but not too much—just the right amount to look like a person who enjoys life.

She couldn't figure it out. Everything else about him was the same. He really was handsome: he had the same long ears-that some troll would be proud to have; the same long neck; and yes, the same long fingers that she admired as if she were a piano.

"When we had just moved here, I conducted a guided tour for my children. And you know what? We got lost. It turned out, I didn't remember Budapest at all, even though it is my home town."

"Ah, you were born here too!

But you already know that I was born here, of course!" she said.

"How could I know? I don't even know your name."

"You know my name," Beatrice whispered.

"Do I?"

Beatrice didn't respond.

"What's your name?" he asked.

"Beatrice."

"And I am Jim."

"Oh, You are Jim now?"

"Now?"

"Nice to meet you, Jim."

TAKE 3:

Jim volunteered to walk Beatrice to the bus stop after a few more failed attempts to get their work done.

"If I can't make something work, it's better to just take a walk," Jim said.

Beatrice agreed, but right now, she'd agree with anything coming from him. They eagerly passed the bus stop, made their way down the hill, and found themselves near the river "The Green Bridge."

It was late autumn again, but dark and cold as in winter. Autumn had no doubts that its days were about to be over and was waving goodbye with strong gusts of wind.

Beatrice noticed that the people out on the street seemed not to be aware of the season changing—the crowd manifested all four seasons at once. While some people flaunted shorts, others wrapped themselves up in thick coats. Since the morning, premature Santa Clauses had appeared in shop windows side by side with overripe Halloween pumpkins and glossy, black-eyed mannequins who promised a wild yet slightly distasteful summer bikini party.

Someone asked Beatrice in Hungarian for directions. She excused herself for not speaking the language.

"In the very beginning, I thought I could easily speak Hungarian," she said to Jim. "I guess it's because I was born here, and my Hungarian father, whom I hardly remember, would give me the language by default."

"You are funny," Jim said.

"It's funny you call me funny," Beatrice said. "But what were you asking me about?"

"I didn't ask you anything," Jim said and cleared his throat.

"Ah, how we moved here!"

"But I didn't..."

"Well, to make a long story short—we are ordinary people. And not significantly successful. You know me, and my husband is a mathematician against his will. He keeps saying that if he had another name he would have become someone else. He was named after Leonhard Euler."

"Who?"

"No one knows the guy! You know, he was a famous mathematician. I guess my Leo feels obliged to his famous and forgotten namesake."

"Okay."

"So I wanted a fresh start. I wanted to do something less ordinary. So I chose film editing."

"I am sure you will do fine." Jim patted her shoulder.

The sun suddenly came out of the clouds and blinded Beatrice. For a moment, she could see only the outline of Jim.

"I am taking a bus from here," Jim's silhouette said and probably left, though his shadow was so long that for quite a while, it seemed that he stayed.

When Jim disappeared from her sight, Beatrice found herself on a bus stop with a half-empty paper cup in her hand. She must have gotten coffee somewhere, but she couldn't recall.

TAKE 4:

The next week was a blur. Only some random bits of the following week were kept in memory: work shifts editing more film, chickenpox spots, Lily staying home from school... And at the end of a tiring and meaningless week, cycling a velomobile on Margaret Island with her family.

It was, most likely, Saturday, a very quiet day. Even the crows in the treetops thought twice before cawing. Leaves were rustling quietly too, the only thing that disturbed the silence around would be someone's occasional short chuckle, which sounded ominous in the hush.

"Who are you texting?" Leo asked Lily, without any chuckle at all.

They were cycling to the duck pond where Hedgehog was supposed to feed ducks.

"Some friend," Lily responded.

"You've been at the new school for what like five minutes, and you've already got 'some friend,'" Leo said, pedaling faster.

Bea paid a worried glance. "How are you, Leo?"

"Have you decided which judo section yet?" Leo accosted Hedgehog.

"I don't want to do judo," the boy said with a sigh.

He had a bunch of leaves in his lap and was trying to make a wreath.

"Oh, what do you want to do?" Leo cried out.

Despite all this arguing, they had reached the pond.

"Lily, go over to the cafe with your brother and get us some két jégkrémet," Beatrice rather commanded than suggested.

"What's going on with you?" she demanded once the children went for the ice-cream.

"We are having a mid-term party for work at some spa resort where you are forced to wear robes instead of suits. I have no idea if I am welcome to come," he said.

"People at work don't like you?"

"I don't know. I am not sure if I want to be liked at my age."

"No one likes grumblers," Beatrice said in a low voice and hugged him to her.

The children came back with their treats. Lily was texting again, and Hedgehog was scratching chickenpox marks.

"What is 'longer' in Hungarian?" With her phone, Lily looked like a stenographer in the middle of urgent work.

"Why do you need to know it in Hungarian?" Leo asked

"I want to find some acorns," Hedgehog said. "For my projects."

"Sure," Leo said, glancing angrily at Lily.

So they stayed and searched for acorns, stuffing their pockets with so many acorns that one could open an acorn craft workshop. Beatrice picked those that looked similar so that even if mixed up in her pocket, one could easily be replaced with another. Leo gathered those that were enormously big, rotten, or missing the cap. Hedgehog gathered all that he saw. Lily didn't gather any at all, she sat and stared at the sunset.

TAKE 5:

When they crossed the bridge, they were home. Their flat was in a building on the border of the 5th and 13th districts. Beatrice had foreseen the place in her Tarot cards. When she actually saw the flat, she had instantly recognized it. This was a good, but not too expensive, neighborhood. The flat was spacious and light and had a loft, where Leo and Bea placed their bed. When they compared this flat (and they compared a lot!) with the dark and shabby half-house they had had in the suburbs of London, Budapest seemed a very right way to go.

But she remembered that it has been back in England when it had begun. Once while traveling on the bus, Beatrice realized she only had one thought running through her mind: when did things begin to rattle?

At first, they were having fun. It had been fine when they were dating. When they traveled, it was fun. When making babies, it was fun. They even used "making babies" as a good excuse for not taking out a mortgage or buying furniture. "We'll figure it out later," she and Leo would say, messing around with pleasure. It continued for quite a while, considering the age difference between their kids.

But then something happened that Beatrice couldn't exactly name. She remembered one night they were returning from their friends' house, and Leo was upset because of something unimportant. There was one day when Leo admitted that mathematics was not the profession he wanted, it had simply become a battle. Beatrice hated both—choices and battles. If it was up to her, she would never choose, but would only take everything that came her way in life.

Beatrice kept recalling episodes, moods, and situations, in hopes of catching out a particular, one-and-only moment when the picture started missing its pieces. She even took public transport for this reason to get outside the scene and did so an endless number of times. Still, the more effort she put into concentrating on the picture, the more out of focus it became.

Once, while putting on her sneakers, she looked around for the right one. But she found the right sneaker was already on—she had kind of missed the moment.

"Ah," she thought I'm missing something. Still, after coming to Budapest, the city seemed to fill her mind completely, its beauty having replaced other thoughts.

TAKE 6:

"They are having a party this Friday," Leo announced when Beatrice, radiating from sitting long hours in front of the monitors, showed up at home.

Leo was still working on his laptop. The children were staring at their tablets.

Beatrice kissed Lily on the cheek, and Lily covered her tablet with her palm. Next, Bea kissed Hedgehog too—all around the face. Then she kissed Leo on his forehead, which was moist and warm.

"Are you OK, sweetie?" she asked.

"Whom are you referring to?"

"Well, you."

"I'd feel better if I understood what's going on," he said and frowned.

"Where?"

"Everywhere."

"That's a bit too demanding a request," Beatrice said with a semi-fake laugh.

"Something your cards are dealing with, right?" Leo asked with the tone that could be equally interpreted as despair and sarcasm.

"Should we eat? I am making spaghetti with meatballs."

"Meatballs!" both children shouted with anticipation.

"Meatballs!" Beatrice shouted some minutes later. "Laptop, tablets—off!"

The four of them gathered together around the table. The pasta smelled nice, the steam warmed up the air, and the meatballs were juicy and just the right size—you could put a whole meatball in your mouth and still say something nice.

"Did you even eat today?" Beatrice asked, observing their enthusiasm about the food.

"You know, we just love when you cook," Leo said, smiling.

"You are cute when you cook, mum," Hedgehog said, and Beatrice thought that she should work less to spend more time here with them.

There were times when she spent hours in the kitchen without questioning what the hell she was wearing an apron for and what kind of magic she was creating with an apple crumble. It was fine as it was, and a part of Beatrice wouldn't mind going back to that.

"So what about the party? Who is having the party?" she asked joyfully.

"The school. A Mikulás party."

"How come it's already Christmas?!" Beatrice exclaimed.

"December follows November," Hedgehog said.

"Thank you, sweetie, I was always bad with calendars," she said, smiling.

"So they ask parents to volunteer and come in Christmas costumes too, whatever it is, or just smart casual style. They're short on volunteers, apparently."

"Just say we are too busy."

"But, I already said yes," Hedgehog wailed.

"But why?"

"Because with the school discount they gave to us, I considered it would, at the very least, be polite to pay them back somehow."

When the dinner was over,

Hedgehog went back to his room, or more precisely, their room. The space was divided into two by a bookshelf.

"I'll read to you!" Beatrice said.

"Not for me!" Lily said, heading to the bathroom, her face looking pink.

"Are you okay, Squirrel?"

"I am not Squirrel!" Lily replied from the bathroom and turned on the water at full capacity.

"I should talk to her," Beatrice said while trying to figure out if she'd talked to her daughter lately.

"So, are you going?" she asked Leo.

"I thought we were both going," Leo said. "It will be fun."

"But I have the evening shift."

"Shift the shift."

"There is no one to switch with."

"So, what are you suggesting?"

"You go and take plenty of photos. Besides, do the kids even have parts in this unexpected Christmas fiesta?"

"Well, Hedgehog is afraid of small devils, and Lily is certainly not an angel. So—no, they passed. They will be watching."

"Then what's the fuss about?"

Beatrice said lightly. "You will be the best dad, I will be the mediocre film editor, and someday we will switch."

TAKE 7:

"Marriage is about feeling someone's pain as though it's your own. If you hold someone's hand—just hold it."

Beatrice felt like she was saying random words, that, if combined, made some sense. People were listening, at least. She was talkative at the work party that had been spontaneously thrown by their director, who had returned from Heviz and smelled of hydrogen sulfide.

There was wine, cheese, a few unknown people, and classic rock on the stereo. Someone was already drunk. Someone was sitting on someone's lap. All together, it set a mood of dormitory fun. There was a blond girl on set texting all the time with a face so light and thoughtful, it was like she was inventing an elixir for eternal youth. There was a long-haired guy who kept winking at Beatrice until it hit her that the guy had a glass eye. There was also a small dog that barked when people clinked glasses.

Beatrice stood closer to the cheese plate; from cheese to Jim was a hand's distance.

When the blond girl grew tired even of texting, she turned to Beatrice and appeared to be a careful listener. She even posed some questions—like, What brought you to Budapest, Beatrice?

"I will tell you," Beatrice said enthusiastically. She told them about her long-lost relatives in Hungary, whom she had tried to reach when they'd just arrived. Their numbers still in her notebook–a present from her dear husband, because Leo liked it when things in order, written alphabetically. Bea felt she couldn't be more grateful for that. "Your aura changes when you live in a family," Beatrice said, splashing and splattering her wine. "You transfer your energy and get some energy back. You become another person, in a way, and another person becomes you."

Beatrice realized that she thought she was talking to the blond girl, but there was no girl around. Finally, she saw her coming up to Jim, hitting on Jim,

taking Jim's hand, holding his hand. Holding his hand. Holding his hand. Jim looked confused but pleased.

Beatrice looked around and noticed that the mise en scene has changed while she was talking and drinking. For one, there was no dog in the room anymore, and the good old rock was replaced with a Hungarian pop singer with a high-pitched voice. A long-haired guy now got a blindfold on his eye.

"Bitch," Beatrice said a little too loudly, but at that party, it could have been referring to anyone, including the little dog.

Jim and the blond girl left together.

That evening, Beatrice went through the pictures from the school party again and again, trying to memorize all the details of who did what, and who liked whom. She hugged Lily, she kissed her boy to sleep, she held Leo's hand and talked, and talked all good, kind, loving words to him until he passed out.

TAKE 8:

"What do you know about the

river effect in life?" the man once said when they were standing by the river; it was winter. In winter, the river absorbs light and colors from the outside and thus becomes darker. The river, when not covered with ice, is not transparent, but more like a dark jellylike substance that sometimes glares yellow and sometimes remains thick and brown. The river in winter doesn't flow—it trembles.

So did Beatrice. She stood freezing while trying to hold the man standing by her side—for warmth and for the response. But her arms seemed too short for this—no matter how she tried, the man's neck, or his chest, or shoulders slipped away from her hugs each time.

"Once I was fatter, but now I am slim," she said. "Once I had lighter hair, but, you see, now I am a natural auburn. Once I dreamt of going to Australia, but then I changed my mind."

"What are you talking about?"

"I just want you to know more, to know things about myself," Beatrice said.

She found a flask in her pocket and anticipated a bitter sip.

"Everything goes like the river flows," the man said.

Beatrice looked down at the non-flowing river and felt dizzy and sick.

"It doesn't flow," she stated.

"Oh, yes, it does," the man said in a tender voice and took one step back from Beatrice. "And everything does. You'll be surprised how different your life will be in a short time."

"What do you know about time!"

TAKE 9:

On one day that winter, Beatrice hopped on the bus. It was the middle part of the Budapest winter when warm sunny days were still taken as a gift. The Christmas party at Leo's work had passed and was almost forgotten, but then St. Valentine's heart-shaped nightmare became a reality, and Beatrice wished to share this time with Lily. While Beatrice could handle Leo's colleagues, maintain a charming conversation about her ancestors and descendants, she couldn't do anything for Lily. Lily, waiting for cards of love from a person who had opted for silence.

"I know how you feel, it once happened to me," Beatrice said to the academics. They accepted her in their arms, simultaneously giving higher scores to her husband, Leo.

"I know exactly how you feel, it's happening to me too," Beatrice said to Lily, but it wasn't relevant at all—like the wolf was mentoring the sheep.

Lily was kind of deaf and dumb lately: she was always wearing earphones and was always chewing something bready. While doing this, Lily was losing substantial weight and, therefore, couldn't take her eyes off herself in the mirror.

"You are a beauty," Beatrice would say, but Lily would just turn away and sniff, so there was no doubt that compliments from a mother earned zero.

Once Beatrice caught her daughter hostage while she was showering and, therefore, earphones-free.

"Any special plans for St. Valentine's?" Beatrice asked over the water.

"To wash my hair," Lily replied. "And to get you out of the bathroom."

Beatrice didn't feel that she could do much here. She had to do some final cuts at the studio, and she took her time waiting for some news from producers who were now out skiing.

Beatrice considered it would be impolite to stay aside from the group on the bus. There were just a few passengers. A couple of old ladies who were whispering and laughing. A tired, greasy-haired office worker in a tie and dusty shoes. A man carrying a baby and a woman was napping next to them, having nuzzled her forehead against the window. An unrecognizable creature in multi-layered ponchos and fur cloaks, wearing two pairs of gloves on each hand and a clownlike hat with a bobble.

Beatrice sat by the window, deep in thought, though she couldn't help noticing that the poncho lady was mimicking her. She was sitting in the same position, her face was also pink and her eyes sparkled with an eerie shine. Suddenly, the poncho lady giggled.

"Tudom, hogy ki vagy! Te vagy nekem. Vagy nekem te. Csak nem most. Megértetted?"

Beatrice nodded.

"De ha jól gondold meg, talán nem én leszek. Lehet, hogy én beszélni baromság, mert meg fog tenni, hogy baromság."

60

Beatrice didn't understand a word of what poncho was saying. Not a word. Beatrice got off at the next stop and inhaled and exhaled many times deeply.

TAKE 10:

"So, what's the fuss about? You will be the best professor and a super dad, I will remain the mediocre editor, and the next day I will join you guys," Beatrice said.

It was some days later. She and Leo were having a late evening tea with ginger Christmas cookies that, for some reason, were still on sale in few shops. For some reason, they tasted even better than when eaten during the holidays. For Christmas, they had bought some new stuff for the home such as lamps, coasters, nice cups. Round items mostly.

"Predictably enough, I sense completeness when I sit here with you," Beatrice said, trying to change the subject. But then she realized she hadn't said it out loud.

"As you wish, sweetie, but keep in mind that your kids may witness their super dad getting fired," Leo said, putting the cup with circles on it on a round coaster and sighed deeply.

Leo recently started a new semester and, in his own words, was already tired.

"You are misreading the general idea of parties, darling. Parties are for fun, not for firing," Beatrice said.

"You never know. Maybe we were just lucky to be kept alive for the new year."

"I know. Cards know. Stars know. You will be fine."

"But don't you think that the idea of dragging mathematicians deep into the Hungarian woods for chilling out at a mid-term party is a genuinely odd idea?" Leo pronounced every word of the sentence with a deep hatred.

Beatrice shrugged.

"It sounds like a good idea. For all of us. To refresh."

TAKE 11:

Something went wrong during her shift. Something with the electricity or the computers, or, most likely, with both. While Beatrice was taking her time with the final cuts, where the main character was wading through the burning sun towards his destiny, the lights went off.

"Hi, there," Jim said, peering through the door into the room.

"Did you do that?"

"There is construction, and the workers are no good," Jim said.

She decided to go home.

Oddly the busses were only going in the opposite direction, and somehow the trams stopped operating as if the building site nearby could affect it. Beatrice was alone in the city.

"I can't get home," she said.

One thing led to another, and somehow, the only place that was reachable was Jim's.

Jim's place was dark grey and squared shaped. It had a perfect lighting system—the primary chandelier on the ceiling and one lamp in each corner.

"Am I on the stage?" Beatrice said, standing in the middle of the room.

"Just as long as you like," Jim replied, and pulled from the shelf one more lamp, portable and dim.

"That's for backstage," he said and laughed.

The flat was abnormally clean too—no dust, no dirty cups, not even a hair. As if all the accidental traces caused by human beings had been urgently removed.

"Do you want wine?" Jim asked, and, without waiting for a reply, poured some into a perfectly shining glass.

Beatrice took a sip and, at the same time, saw herself, already in bed, covered with pristine white linen, and side by side her was a man with long dark hair and an athletic body. For some reason, when lying in bed, she was wearing glasses and long red nails, and that was all she was wearing.

"You make me wanna dance, Jim," she said to him.

He turned to her, but he was not exactly Jim. His ears were smaller, and his hair was way too long.

"You are funny," the guy said. "But I am not Jim, I am Morrison."

"And who am I?" she said and laughed.

Beatrice took another sip, and the bottle was gone.

She and Jim, now definitely Jim, were lying in bed, covered with fresh white linen. Their eyes were open, then shut.

While they had their eyes shut, a huge, vicious man with

a sharp hunter's knife appeared from the wardrobe.

He was big and red. Bea opened her eyes and faced the killer. There was a bright red blood all over the perfect bed and marble-like walls, and Jim looked awfully dead. Bea screamed out as the killer approached her.

Then she woke up again. She was near Jim, and everyone was alive; there was no killer in the wardrobe.

Beatrice jumped out of bed and hurriedly pulled on her clothes.

"What are you doing?" Jim asked half asleep.

"I have to go before the killer chases me," she said.

"What killer?"

"The one who can kill me."

She rushed out of the flat, swallowing fear.

The street was foggy. No buses seen, no certain way to go. Beatrice landed on some curb next to the bus stop. At some house on the hill she noticed a person on the balcony. Not even a silhouette could be seen, just the top of a head sitting in a chair, seen from behind. She could see the tiny cigarette light that slowly burned and faded. Bea continued looking

and looking and ended up with a lightened cigarette in her hand as well. Bea took a puff or two. She saw birds flying from the trees, she could hear someone shout "Jó reggelt!" in distance.

Eventually, the silhouette stood up, and she saw her Leo.

"Why are you not coming inside?" he said. "We are all starving. Did you buy enough cinnamon buns this time?"

"They didn't have cinnamon buns," Beatrice said without realizing what she was saying, "I've got some with cottage cheese and with poppy seeds."

And as if it could prove her words, or as if it could prove anything else, she showed Leo a paper bag from the bakery.

TAKE 12:

"Lily is missing," Leo said over the phone.

"Missing?" Beatrice mechanically repeated and looked out the office window into the warm early spring evening.

"It is evening," Beatrice said. "Where could she be?"

"Yes, and Lily was supposed

to go the pool after school and then to drama class," Leo said with irritation. "That's kind of funny that you are not aware of your daughter's schedule."

"I am."

"Then maybe you can tell me where she is. I already called the teacher, her two best friends—god knows where she dug them out from, they are pathetically stupid—and now Hedgehog and I are driving around the city and I have no idea what we're doing or what we should do."

"Meet me somewhere," Beatrice said.

"Where somewhere?" Leo asked nervously.

"I know where she is," Hedgehog said, daring to raise his voice from the backseat.

"What? What is he saying?" Beatrice said.

"What? How do you know?" Leo said at the same time.

TAKE 13:

A couple of days before, or whenever it was, she had said that same, "meet me somewhere," to Jim.

He did meet her, along with other crew members. They chose a beer garden for the meeting, one of those beer gardens that are so numerous and identical that Beatrice could never memorize their locations or names.

The beer garden had just reopened after winter. In essence, the tables were stable, the bartenders new, the burger corner still on vacation. The chalkboard offered house lemonade along with beer of different shades; Beatrice thought she should take both.

The air in the garden was fresh too—it would take a couple of months for it to fill with smells of tobacco and fried food. There were a few people organized in small groups, including Beatrice and Jim, and others, who were occupying one of the corner tables that was hidden behind some small bushes. People were talking in low voices, but laughing at a loud pitch.

Beatrice and Jim didn't laugh, though. They talked about some work stuff. Beatrice had just finished editing a commercial series and was about to start a new film.

"That László guy is not so bad after all," she said. "He gives work to people. Once we had a private talk, just him and me, and, you know, he revealed himself to be a sympathetic, deep guy. So, I am for him now."

Jim laughed then, and it was not a good laugh.

"It seems like you like keeping yourself busy," Jim said.

"I do," Beatrice replied, ignoring his sarcastic tone.

"Well, I am done."

"You are done?"

"Yeah. Want to try something else. Stage maybe."

"Stage?"

"Why are you echoing me? Stage design. Is it difficult to get?"

Jim leaned back and put his hands behind his head. He was looking around, and Beatrice could see he was bored.

The street lamps turned on. A group of people in shiny clothes entered the garden. The ladies' hair sparkled with silver and gold, and the sleeves of their clothes were wing-wide. The men were clean-shaven, and some were wearing hats. They were all remarkably tall and skinny. Right after they entered the garden, the garden started to smell powdery sweet like some outdated perfume.

One lady's nose began heavily bleeding. The blood ran down her chin, but she kept laughing. One gentleman from the group kept trying to make her sit down.

"Who are they?" Beatrice asked.

"Stag party?" Jim suggested.

"Look carefully!"

"What language do they speak?" Beatrice asked.

"English?" Jim said.

"Listen carefully!"

"Ancient Greek?"

"What are they doing here?" Beatrice kept wondering aloud.

"Hanging out?"

"Think carefully!"

"I don't know! What are they doing here?"

The group of people surrounded Jim and Beatrice and, for some seconds, black flat hats covered them, and wide sleeves embraced them. Music and talk fused into a not disturbing buzz. Beatrice looked at Jim: his face was illuminated by the street lamps so brightly that she couldn't tell if it was bored Jim, sitting next to her, or if it was someone else. She preferred to think it was Jim.

Both of them were sitting,

stuck to their chairs, remaining in light and silence, while these human-like creatures whirled around them.

And then an actual stag party actually entered: fake boobs, fake lips, fake girls, but real drinks.

Beatrice went home, and nobody stopped her. She actually couldn't see Jim in that crowd.

She met her husband Leo on the corner and got into the car.

TAKE 14:

Hedgehog was sitting in the back, Beatrice was tapping her fingers on her lap and Leo's lap. Leo was driving.

"Where am I supposed to turn here, Hedgie?"

"I don't know, Dad. I've only been there once."

"You've been there...?"

"Once."

"So, where I should turn?"

"Try GPS, Dad. I just know what the place is called. It's where Squirrel goes when she feels bad."

"Squirrel?"—that was from Beatrice.

"That's her pet name, didn't you know that?"

"I gave her this name! But I thought it was banned now."

Hedgehog shrugged.

"I don't know. I call her that, she seems fine."

"So, if you've been there, does it mean that you've also felt bad? You felt bad together?" Beatrice said, probing.

"No, she was upset, and I just went out of curiosity."

"I see, Honey."

"Sometimes her boyfriend joins."

"Which one?" Leo asked.

"She's only got one."

"Is there water?"

"What do you think: if it's an island, is there water?"

TAKE 15:

They arrived at the island on the north side of Budapest. Népsziget—a place that once flourished, but later was shunned and forgotten by everyone except for those who could see beauty in desolation.

That's what Beatrice read on her phone while they were driving there, and the description alone disturbed her.

It was not even late in the evening, but for Beatrice it looked like the dead of night. She noticed a lonely silhouette walking in the water, very close to the shore.

It was Lily.

They stopped the car and Beatrice rushed out.

"Where are you going, Bea?" Leo screamed out. "Here she is, here is Lily!"

But Beatrice ran into the water. Perhaps, she ran too fast, or she was too scared, or she couldn't see well in her personal darkness, but somehow she got her clothes wet and appeared to be much deeper in the water than Lily was.

"Lily! Squirrel! Honey!" she cried and splashed back.

"Why are you here? I'd have come home," Lily said calmly.

"But, sweetie, it's cold. Your legs will be in pain."

Beatrice's face was burning and she could see her breath. She looked at her daughter, and her daughter's breathing was loud, unlike her voice, and her face was burning from the inside.

Suddenly Beatrice saw a baby, who was very tiny and thin and cried all the time as if she was constantly unhappy. Then she saw a little girl, who gained some weight and had learned how to smile, who was forced to wear flowery dresses. Then, she saw a five-year-old girl digging into her mother's purse with the passion of an archaeologist.

Beatrice and Lily, both with big eyes, bad hair, rough skin, were sitting on the river bank, both covered in blankets, though not wet at all.

"You will be happy, and smart, and gorgeous," Beatrice said. "And happy."

TAKE 16:

Four of them, a man and a woman, a girl, and a boy, were lying on the same bed, glued to each other by palm, foot, ear, or back. Hedgehog was hugging Beatrice in his sleep with both of his arms and both of his legs.

Lily breathed with her face in the pillow, leaving on it a bit of her mascara, her saliva, and some indistinct sighs.

Both Beatrice and Leo closed the composition: Beatrice from one side, Leo—from the other. Beatrice was trying not to move and, instead of breathing, was picturing what it would be like if she was not a woman, but water herself. Leo was patting Lily's back and was murmuring something about the water that flows and something about time, and about something that matters, but Beatrice couldn't hear what it exactly was. ◉

The Editing Room

Anne-Marie Yerks is a fiction writer, essayist and digital journalist from the Metropolitan Detroit area. After earning an MFA from George Mason University, she contributed to magazines, journals, and websites while working as a multimedia designer. She has been teaching all forms of writing, creative and professional, for over twenty years. Her novel "Dream Junkies" was published by New Rivers Press in 2016, and she continues to publish short stories and articles regularly. Her work has appeared in "Good Housekeeping," "Redbook," "Marie Claire," and in literary journals like "Juked" and "Streetlight." She loves attending writing conferences and traveling to literary destinations. Find her on Twitter @amy1620. Anne-Marie is represented by Vicki Marsdon of High Spot Literary Agency.www.dreamjunkies.nyc.

Godflash

Anne-Marie Yerks

*L*eShey sat at the kitchen table and tore open the package from NegePet, pausing at the photo of a smiling white dog. She unfolded the instruction infographic, flipped to the cat side, and carefully detached the information card.

"Paisley?" Her daughter was upstairs studying for a music theory test. "Bring Domino down for his DNA sample."

She waited for any sounds upstairs, picturing her son Walter lying sideways on his bed, fantasizing about that skinny girl – what was her name? Cleora or Kissie or something trashy. Her son liked loose girls, the ones who dyed their eyebrows, sometimes even their teeth, and wore mesh-metal panties with vibrating sensors in the crotch. LeShey admitted to trying on a pair of them herself once but found them difficult to clean. They were now hidden in the bottom of her bureau drawer.

No Paisley. She found a pen and began filling out the card, hesitating at "Age of animal?" Domino might be a few months over the limit, but who would know? And would it make a difference? These genetic companies probably played it in the safe range. LeShey's sister, Dreama, had done a Labrador when he was a year over the limit. A woman from the child therapy center had copied a two-year-old hamster.

But weren't all hamsters already the same? Maybe some had better fur textures or pinker noses. Maybe some ran faster in the wheel. LeShey went to the refrigerator to access the family calendar, scrolling back five years to find "Visit animal adoption agency" on February 20, 2045. By subtracting six weeks, she determined Domino's true age and shaved off a few weeks.

Love was love, she supposed, writing the fraudulent age onto the card. Even for a rodent.

The refrigerator calendar flickered into a live feed from Walter. "Mom," he said in his pretend-nice voice. "What am I eating for dinner tonight?" He was too close to his camera, appearing as a plump red mouth over a squat chin. LeShey noted with worry the darkening fuzz over his top lip. Raging hormones. Why couldn't he be more like his father, a smooth-skinned man with a moderate sex drive?

"I hardly know yet," she told Walter. "Check the menu."

"It doesn't work in here. Can I come down?"

LeShey found the kitchen remote and changed the channel to the recipe bank, choosing "Dinner | Wednesday | Walter Krigen," from the list. She sent the page to Walter – spicy soy loaf, heritage corn, and blue avocado salad – and blocked him from live-feeding for an hour. He was grounded from everything except meals and therapy sessions. He was locked in his bedroom with books and no technology except the family network, which he could use only through the ancient stereo system. On schooldays, he used Paisley's computer to attend classes remotely, returning it to her when she returned from the gymnastics academy.

Paisley finally came down with the cat pressed against one shoulder, his head tight and tense as she walk-stomped through the hallway, activating the safety light. "I had to look all over for him. He was under the guest bed, way way back. I think he knows we're doing this, and he doesn't like it."

"It won't hurt him." LeShey took the black-and-white cat's warm body into her arms and adjusted the squirming feline into their favorite position – back legs resting neatly on her forearm, her hand cupping his breastbone. She tickled him under his chin, kissed between his ears, and sat down at the table with the paperwork. Paisley joined her and helped capture the animal's DNA, forcing Domino's mouth open. LeShey swabbed the back of his tongue with a tiny swab that retracted into a plastic case imprinted with their ID code. They snipped off a bit of hair, a toenail, and printed a photograph from the kitchen station.

"Mommy," Paisley inserted the

photo into a slim cardboard case and added it to the pile, "Can Walter come to my birthday party? Pretty please? I really want him to be there."

LeShey smoothed back her daughter's hair. The coarse, kinky strands were so different from her own silky fine hair, one of her best features due to its gentle waves and honey-apricot color, both completely natural. Paisley's hair was a dull brown. She had big bones, a thick build with wide hips and thighs as big as hams.

The birthday party—LeShey had temporarily forgotten about it.

"He will be all over the girls. Forget it."

"He doesn't like any of those girls." Paisley attempted eye contact to intensify her plea. "Mommy, he didn't do it. You should believe him like I do."

"You know he likes every girl, Paisley."

LeShey escaped to the bathroom, shut the door, and mouthed "Party Chart" into the mirror. Intently reviewing the infographic, she scanned the details of the party they had planned seven or so months ago. The supplies were already ordered: invitations sent and received; entertainment (a piano player); ice cream maker, and an I Ching reading machine. All arrived. It was done– all scheduled and paid for. LeShey checked the RSVP list. Only two girls had answered yes to coming.

She turned off the chart. They might have to include Walter just to make it seem like a party. The flowchart faded to reveal her reflection, a thin face pulled with guilt. Raising her shoulders, LeShey pursed her lips and looked down her dainty nose, another of her best features. Back when they were in their twenties, her sister Dreama had her own pig-like nose surgically sculpted into its replica.

Would you like to compare today's image to a compilation of last year's? The mirror read in a thin blue font.

She said "yes" and waited while the mirror drew a frame and prompted her to position inside it. The frame contracted into a whorl of colored pixels, sharpening into a photo-memory of LeShey from a year ago. A translucent layer of her current face fell over it. She scrutinized the composition and decided she looked the same, hadn't aged a day. Perhaps her eye serum was working.

Would you like to view a series of predictive images of yourself in ten, twenty, and thirty years?

"No," she said firmly and cued the mirror back to default. Out of habit, she pressed the scent spray button before leaving the bathroom.

In the kitchen, Paisley had abandoned the cloning kit, leaving its contents spread out on the table. LeShey rustled through the shallow box to find the padded envelope for the samples. A folded paper lay on top, a long-printed list of physical and behavioral attributes of typical felines.

"Please check up to three attributes you would like to modify," the instructions read. "Use the subcategory list and comments box to more precisely tune desire modifications in your cloned pet."

LeShey focused on the "PURRING" section. Domino's purr was very soft, so soft they had to hold a hand on his vocal cords to determine if he was even purring at all. Was that a flaw? She folded the card and tucked it under the sample syringe, uncertain.

They would need flowers for the party – a gigantic bouquet of colored daisies, maybe. Or maybe black roses. Paisley would be fourteen, so the party should celebrate her maturity. They always said she'd been born an old soul.

The house was silent except for electric ticks coming from the appliances and a wail of violin music, the background of Paisley's instrument practice exercise. LeShey pinged her sister's kitchen camera at her house, but Dreama wasn't there or in her other rooms. So she pinged Walter's room. Her son was dressed in old blue sweatpants, no shirt, spread sideways on his bed, huge feet hanging off, staring blankly into the wall. All those books they'd given him were certainly untouched, not even opened. He probably hadn't even looked at the titles, maybe hadn't seen she'd included a funny guidebook to dating and a comprehensive history of the old cartoon South Park. He liked magazines about science instead.

She blamed the nuts. LeShey had eaten too many synthetic pistachios—known for producing logical kids—when pregnant. Maybe he was this way because she had fed him formula instead of breast milk. He'd sucked so hard on her nipples, she couldn't bear the pain.

Down in the basement, she slipped off her silk cardigan sweater. She opened the door leading to the heated hydroponic garden. Domino tried to exit with her, she pushed the cat back in with a foot and closed the door on his inquisitive little face. Usually, he liked chasing the butterflies and mussing the plants by jumping through the neat, tight rows.

LeShey checked on the microgreens and herbs, snipping what they could use for a salad that night. The only flowers in bloom were tiny white chrysanthemums and the blossoms of drooping sweet peas. They would have to find prettier flowers for the party. The lights flickered a warning. She rushed to the door, spilling the greens from her apron, her hand on the lever just as the nutrient mist hissed over the garden, dampening her clothing and hair.

On the other side of the glass door, Domino meowed insistently. Peeking through the window and following the cat's intent gaze to the ceiling, LeShey gasped. A skinny gray rat with a long hairless tail scooted along ta pipe. Following it through the basement, it looked down just once, long enough for her to communicate fear directly into the rodent's beady black eyes.

* * *

Saturday, the day of the party, arrived. It was wet and cold. Wind wheezed through the front trees and tossed green walnuts across the street. Standing at the kitchen doorway, LeShey took in the majesty of her humming appliances and glinting countertops, the efficient choreography of meters and gauges, the heady hiss of hot coffee pouring into the insulated carafe, the spotless white floor. Domino was curled onto a red velvet pillow, a furry circle of comfort centered in the wide window seat. She made strawberry frosting with the intuitive whisk she'd gotten for Christmas then shouted for the kids to come and help her.

"Mommy," Paisley called from the top of the steps. "Can Walter come down now?"

"We discussed this. Walter has to shower first and put on his suit."

After a long period of silence,

Paisley returned with Walter in a pair of brown tweed trousers and a white polo shirt buttoned to the top. A gold and green striped tie hung in a sloppy knot several inches below his neck.

The doorbell rang – it was the piano player, a lanky man with a heavy accent who looked exactly like his photo in the advertisement. LeShey pointed to the white baby grand in their foyer; within a few minutes, the silent house echoed with a montage of Monet and Beethoven bests.

Alone for a minute, LeShey spoke into the bathroom mirror.

"Paisley."

It produced a photo-memory collage of her daughter's life: baby footprints, toothy toddler grins, school portraits, crayon compositions, Santa letters, medals, certificates, music school group shots. The timeline ended with a screenshot of her latest accomplishment – the summer tour with her gymnastics club.

LeShey sent the scrapbook to the kitchen publishing station, glancing again at the gymnastics photo. How had she, LeShey, a petite as well-proportioned as a porcelain doll, given birth to a daughter with broad shoulders and chubby knees?

Paisley was at the table, curly hair flattened to her temples with black ribbons, a plate of strawberry cupcakes, and the cat cloning kit still before her.

The piano player began a different montage, something smoky jazz and blues. Walter sat at the bar, rocking back and forth on a stool, eyes transfixed on the counter. He'd been assigned the job of arranging the black roses–hunted down at the market that morning by Daddy–into a gold vase. Daddy was now in the basement to get away from the commotion. Walter stood still. He'd done nothing but untape the paper cone.

"Why didn't we send this in yet?" Paisley asked her mother. "We have to do it before Domino gets too old. He's already close."

LeShey checked the cabinet for glasses and pulled out six. "Did you see it's snowing?" She handed a pair of floral shears to Walter, avoiding eye contact with her son.

"Cut the ends and put them in water."

"Am I OK now?" he asked. "I want to be OK again."

"We've got to send it in, Mommy," Paisley said.

LeShey spread a cloth onto the dining room table and set the freshly-printed scrapbook in the center. They arranged the cupcakes and roses behind, creating an altar of Paisley for guests to enjoy.

"Maybe," LeShey replied. "But I'm not sure this is a good idea about Domino. Copying him. What if they don't do it right?" She remembered a very old book she'd read in high school about a man whose cat returned to life after being buried in a magical cemetery. The cat in the old book had been evil and demented after its resurrection.

They all looked over at their family feline, still asleep in the window seat.

"No, Mommy. Please send it in. If I get nothing else for my birthday, I want this. We have to keep Domino forever." Pink blotches of anger appeared on Paisley's cheeks.

"We'll just get a new cat after Domino," she told her children. "Besides, he's only five years old and will be alive for much longer. You won't even live with Daddy and me by the time you would need a new cat."

"That will be nice," Walter said as the doorbell rang.

On the step stood a girl, shivering either from nerves or the cold, black hair and cotton-white skin, slender body buttoned into a wool car coat. She announced herself as "Elaine, the I Ching reader."

"I thought it was a machine," LeShey said to Walter. "Let her enter."

"I ordered an I Ching reading machine, not a person," she said to the girl.

"Oh, sorry. My company's owners don't speak English well." She sat down at the table.

Walter sat down with her and taking her tiny bag of coins, shook them out over the surface while Elaine studied the formation in surprise.

"Did you know," Walter whispered loudly. "There's a point in space, PR209, where radio waves repeat with high intensity," he told her as he pointed to the coin formation. "Researchers at MIT spent a quarter of a century trying to find out what it was. Turns out, they call it a godflash."

Elaine took a picture of Walter's coin formation on and printed an I Ching fortune from her tablet. "What's a godflash?"

"God pleasuring himself,"

Walter said, smoothing his tie.

"Walter, Stop it," LeShey warned.

"Oh, really?" Elaine said smartly. "Who knows that Sentient Being PR209 is male? Or that it's even a God?"

"I know," Walter said. "I know it for certain."

Thankfully, the doorbell interrupted them. It was a group of Paisley's friends—none of whom had RSVP'd, LeShay noted. Behind them were the two who had.

The house was soon spilling over with young girls giggling and directing slinky glances at Walter. LeShey ordered them all back into the kitchen, seating each guest before a pink lemonade cupcake and glass of fruit punch. They sang "Happy Birthday" over the piano montage and viewed the electronic version of Paisley's scrapbook scrolling on the monitor. The girls each had their I Ching reading, shaking the coins and listening with respectful silence to Elaine as she read their esoteric forecasts.

Domino scampered into the kitchen just in time for birthday candles and another song. Jumping on the counter, he began to lick a forgotten mound

of cream cheese.

LeShey pushed the cat off the counter and began to clean. She was relieved the party was going well. The kitchen was a mess, but the snow had stopped, and the sucking sounds of the hydro-ports taking in the snow would soon end. Then the solar fans would blow the yards back into the deep gossamer green the neighborhood beautification committee had selected years ago.

Suddenly she heard gasps and embarrassed giggles.

"Mommy," Paisey said. "Mommy, turn it off."

She turned to see that the kitchen screen had stopped playing Paisley's scrapbook montage, and one for Walter was now scrolling before the party guests. The major events of his seventeen years played inside a dark blue and green theme fringed with soccer balls and checkerboard flags.

"I never published this," LeShey said. "Why – "

"Oh, I didn't know it happened that way," one girl said.

They were looking at a photo of Walter in the hospital bed. At eight, he'd taken a head-first dive into their neighbor's swimming pool and shattered his skull. The respirator shown in the photo had held him a coma until Dr. Griston had arrived from Chicago with his round eyeglasses and smooth, warm hands.

"I can restore Walter with essence QT673 – a synthetic version of who he was, of who we all are, a seed from space to regrow the core consciousness that slipped away."

LeShay remembered his warm hands. Round glasses. Thin lips pressed into a tight line.

But it's a clinical study? she had asked?

Do you have a choice?

The Walter scrapbook continued with a lighthearted, jingling tune clashing against the deep bass notes of the piano in the living room.

They watched him: his return to school, head bandaged like Frankenstein; a wide smile from the seat of an Adirondack on the beach the following summer; soccer games, a spelling bee, band camp; hugging his best friend at a bar mitzvah; singing in a school musical. It all looked so normal in hindsight, but of course, it hadn't been.

"He tried to lick my boobs that day," one girl said as the class

photo taken at the aquarium scrolled by.

"Mommy, turn it off," Paisley demanded. "You know what's –"

Already it was too late to stop. The horrifying news story appeared as a headline tucked inside a zigzagging blue frame. Animated bolts of comic-book lightning playfully struck the bold letters: "Local Boy Accused of Vicious Rape."

LeShey stood with the girls, frozen, as the subsequent pieces played. There was the girl, an exchange student from Germany named Eve, crying on the court stand. There were photos of bruised ribs and bloody gashes, her angry parents at the airport, the passionate attorneys. Finally, the pale and hollowed-out Walter, hair flattened from nights on a cell cot. And the sentencing scrolled by last: "Local Boy Guilty, Sentenced to 75 Years."

LeShey saw the girls' faces: wondering how Walter was instead in the other room, debating the theory of mirror worlds with Elaine, the I Ching reader.

Paisley scrambled to the bathroom and paused the projector.

"You messed up the settings,

Mommy," she accused, blinking wet eyes.

"Don't cry," one of the friends took Paisley by the waist to calm her.

"He didn't rape Eve," Paisley insisted. "She wanted to try rough sex then got mad when he hurt her."

"Let's go outside!" LeShay sent the somber girls into the yard for sparklers and a photo shoot before their pop-up green screen.

While she cleaned cupcake crumbs from the counter, LeShay let the Walter show play on in silence. Not much was left, just the news story about the high court's resolution. Walter was mentally incapacitated due to experimental surgery, a lab rat gone wrong. He must permanently be banned from school with other children. Not a criminal, not a citizen, he would live as a ward in his parents' home. The show ended with the phrase Walter must have typed in, "To be continued," bouncing like a tennis ball from the monitor.

A commercial for NegePet followed, and LeShey remembered the cat cloning kit, still opened on the table. There was enough time still to send it into the mail chute.

"Outstanding party, and a lovely day in the end," The piano player called as he came into the kitchen to shake her hand and receive payment. She pressed the flat disc in her thumbnail, which sent the money to his bank account. "Lovely party, lovely teenagers. That boy of yours is remarkable in his understanding of music theory. And the I Ching fortune teller –an unusual idea." He winked at her before leaving.

Outside, the girls had forgotten about Walter and were giggling on the lawn, posing in front of backgrounds on the green screen: The cliffs of Dover, a Japanese garden, the old White House, a whorl of tie-dyed galaxy dust, the mouth of a lion. Their photos printed on the kitchen station. An efficient chugging from the wheels and sliders produced a vibrant depiction of Paisley standing alone in the Sahara Desert, arms out to her sides. Was she getting prettier? LeShey saw only a hint of her own face in her daughter's.

"Daddy?" LeShey called out to her husband as another photo printed – Paisley at a 1970s discotheque. "Daddy?"

"I'm in the basement," her husband called. "Mopping some

water down here. Goddamn storm."

LeShey flicked on the refrigerator's live feed and saw her son and the I Ching reader sitting together in his bedroom, both fully dressed on his twin bed, reading from the pages of a science magazine.

"See this," Walter said, pointing to an illustration of the repeating radio waves from the godflash beckoning. "It's a portal in the bubble holding us in this universe."

"But how would we get through?" Elaine asked.

"You'd have to have the most powerful orgasm ever," Walter said, the magazine slipping from his lap. "A real mind-bender."

LeShey held in a breath as their mouths merged, the smacking sounds of the kiss passing through the speakers, each one like a slap against LeShay's flaming cheeks.

She was about to interrupt with a voice command but stopped. Her son ran a hand through the girl's obsidian hair, circle her small ear with a fingertip, then lower his mouth to caress the top of her cleavage. The pair clasped their hands together, eyes locked fiercely. Elaine

giggled in a way that reminded LeShey of bubble baths.

"Where's your mother?" she asked.

"Probably watching us through the camera." Walter looked into the lens and waved.

Hands shaking, LeShey turned off the screen.

She turned, signed her name on the cat cloning disclosure form, and dropped the sealed package into the mail chute. Domino would live again, bulge from the laboratory flesh with a louder purr and greener eyes.

"LeShey?" her husband called up. "Are you ready to stop this? We've been playing this for a while now. It's getting uncomfortable, don't you think?"

"If we stop—" she turned to watch Paisley through the sliding glass doors. "Will they be gone?" Paisley danced and jumped with her friends, and they sang Ring Around the Rosie.

LeShey's husband put a hand on her cheek, turning her away from the curly-haired girl on the lawn. "It's just not working well," he coaxed, circling around her. "They don't look like us, and something is off with the boy."

* * *

LeShay looked over at the simulation printer sitting unnoticed on the buffet. It ran, grinding the "parenthood" chip inside its metal teeth with such intensity, a veil of heat hovered around the casing.

"We can try playing again in a few weeks... get some peace and quiet around here."

Her husband's finger hovered over the END button as he looked at her, head cocked, eyes pleading but playful. "Oh, I see you are sad." He hesitated. "But you don't really want these two, do you?"

"Maybe just her... And maybe him too... I don't know."

He punched the button with force, and LeShey watched the scene of the girls out front crystallize into an empty lawn and patio. They were back in their home, the lonely blueprint of it where she was always hungry.

"Don't be cross, darling." her husband said, holding out a hand.

"Come on, let's enjoy being young a little longer." ◉

Jackie Kenny graduated in 2018 from the University of North Carolina with a degree in English and minors in Creative Writing and Comparative Literature. Her passion for ethical food-systems has led her to work in some amazing places in the past two years: a raw milk goat farm in Washington State, a 214-acre biodynamic farm in California, a small Hawaiian coffee farm built on volcanic soils, and an Alaskan homestead supported by its eco-kayaking tours. She's currently working on an organic vineyard in Tuscany and learning the ins-and-outs of wine making, pizza eating, and building daily fires in a finicky wood furnace. Her writing is inspired by the natural world and farming communities; she's fascinated by the powerful, complex interconnections between all living things. You can find more of her work in *Allegory Ridge*, *Atlas and Alice*, and *Qu!*

Little Moons

Jackie Kenny

*I*t was August, and the night sky was often lit with the blue streaks of falling little moons. They fell in all sorts of weather. They fell when grey clouds broiled low and steaming across the horizon, and when stars clustered like white cockleshells in a tide pool. They fell when the air was as hot and wet as the water itself, when the wind beat the rising foam off the waves. Sometimes, they did not fall at all, and the sky would remain dark and still

During the week, Claire watched for falling little moons from her gabled roof. When the roof tiles were slippery or cold, she would spread out a towel and wrap herself in a thin beach shawl. She sat alone and tracked the little moons as their light whistled into the sea.

On the island of Lysonia, it was said that if you took a little moon and hid it in the home of unrequited love, it would slowly, night by night, coax your lover's dreams around to love for you. It was infallible, people said. Claire's grandmother was a particularly firm believer.

The little moons were attracted to the water, people said. Or maybe it was just that the ocean was much larger than the island of Lysonia, and that the few moons that fell onto the ground never survived impact. Even the white billowy sand dunes were not soft enough to catch and cradle a falling little moon. Every now and then, Claire would see shattered moon shells by the edge of the road on her morning walk to middle school. By afternoon, the jagged pieces would be gone, crushed into powder by the force of a few passing cars or the heat of the sun.

Broken little moons were useless. Their beauty lay in their polished glow, the soft blue burn that could seep between the spaces of cupped hands or shine faintly underneath layers of swaddling. But with the very first crack—even if it was the smallest, most minuscule crack—the glow would gradually leak out of a little moon, and it would become as dull and grey as a plain stone. Without their glow, it was said to be impossible for the moons to inspire love.

* * *

By September, Claire had seen enough little moons fall to justify telling her best friend Liv they could start taking out the skiff. Because the moons generally only fell in the last months of the year, it wasn't worth the time to go any earlier. Claire and Liv, along with the few other moon hunters, had picked the prime spots bare the previous gathering season. It was Claire's job to know where the moons fell because Liv's house was in the very center of Lysonia and did not have a clear view of the ocean. Liv's job was to be in charge of everything else.

As she had grown older, Claire started to doubt whether little moons worked the way that people claimed. It wasn't like she had any evidence that the moons didn't inspire love; it was just that there wasn't any solid proof that they did. She never voiced her doubts to Liv, half-afraid that if she said anything, Liv would tease her, or even worse–give up completely on looking for little moons.

Their first night out, Liv showed up on the stroke of eight in a rubber coat that went past her knees. She had a styrofoam cup of black coffee and carried a wooden paddle.

"Hey, Claire," she said. "Let's do this."

It was easiest to find the little moons at night. During the day, their blue glow was not strong enough to overcome the sun, but in the dark, if you knew what to look for, you could spot their soft illumination in shallow water. Since Claire was thirteen this year and Liv was a few months older, their mothers had agreed to let them stay out in the skiff till ten. Claire's skiff—given to her by her grandmother—was tied underneath the old wooden dock and rested high on the sand. It took them a while to shove off into the water. . Once they were floating, Liv used her paddle to push them along until it was deep enough for the motor.

The night was cool, and their spotlight shone on a bobbing grey pelican as they passed out of the cove. When they first started hunting in the skiff the year before, Claire and Liv had eventually discovered that the offshore sandbars were the best place to look for little moons. After eight unsuccessful hunting trips in a row, they spent a week huddled over books and maps in Claire's attic bedroom, learning the coastal currents and riptides. This time, they were ready with a sketch of the undersea hills of sand where the freshly fallen moons might gather.

The little moons had a scientific name, of course, and an explanation that no one really cared enough about to pay attention to. All that mattered was that they were lovely and delicate and rare, rare, rare. They did not show up on thermal radars, metal detectors, or sonar scans. Smallbut heavy, they escaped even the trawling nets of deep-sea fishermen. Little moons had to be found the old-fashioned way: one by one, with bare human eyes and hands.

"There," Liv said, about forty minutes in. She cut the engine. They were off the eastern edge of the island where the mangroves crept into the bay. As the motor sputtered, Claire rolled up her sleeves and peered over the side of the boat. Below the spitting, salty waves, she could see a pale luminous circle about the size of her fist.

"That's a deep one," Claire said.

"You can go first," Live said, without looking up, already pulling out the applewood basket from underneath the bench to coil and fluff the red towels that lined the inside.

Claire groaned. She pulled her sweater over her head and let her shorts drop to the floor of the skiff, where two untouched lifejackets lay. The sea wind bit at her bare stomach. She drew her hands down her thighs, rubbing out the rising goosebumps. Then she stood and curled her toes on the gunnel, shivered again, and held her arms out for balance.

"Just dive, Claire, dive," Liv said. Claire could hear the grin in her voice. She didn't have to see her to know that Liv sat behind her on folded legs like a young bird hiding its cold feet. She knew it, just like she knew that Liv would be tucking her thin hair behind her ears every time the wind blew and that her cheekbones would be flushed high with excitement. Her hands would be white and eager, fiddling impatiently with the red towels, and her shoulders would be drawn tight, the freckles on her neck speckled and scattered like cinnamon—

Liv shook the starboard hull, and Claire teetered.

"A flip, Claire, a flip! Do a summersault!"

"For God's sake," Claire said, laughing. She jumped.

Later, after Claire and Liv had both swum down twice more to pick up little moons, they turned the skiff back towards shore. The applewood basket glowed and clinked. Claire placed her feet on either side of it to keep the little moons from spilling over the edge.

* * *

When Claire was six, her grandmother had told her that it was wrong for a girl to love another girl. They had just come back from collecting seashells, and Claire was sitting cross-legged on her grandmother's front porch, sorting auger twists, rough scallops, and keyhole limpets into piles for threading necklaces. Her grandmother was standing behind her, watching. Her grandmother had many passions, but cookies, the youth group that she ran, and seashells took the main stage. She also had the longest hair out of everyone Claire knew: straight, smooth, grey hair that went all the way to her waist. When she was in a good mood, she would let Claire and Liv take turns brushing it all the way through. At the end, if they had brushed it carefully enough, it would slip through their fingers like silver water.

Claire had just finished separating the shells into their respective color groups when she felt her grandmother's body tense. She looked up.

Two girls were walking down the sidewalk that curved past her grandmother's house. They couldn't have been older than fifteen, and they were holding hands. One girl was especially beautiful. Her black hair was pulled back into a single braid and entangled with small, newly bloomed white flowers. The other girl wore an orange and gold sundress that grazed her knees. They walked past, swinging their hands back and forth, and then stopped underneath a palm tree that grew a few houses away. Stripes of shadows and sunlight fell onto their tan skin.

The girl with white flowers in her hair kissed the other girl on the mouth. She ran her fingers through the sundress girl's sandy blonde hair. Claire's eyes widened.

"Well," her grandmother said, with a sharp intake of breath. "That's not right, Claire. Not right at all."

"Why?"

Her grandmother didn't seem to hear. She was narrowing her eyes at the two girls, and her arms were folded across her chest. The girl in the sundress nuzzled the shoulder of the girl with the flower braid. They both were laughing. Claire strained to hear their words, but they were too far away for her to understand what they were saying.

"Something like that will just end poorly, my dear." Her grandmother sighed and unfolded her arms, shaking her head. "I'm not sure what they're thinking." She bent down and straightened one of Claire's shell piles. "There, Claire. Just don't give it your attention. Do you need help with cutting that string?"

Claire let her grandmother take the scissors and the ball of twine. As her grandmother unwound and measured the string around Claire's neck, Claire stared at the girls, who had resumed walking. Their hands were still intertwined. Claire imagined their palms to be sticky and warm with sea salt. Right before they turned the corner and disappeared, the white flower girl brought the sundress girl's knuckles to her lips and kissed each individual finger.

Claire blinked and shifted her gaze back towards her shells.

That same year was when Claire first saw a little moon fall. She had been down by the water with Liv, digging in the dusky, soft sand for coquinas. The tide had been low, and the beach stretched into the distance, long and wet until the shoreline turned a sharp corner and disappeared. A pink plastic bucket halfway filled with sand and water sat between them. Inside the bucket, six coquinas— Liv had been insisting that they only collect the red ones— poked the tops of their shells out of the sand, their white siphon stalks like still, unwavering sails. A few hundred yards back, Claire's mother watched from the back steps of their house, and the porch lights spilled buttery between shadows onto the patches of salt meadow rush growing in the yard.

Then Liv grabbing her hand, saying, Claire, Claire, look, and pointing as a thin celestial glow, as blue and soft as the hem of her grandmother's dress, slid through the sky and into the waves. From the corner of her eye, Claire could see Liv looking at the water. Out of everything—out of the remnants of the little moon's glow, out of the small, speckled stars, out of the yellow lamps on the boardwalk—it was the wonder on Liv's face that shone the clearest.

* * *

Claire couldn't remember a time before Liv.

Liv had golden eyelashes as pale as the translucent guso that washed ashore. She was too angular and knobby to be considered typically pretty but was interesting enough to escape ugliness. She had a temper that could only be checked by Claire's grandmother. Claire had a vivid memory of a seven-year-old Liv refusing to eat for two entire days because she was upset that her mother wouldn't allow her to get a dog. Eventually, her grandmother walked to Liv's

house, took Liv by the ear, and didn't let her leave the kitchen until she drank a glass of orange juice.

Another time, when they were in third grade, Liv told their teacher that she was explaining fractions wrong and got up from her desk to redraw the example on the whiteboard. When the teacher tried to take back the marker from Liv's hand, Liv gave it to her, but then walked out of the classroom, out of school, and all the way back to her house.

Once, when they were nine, Claire and Liv had woken up before the sun and gone swimming in the ocean. The sky had still been a wet grey, and the water was warm and bath-like. They had moved out just far enough so that the sea came up to the tops of their bikinis. Claire was floating on her back with Liv standing beside her when the stingrays came.

"Don't move, Claire, don't move," Liv had said. "Don't put your feet down." She put her fingers under Claire's shoulders. The tips of Liv's blonde hair drifted and curled in the thin layer of water above Claire's chest. Claire stared at the sky and took a slow deep breath. She had seen packs of stingrays glide along the shoreline before, but only from the safety of the beach. She imagined the tips of their wings just beneath her, their slick brown and grey bodies skimming over Liv's bare feet. When the last stingray finally passed by, Liv took her fingers away. The clouds were just beginning to turn pink.

Liv was just like that. Even though she was only two months older than Claire, she somehow knew everything first. She taught Claire how to boil live coquinas and pick them apart so that only their butterfly shell remained. She taught her how to spell archipelago and when to step around unmarked turtle nests. She could grill chicken without her mother's help, showed Claire how to squeeze the nectar from red honeysuckles, and tried to teach her how to carve whistles out of coconut shells and kamani seeds. Claire could never get her whistles to work.

But it had been Claire's idea to go looking for the little moons. They were eleven and watching a man pulling a hobie-cat boat with green and white sails onto shore. A little moon rolled and glistened in the leather sling that the man wore around his neck.

"My grandmother could give us her boat," Claire said suddenly.

"What?" Liv asked her.

"Her boat, Liv. If I asked her, Grammy might let us use her skiff to find little moons. I bet we could find a million more than that guy can."

Claire hadn't doubted her words. In her mind, when she and Liv were together, they were insurmountable. So it didn't surprise her when they spotted their first little moon a year and a half later. Liv had leapt fully clothed out of the skiff before it had even stopped moving and splashed through the waist-deep water until she reached the small, submerged glow. She sank down and when she came back up, clutching the little moon, her whole thin body was illuminated in blue.

It was because of Liv that Claire had trouble making friends. It wasn't that kids didn't like Claire—it was just that she wasn't interested in hanging out with anybody besides Liv. Frankly, the thought of trying to be friends with the other girls in her class appalled Claire. If she were forced to choose, she would rather spend time with a boy. The girls her age were conniving, scheming, shallow, dull, unbewitching things different from Liv's friendship as saltwater from fresh.

Once, when Claire was working on algebra in her attic bedroom after school, Liv burst in without knocking. She was wet and panting, her hands cupped together and stretched away from her body. Before Claire could move, Liv was at her nightstand, bending over the glass cup that Claire always kept by her bed, and opening her hands gently, gently. A thin stream of clear water, a tangle of seaweed, then the smallest green and blue pufferfish, tumbled into the glass. Liv in her white t-shirt, dripping, the afternoon sun coming in through the window, puddles shining on the wood floor.

***

It was after their fourth gathering trip in that September that Liv met James. Claire and Liv had set up a booth on the rim of the town square, right in between the bookstore and the sweet shop, to begin selling off their collection of little moons. Claire had yet to decide if she and Liv had gotten lucky or were just extremely talented. It was only three weeks into the season, and they had already found eleven little moons. It

was a pretty decent number, considering that most hunters had difficulty finding more than one.

The day was hot, and the sun burned on the stone pavement. In the middle of the square, the rushing of the town's mermaid fountain blended in with the rumbling of the sea. . Shoppers roamed, peered into shining windows, fanned themselves with the weekend edition of Lysonia Life, and argued over papaya and kiwi prices at the organic farmer's stands. Bells chimed whenever the jewelers' door opened, and the radio in front of Marvin's Grocery crackled out classical music. A freckled woman painted seascapes and mountain ranges in the shade of a mango tree, and a boy sat outside The Lion's Paw Café, eating a pumpernickel bagel.

Claire had covered the wheelbarrow full of their little moons with a striped towel and set up a beach umbrella for extra shade. Liv stood closer towards the Sunday crowd and held their sign out proudly.

Their first customer was a tiny girl in a calico dress who ran ahead of her mother. She passed over thirty dollars reverently and squealed when Liv placed a little moon gently in her hands. People came up and passed in quick succession then; an old man with a red bowler hat, a sunburnt teenage surfer boy, another boy with wild, curly hair, and a middle-aged woman with a silver nose ring.

"Sometimes I wonder," Claire said after three giggling girls had paid for their little moons and flounced away. The words had slipped out before she realized fully what she was about to say; perhaps it was the three girls, who looked so confident and hopeful, that had prompted the words she had only thought about for so long.

"Wonder what?" Liv had given up on standing and was lounging on the ground. She picked a dandelion out of a crack in the sidewalk and blew its seeds away. Claire hesitated, but she couldn't think of anything else to say besides the truth.

"The whole moon thing is just a bit ridiculous, that's all. If you think about it." She watched the seeds break apart and spiral towards the mermaid fountain. Two white puffs settled into the fountain's basin and were pummeled under by the churning water.

"What? Why?"

"I don't know," Claire said. "Just—how so many people actually will pay for them. Sure, the moons are pretty, but they can't really do anything, right? Love-wise, we don't know that they really work—

Liv wasn't listening. She was staring at the boy who had risen from his chair outside the café and was walking towards them. No, Claire thought in irritation, completely forgetting about the moons. He's not walking, he's sauntering. As he got closer, she saw that he was beautiful and that his hair gleamed like copper wires. He looked familiar, and Claire thought he might be a grade or two above them in school—he looked around fifteen. He went straight up to Liv and stuck out his hand.

"I'm James," he said. Claire noted with pleasure that his voice was high for his age. But Liv, stupidly, was blushing.

"Olivia," she said.

"That's a nice name," he said. He had the beginnings of stubble on his chin. He nodded at their emptying wheelbarrow. "You have a pretty good business going here."

"Oh," Liv said. "Yeah. Yeah, it's

all right. Thanks."

"It's more than all right," he said. "I had never seen so many moons in one place before."

Claire stepped out from behind their table. She felt a strange urgency to block Liv from James' view. "Would you like to buy one?" Her right hand drifted towards Liv's sleeve to pull her backward, but then she stopped herself.

"No thanks," James said. He didn't take his eyes off Liv, who kept flicking her own gaze from him, to the moons, to him.

"It's just that I was about to head down to the beach for a walk. Would you like to come with me, Olivia? If you need a break?"

Claire's pulse quickened. Liv blushed harder and hesitated. For a hopeful instant, Claire thought that Liv might refuse, but then James smiled at her— white, bright teeth—and Liv gave in.

"Sure," she said. "That sounds nice. My friend can watch the rest of the moons for a little bit. That's okay with you, Claire, right?" Both of them turned and looked at Claire. Two sets of amber, eager, distant eyes.

"But—

"You're the best. I'll be back soon," Liv said. She knelt on the sidewalk and tightened her bootlaces, her blonde hair swaying in thin strands across her cheekbones. She stood, smiled briefly, nervously at Claire. As they turned and walked away, Claire saw Liv look up at James at the same time that he looked down at her. Claire's stomach dropped, and she bit down on her tongue hard enough to draw blood.

Claire waited. An hour passed. The sun sank lower in the sky and cast long shadows into the streets. She sat beside the wheelbarrow, braiding blades of grass together that came apart in her hands. After another hour, the plaza emptied. Ladies with their full, rustling shopping bags and swinging purses trickled out slowly. A group of yelling boys in wet swim trunks pedaled past Claire on their bicycles. The grey-bearded man who ran the sweetshop locked its doors and walked away, whistling.

The boardwalk where Liv and James had disappeared remained vacant. After a young woman in a hat brimmed with sunflowers bought the second to last little moon, Claire packed up. She didn't feel like waiting around for the last one to sell.

She folded their table and put it into the wheelbarrow along with the umbrella and Liv's sign. She pushed the wheelbarrow home alone and tightened her grip whenever its wheels thumped over a gap in the cobblestone path.

Later that evening, Claire curled up in bed, her legs sliding and turning under the cool covers. The sky had turned a pearly grey and was steadily darkening. She wasn't planning on falling asleep. She thought she might get up soon to go sit on the roof—she could hear her mother cleaning the dinner dishes in the kitchen below, the rush of the sink going on and off—but the next thing she knew, she was being roughly shaken by a familiar hand. The room was dark, and the night outside was still and quiet.

"Claire," Liv whispered. "Wake up."

Claire sat up slowly. She propped herself on her elbows. Liv was sitting at the end of the bed, facing the window. Claire could tell that something had happened to her. Her voice was strained.

"Do we have any moons left?" Liv asked, still in a whisper. "Are there any left?"

Claire blinked. "There's one in the basket—

"It was amazing," Liv said, scrambling off the bed and leaping towards the applewood basket that Claire kept by the side of her bed. It took Claire a second to realize what she was talking about. "James, he's amazing, he goes to our school, did you know that? He's on the baseball team, but he only really does it 'cause his dad wants him too, he actually loves inventing things, that's his real passion and someday he wants to leave Lysonia so that he can go to a really good engineering school—

"Wait," Claire said. Liv was picking up the last little moon from the market and sliding it into one of Claire's canvas backpacks. "What—what's going on? What are you doing?"

"I've never felt this way about anybody, Claire. Never," Liz said in a hoarse whisper. "I can't take chances. You understand, don't you?"

"About James?" Claire said, disoriented. Liv was talking about the guy from the boardwalk? Liv liked him this much, so soon? How? What time was it? The whole room reeled.

"Yes," Liv said. She stood up and began to shrug the

backpack with the little moon onto her shoulders. The gesture shot a terrible pain through Claire's chest. In one motion, she scrambled upright, leapt off the bed, and grabbed the backpack strap before Liv could put it on all the way.

"You never came back to the market," Claire said. "You said you would." Her bare feet felt cold on the wood floor.

Liv stared at her. "I know." Her eyes gleamed in the shadows. "I'm sorry. James and I were having such a good time, and I didn't want it to end."

"Such a good time that— you forgot about me?" Liv had never abandoned her before. If anything, she was always the one to make sure that Claire was okay. And up until now, she paid as much attention to boys as Claire did, which was zero, nothing. Boys—especially boys as crushes—weren't something that Liv and Claire talked about.

"I'm sorry," Liv said again. Her voice was calm, but Claire could still sense the excitement straining behind it, and Claire thought of the way the ocean tide pulls back, hard, before a large wave thunders into shore.

"You're right, I should have come back. But listen, Claire, come with me now, okay? Come help me do this." Liv took the backpack off, placed it in Claire's arms, and without waiting for an answer, walked out of the room. The door remained open behind her.

Was it a dream, the way that she quietly slid on her sandals, followed Liv down the stairs and out into the warm salty night, the backpack heavy on her shoulders? A dream, the way that the island was black and grey under the full silver moon, the coconut trees tall and sentinel-like, the cobbled streets deserted and motionless? Life seemed frozen, and if she didn't know the island as well as she did, she might have been afraid.

It had to be a dream: Liv was beside her in the empty streets whispering directions, in a night that was unlike any of the nights they had spent together on her grandmother's skiff, occasionally murmuring to Claire something about what she and James had talked about, what James was like, and when she was going to see James again, and Claire couldn't listen to anything except his name, which was like a stab each time: James…James…James. It couldn't be real.

Later, Claire couldn't remember when they had found the white house that James had shown Liv. She wasn't sure how exactly she and Liv crawled on their bellies through dense bushes to get under James's window, or how long it took to dig a hole big enough to bury the little moon. She just knew that her resentment built with each movement of her shaking hands—this wasn't James's moon to have.

After the moon was buried, Claire and Liv sat in silence, staring at the lumpy ground. Claire wondered if Liv was thinking about how close James was. They could probably peek in the window and see him sleeping.

"Don't tell anyone," Liv whispered suddenly, squeezing her arm so hard that it hurt. "Promise?"

Claire ground her teeth; she felt loose grains of sands roll around her tongue and wanted to spit. Instead, she pressed her lips together.

"Come on, Liv, who would I tell?" She said it louder than she meant to. The only person she ever told secrets was Liv. Now she wanted to grab Liv by the shoulders and shake her

and hiss—snap out of it, look at what you're doing, how does this random boy mean anything to you?

Liv grinned and released Claire's arm. "Right, she said. "Let's go." She turned and began to crawl away through the bushes, twigs snagging on her hair and her shirt.

"It's just I don't think it's worth it," Claire whispered. "It's a waste of a little moon, that's all."

The night air was still, empty of a response except for the soft roar of the ocean and the whir of crickets. Claire sighed and began to crawl after her friend— but then doubt began sliding around in her head. What if, she thought, her left knee hovering right above the ground, the little moons really are completely powerless?

In that instant, watching Liv creep away without even looking back for her, Claire convinced herself of what she wanted to believe. This little moon was only good money buried in a sandy hole and nothing more— good money that she and Liv had worked hard for. It would do nothing under James' window. Sure, it was fine for those other people to buy moons if they wanted to; that was their personal business. But for Liv to just throw away a moon for James' sake when it wouldn't work anyway—well, it just wasn't right. Liv shouldn't be suckered into putting hope into something foolish, and this little moon would do much better in a wheelbarrow at the market. Then they would actually have something to gain.

Quickly, faster than she thought she could, Claire whipped around and dug her hands back into the ground. She scooped at the sand until her hands felt the cold, smooth surface of the little moon, and then she wrenched it up and threw it into her backpack. She zipped the backpack closed around the shining blue light, her hands trembling, and filled the hole back up, patting the sand so it looked like it had when Liv had left.

"Claire!" The whisper came around the corner of the house. Claire jerked her head , but she couldn't see Liv through the bushes, and the guilt that had rose at the thought of being caught subsided. You're doing this for Liv's own good, she reminded herself as she crawled away from the window towards Liv's voice. Branches scratched at her back. The backpack was heavy and dug into her shoulders. Once she was out of the shrubbery, she stood and dusted her hands off on her knees.

It wasn't until about fifteen minutes later when Liv turned on the corner that led to her street and Claire continued alone, that her stomach dropped. She realized with a bolt of fear that Liv would definitely know the difference.

"Stupid," Claire groaned under her breath to the dark, shuttered beach houses. Her heart was beating fast again. "Stupid, stupid." Of course Liv would notice if the little moon just showed up in the wheelbarrow. What was she thinking? The little moon had been the last one left, and Liz knew it. She rubbed her eyes with the heel of her hands. All of a sudden, she felt very tired. All she could think of was the way that Liv had looked up at James. She felt that Liv was leaving her for a strange place where she could not follow.

Claire could try to sneak the moon into their next cache when they went hunting out on the boat, but Liv was a stickler at counting the moons as they went into the applewood basket. She could just walk down to the boardwalk now, wade into the ocean, and throw the moon out into the dark water, but that would be a waste of a good moon too. And the thought of sticking it back under James' window—a whole shudder ran down her spine—was absolutely repulsive.

Slowly, her feet heavy, Claire turned around. She didn't feel like thinking it through. The street was shadowy, empty. The night breeze picked up and ruffled the yellow jessamine vines along the houses' wooden fence posts, leaves rustling like tiny whispers. She could almost hear it within the leaves, the voice that always uncurled inside her whenever she didn't know what to do:

Go to Liv.

It was natural. It was easy. She stumbled back towards Liv's street, where she had seen her friend pass only a few minutes ago, the streetlights gleaming on her golden hair. She didn't really know what she would do if she caught up to Liv, how she could explain herself, or even if she would show her the moon, but this, tracing Liv's footsteps, was what she knew how to do. She knew above everything else that she did not want to be alone.

Liv's house, like all the others, was dark. Even her bedroom light wasn't on. She must have slipped upstairs already and climbed into bed. Claire didn't have any doubt that she was asleep. Liv was the type of person that knocked out cold. At all of their sleepovers, Liv would fall asleep seconds after she and Claire finished their whispered conversation, while Claire would lie awake next to her and stare at the ceiling.

Now, looking up at Liv's second story window with its familiar blue curtains pulled tightly closed, an idea began to tap at the back of Claire's exhausted mind. She shook it away at first, like shaking water off after coming out of the ocean, but the idea swelled right back and clung.

What if... Claire frowned, tried to shake the idea away once more, but in its absence, another image barreled in: the nervous, unfamiliar smile that Liv had given Claire at the market.

Claire hunched her shoulders, tightened her grip on the backpack straps, and walked through Liv's front gate. She knew the yard by heart; even in the dark, she had no trouble stepping around the flowerbeds and the small rock pond. She knelt under Liv's window, and exactly like she and Liv had just done, dug a hole in the soft soil with her hands. This time, her hands didn't shake; she felt eerily calm.

She unzipped the backpack and pulled out the little moon. Its blue light spilled over the ground, illuminating scattered twigs and pebbles and a small line of black ants scurrying along the house's foundation. She placed the moon in the hole and covered it with dirt. Burying the moon under Liv's window was the right thing to do. Here, whatever happened, the moon would be harmless and she could protect Liv from putting too much false hope in James. It wasn't like she was trying to make the moon do anything to Liv; it just would be safe here until she found a good way to sneak it to market. And well, if something did happen to Liv— Claire sat back on her heels and took a deep breath—then she would know once and for all if the moons had any power.

When Claire got home that night and fell into bed with her dirty clothes on, she couldn't get the little moon out of her mind. She tossed and turned. The pillow grew hot and sweaty under her neck. When she finally fell asleep, she dreamed that she was out with Liv in the middle of the ocean and her grandmother's skiff was overflowing with little moons. The moons were rolling and clanking and the waves were swelling and tossing and Claire couldn't stop them—the moons began to roll out of the boat and sink down, down through the deep water. Liv sat by the bow, with her hands folded, unmoving. Help me, Claire said to her, help me, but Liv smiled and did nothing and with an ugly twist, her face shifted into James' face, and the moons continued to slide into the water, their light flushing everything— the velvet black sky, the freckles on James' neck, and the foamy rocking waves—with an intense tormenting blue, like the whole world had turned into lightning.

* * *

When they met to walk to school in the morning, Liv didn't talk about James or how they buried the moon under his window. Claire waited through the next couple days nervously—what if Liv decided to check on the little moon and discovered that it was missing? But Liv didn't bring the moon up. She was oddly silent, and

Claire couldn't help but wonder if the night really had been just a dream.

Three days later, while they were eating lunch outside on a picnic table, Claire asked tentatively how James was doing. Claire had been keeping an eye out for him at school but hadn't seen him. Liv turned red and said quickly: "Nothing, he hasn't texted me yet," and Claire felt such a fierce rush of relief that her fingertips tingled. She stopped herself from smiling at her turkey sandwich.

She watched Liv carefully the rest of the week, trying to decipher if Liv had changed in any significant way. She told herself that Liv was acting normal—if a little quiet and jumpy. But most importantly, Liv didn't mention James, and neither did Claire. In the gaps in their conversation and in the moments when she least expected it—brushing her teeth, staring at algebra equations, knocking on her grandmother's door—Claire's mind filled with the image of the little moon, shining blue under the dark soil by Liv's window.

She couldn't help it. The secret part of her that wanted so badly to believe in miracles, in inexplicable powers, and in life remaining good and happy with Liv forever, grew stronger and stronger each day. When she crawled under the covers at night, she would think hopefully: Maybe it's working. It's working.

* * *

A week passed. It was going to be their first night going moon hunting since the market, and Claire spent the day beaming, involuntarily bouncing on her toes. The thought of being on the ocean again with Liv sent shivers of anticipation down her spine

"You look happy tonight," her mother said, looking up from the pan of vegetables she was stir-frying. Claire shrugged, grabbed a handful of pretzels, and ran out the door.

"Remember, be back by ten!" her mom called.

The black sky curved like a bowl of smoke. Claire got to her grandmother's skiff right at eight. Five minutes later, when Liv still hadn't shown up, the happiness inside of Claire dimmed. Liv was never, ever late—not for moon hunting.

After twenty minutes of pacing back and forth on the sand, chewing at her nails, and kicking shells, the happiness was completely gone and replaced by an uneasy, slithering feeling. Where could Liv be? Could she have forgotten? Could something bad have happened to her? Was she grounded again? Could she be with—

Liv materialized out of the darkness. She had strolled up to the skiff so casually that Claire hadn't heard her approach.

"What's up?" Liv said and Claire was at once so happy to see her and so stunned by her lack of apologies or excuses that all she could say back was: "Nothing." Together, they pushed the skiff into the water.

As they steered towards the sandbars, Liv didn't talk. She hummed instead, and she kept turning her face away to smile. Claire tried multiple times to start a conversation, but Liv just nodded and smiled wider each time, as if she was thinking of something secret and wonderful. After Liv dived for the first little moon and cradled it in her hands instead of putting it in the applewood basket, Claire couldn't take it any longer. She yanked the motor to idle and crossed her arms.

"Liv!" Her voice sounded loud to her own ears. "What happened? Why are you acting so weird?"

Liv looked up. She tucked her hair behind her ears, and the proud look in her eyes made Claire think that Liv had just been waiting for her to ask.

"James," Liv said, like she was savoring the name. Claire's stomach plummeted. Liv looked at the little moon glowing blue in her hands. "He came to my house right after school, after you left."

Claire tried to swallow her anger and failed. It didn't work after all, she thought savagely, and in that moment, she hated every single little moon in the world. "What did he want?"

"Well," Liv said. "He told me that he was sorry that he hadn't texted me all week." Her feet tapped against the bottom of the skiff. "His phone doesn't work all the time, but he said—he said he missed me so much that he had to come see me."

"How do you know he's telling the truth?"

"What? No, I mean, he came to see me."

"So? That doesn't mean anything."

"It does," Liv insisted. "He wouldn't have come if he didn't care. Also"—she blushed and fidgeted, the pride flashing in her eyes—"he kissed me. So. There."

He kissed me. Claire's head felt like it was going to explode. She saw it, the way that James would have leaned in, his copper hair falling across his eyes, how Liv would have put one of her wiry hands on his chest and wrapped the other around his neck—she saw it so clearly and she hated the little moons for letting it happen, she was so disgusted by their stupid, stupid legend, what love could these moons possibly inspire—

"Whatever," Claire said out loud. "I just can't believe that you were late tonight."

"What?" Liv raised her eyebrows defensively, incredulously. "Really? You're upset about that?"

"We have a schedule, Liv, and I don't think you're taking it seriously anymore."

Liv scoffed, but Claire could tell that she was starting to get mad. Her back had stiffened, and her fingers tightened around the little moon. "This was one time, Claire, lay off—also, don't you care? Aren't you happy for me? I just had my first kiss, and you're—

"You must love him so much to come late to moon hunting," Claire said. She couldn't keep the sneer from her voice. She was so angry she couldn't see straight. "You love James."

"I do not," Liv snapped, her color rising.

"You do."

"I don't, okay? I just really like him! He's nice! I'm sorry that I was late, I just figured you would understand since I was having my first kiss—

"You can tell me, Liv, just say it. I want to hear you say that you love him. Say—

Liv rolled her eyes, and furiously, Claire grabbed the little moon from Liv's hands and threw it against the side of the skiff as hard as she could. The little moon exploded in a cloud of shattering blue, and Liv cried out. Tiny chunks of shell, as sharp as glass, were embedded in her right leg. Drops of blood welled around the shells. At the sight of Liv's blood, Claire's anger instantly turned into horror.

"I'm so sorry, Liv, God, I'm sorry—

"You idiot, Claire, what the hell—

"I'm sorry, Liv, I didn't mean it, I swear—

Liv shoved Claire's hands away. She didn't even bother looking at her leg. .

"What is wrong with you—leave me alone! Don't touch me!" She wrenched the tiller around and turned her back on Claire, her shoulders tight.

"I love you," Claire said. The words hung like lanterns in the blue air, bright and laden with desperation. Her fingers shook, her ears roared. The boat rocked, and Claire thought distantly, as if she was suddenly very far away or looking down from the sky at the black silhouettes of her and Liv in the skiff, that Liv would turn and was turning even now. She could see it. Liv's face might be clear and open, that her narrow chin might dip in understanding and acceptance, and that she would take back Claire's hands and hold them until they stopped trembling. Brief flashes of intangible possibilities, like the shining screen of an old silver movie flicking through different scenes: of Liv standing and swaying in the boat with uneven grace, Liv biting down on her red lip and leaning forward fractionally with her wet palms on her wet thighs, Liv tilting her head to consider Claire, her neck a smooth, vulnerable curve, Liv raising her shoulders in a simple shrug and a small smile.

But in the space of a breath, in only the time that it took for Claire to swallow, Liv spoke. She kept her hand on the tiller and her gaze forward over the dark sea. Above, the stars burned thick and white.

"Love you too, Claire," Liv said, as unforgiving and hard as an unexpected rock bed in deep water.

Claire squeezed her eyes shut and then opened them to stare at Liv's unmoving back. The urge to apologize again dragged through her, but she could not find the right words. Neither of them spoke during the rest of the ride back to the dock and when they reached shore, all Claire could hear was the murmuring scurry of the fiddler crabs escaping into their holes. ◉

Little Moons

Con Chapman is a Boston-area writer whose work has appeared in The Atlantic, The Christian Science Monitor, The Boston Globe, and various literary magazines. Writing is not his full-time job, so he has to find time as best I can at the beginning or the end of the day and hope that the muse can find him (assuming he's awake in the morning, and not too tired at night). Readers can find his work on his author page at Gerbil News Network, named after his book on the 1978 Red Sox-Yankees pennant race "The Year of the Gerbil." Gerbil News Network features his fake news, parodies, first-person humor and extremely bad poetry. An empty-nester with two grown sons, he lives in the suburbs of Boston with his wife Laura and their pet Komodo dragon, Fritzy.
(conchapman.wordpress.com).

One of Us

CON CHAPMAN

*R*achel was, without a doubt, the most popular woman on campus. So many of the women were drones, the men horny, that it left her a fairly broad canvas on which to paint her personality. She didn't understand why everybody in Hyde Park had to be so gloomy and studious all the time. She smiled at people because she was a happy person. She'd always been a happy person—why should she change just because she decided to go to a college where everyone had been a high school valedictorian?

Maybe she'd made a mistake attending college, but there was scholarship money available. She hadn't been accepted by her first choice, so she'd transplanted herself from the suburbs of Boston to Chicago–and she wasn't going to stop living for four years just to get good grades. Life would take care of itself.

She introduced a few innovations to the campus social scene for which she'd become well-known, even infamous. She took off her blouse at concerts, a breach of decorum even at a school that had a clothing-optional dance every year on Valentine's Day. It made a lot of people uncomfortable. She had learned from reading Claude Levi-Strauss that even primitive societies impose standards of propriety--still, she didn't care. Rachel's bare breasts would flop about, her ivory New England skin in sharp contrast to the dark gym where the white rock bands and black blues musicians would play. It made other women uncomfortable since her conduct raised expectations among the men. It made many men uneasy when she would try to drag them on to the dance floor, they in their finest dishabille, she in blue jean bell-bottoms and nothing else.

By senior year, she'd flirted with, won, and taken as her lover, a drummer for a group that played there. This was a conquest that set her apart from other campus beauties. They would never confess to be interested in someone as plebian as a rock musician. In his case, however, they were still interested—they just couldn't admit it; there had in fact been a wave of revulsion against the browbeaten academic types into which the women had turned the men on campus, hammering them on the anvil of liberation. Since "her" drummer was on the road a lot, Rachel functioned as a sort of dowager empress to the social scene, appearing at every party and concert, conferring blessings on all. She made the rounds urging people to break down the walls of repression that kept them from feeling and expressing universal love for each other. Other people would write the great novels, or make big scientific discoveries, or run for office. She'd decided that her mission in life was to bring people together.

It was at a potluck dinner at the feminist coffeehouse that she ended up sitting next to Mark and Linda. They were a quiet couple on the fringes of the floating social scene that centered around her apartment, with its four male and one other female occupants. Mark wore his hair Cherokee-style, long, with a headband to keep it out of his eyes. Linda's hair was essentially the same but without the headband. They both wore glasses and were a little paunchy from study and no exercise. Early on in their college days, they had decided that they were soul-mates. As such, they found no reason to join in the drinking and drugs and casual sex that other students indulged in. Others were striving towards . . . something. They had arrived at their destination.

"So, you're into astrology?" Mark asked with a rising tone in his voice as he noticed Rachel's necklace with the Pisces symbol on it.

"Yeah—it's cool."

"We are too," Linda said eagerly.

"There's a lot of stuff out there that you won't learn in class," Rachel said, a phrase she frequently used to put down those she considered too studious.

"For sure," Mark agreed. "I'm doing an independent study on world religions, and I think I'm on the verge of proving how they outweigh a lot of scientific skepticism."

"Wow!" Rachel exclaimed. "I dated a pre-med student last year, and I basically talked him out of med school. He's into holistic medicine now."

"That is so wonderful!" Linda said.

They ate the potluck fare—lentil soup, vegetarian lasagna, and carrot-raisin salad. Rachel was glad for the company—her drummer was out of town, and she felt better having people to talk to.

"Why don't you guys come back to my apartment?" she asked when they had bussed their dishes and were ready to leave.

"Sure—we'd love to," Mark said. He always seemed to speak first, she noticed, but the two of them were so obviously in love she respected whatever order of precedence they had worked out between themselves.

They made it back to her place—it was empty except for Phil, an anthropology major, who was holed up in his room, as usual. "Do you guys want some tea?" she asked; both of them said yes, so she boiled some water and made a pot of chamomile.

They went into the common room, and Rachel put on some soft folk music, figuring it was appropriate for the mood and the company.

"So what else are you guys into?" she asked when they had settled themselves.

"Oh, lots of stuff. Out-of-body experiences, astral projection." He let this hang in the air for a second, then turned a beaming smile on Rachel.

"Really?" Rachel said. "Have you . . . done it?"

"Oh, yes!" Linda said. "It's a totally different world."

"And we're getting into weather control," Mark said.

"Can you really do that?" Rachel asked, trying to sound supportive and not skeptical.

"There are people out on the west coast, in Seattle, who are experimenting with it," Mark said.

"Because of all the rain," Linda added.

"They got together because of politics, but they soured on that, and now they're getting into more cosmic things," Mark said.

"Huh—I see," Rachel said as she sipped her tea.

"I'd like to be able to use it here during the winter," Linda said. "It gets so grey here in the winter. In the spring, it's like you traded in a black-and-white TV for a color set!"

They all laughed, and Rachel got up to change the music. She put on a record whose album cover had a pentangle on it, and Mark picked it up from the floor to look at it.

"The pentagram has magical powers, you know," he said to Rachel.

"That's what I've heard, but I don't know too much about it," she replied.

"The five points represent the planets Mercury, Jupiter, Mars, Saturn and Venus—Queen of the Heavens."

"Mark is very sympathetic to the women's movement," Linda said.

"Unh-huh," Rachel said.

"The Pythagorean version has two legs pointing up," Mark said, as he turned the album cover to demonstrate. "That's where the children of the pre-cosmos were during their gestation before the cosmos to be born. The divine products of the seed of Chronos were deposited in the five recesses."

Rachel looked as he pointed to the album cover. "Do you guys want some more tea?" she asked.

"I'm fine," Linda said.

"I'm okay," Mark said. "Rachel," he said when they had all been silent for a moment.

"Yes?"

"We're glad you asked us over tonight."

"I'm glad you guys could come. You're always so quiet—you just hang back at parties and don't dance or get drunk or anything. It's neat how you're so—self-contained."

"Yes," Mark said, his voice trailing off. "You know, we've been watching you for some time."

"Watching me?" Rachel said, surprised. "Why?"

"With admiration." Linda chimed in. "We think you're so nice!"

"I like you guys," Rachel said. "It takes all kinds of people to make the world go round."

"Precisely," Mark said. "But there are certain special kinds of people who are necessary for the universe to work out its destiny."

Rachel noted a change in his tone; he'd turned serious, rather pedantic as he said this.

"You mean like . . . visionaries?"

"Sort of," Mark said. "People who push the boundaries of convention."

"I'm all for that," Rachel said with a smile, feeling they were back on familiar ground.

"Rachel—we think you're one of us," Mark blurted out.

"One of you?"

"One of the chosen ones. One of the ones who will leave this planet and time-plane, and progress to a higher evolutionary plateau."

Rachel looked at Linda, who was nodding at her, smiling. "I-guess I don't know what you mean," Rachel said.

"Certain people," Mark continued, "are chosen to carry out the will of the universe as it unfolds. We have experienced the life force, and we think you are a living embodiment of it."

Rachel looked at Mark, and for the first time, her face revealed uneasiness. "So . . . what are you saying?"

"We'd like you to join us in our astral travels!" Linda said, smiling even broader than she had been.

"I—that's great. Thanks. I'll. . . think about it."

"You could come over to our

place—we live by ourselves if you'd be embarrassed around your roommates," Mark said.

"That's. . . okay, they're hardly ever here," Rachel said, then realized she might have put herself in a corner, as she now had no excuse if they wanted to start doing. . . whatever they did . . . right then and there.

"You don't need to be in any special place," Linda said. "You just need to have the desire, then overcome the fear."

"What's there to be afraid of?" Rachel asked.

"Some people think once they leave their body, they might not make it back. The truth is, when you achieve separation, lots of times you'll be in such a beautiful place you won't want to come back!" Mark said.

As open as Rachel wanted to be to new experiences, and as nice as Mark and Linda were, getting into particulars of the subject made it all seem slightly daft. She scolded herself that her rational mind was taking over when it should have withheld judgment, but she couldn't stop herself. The fact that her potential fellow travelers' bodies were flabby didn't help; it was hard to imagine fleet souls flying out of them.

"So do you want to try it now?" Linda asked eagerly.

"Uh, I don't think so. Not tonight anyway."

"It can be scary," Mark said. "You may hear radio waves, or you feel them. Or see unearthly beings."

"How would I know? I think aliens could blend in pretty easily with the people around here." They all laughed.

"One night, I'd been trying to get out of my physical body for like a half-hour but couldn't," said Mark. "I lay back and tried again, visualizing each muscle from my feet to my head. I started to vibrate and did the rope trick."

"What's that?" Rachel asked.

"You imagine a rope hanging down to you from the ceiling, then you use your astral body to grab hold of the rope and start climbing," Linda said.

"I could never climb a rope in gym class." Rachel laughed, but this time the other two didn't join her.

"It worked," Mark said. "I reached the ceiling, then exited my body and began to explore the astral plane."

"What . . . does all that mean?"

"Each of us has a physical body, and an astral body," Linda said. "The astral body is separate from the physical body—a good thing in my case."

She smiled. Then Mark smiled as if in reflection of hers, like the moon catching the light of the sun.

Rachel looked from Linda back to Mark. "So . . . what happens then?"

"Your astral body leaves your physical body, and you begin to travel on the astral plane."

"You're dreaming, but you're wide awake," Linda interjected meekly.

"I could see my body from up where I was," Mark said. "I could look down into our apartment."

"So . . . is it just relaxing, or do you feel like you're floating, or what?" Rachel asked.

"It can be a wild ride sometimes," Mark said.

"Like how?"

Mark swallowed and looked at Linda, who nodded at him and said: "Go on–tell her."

"The time I'm talking about? I saw four alien beings in our kitchen. They were faceless, and they wore monk's robes."

"That's. . . creepy," Rachel said.

"Yes but it was . . . pleasantly creepy," Mark said. "My skin was crawling, like at a good suspense movie."

"They didn't mean him any harm," Linda added in a comforting tone.

"They turned and saw my physical body lying in the next room, and they rushed in," Mark said. "Then they began to examine me."

"Like they wanted to help you, or what?" Rachel asked.

"Yeah, like I was some kind of wounded animal or roadkill. It was like they were trying to decide if I was on the plane of existence they'd come down to, or if I'd gone higher."

Rachel felt a gust of wind off the lake blow across her neck from the bay window that looked out onto the street. It cooled the perspiration that had formed there, which she hadn't noticed before.

"So . . . did you come down from the ceiling?"

"No. I heard a voice come out of me—it wasn't mine. I was speaking in a language I didn't recognize—it was gobbledygook, Greek to me–I couldn't repeat it if I tried. They heard me and looked up. They saw me and flew toward me."

"Geez," Rachel said involuntarily.

"They blew past me, or rather through me."

"Mark told me it was like smoke being blown into a bottle," Linda said.

"And . . . you were the bottle?" Rachel asked him.

Mark nodded.

"So something was infused in me that night. Before, I would just stumble through my days, like a bumper car. Hit one thing, go on to the next. Now, it's like I have a new prescription in my glasses. I can see things more clearly, I understand where their boundaries are. I know where they're going to go next."

"Wow," Rachel said, falling back on a simple expression of wonder that she hoped would bring the story—and the evening—to a conclusion. "And you're here today to tell about it."

"The thing is," Mark said, "I think you were there—before me."

"Me?"

"Yes, you. I think the lightning that struck me that night, I think it just brought me up to your level of consciousness."

"I agree," Linda said, nodding her head, her eyes opening wider. "You're light years ahead of where we are. So we want you to join us—and take us higher."

"Me?"

"You have extraordinary powers that you don't even know about!" Linda said with more emphasis than Rachel had ever heard her use before. "The way you bring people together and make them happy."

"We've watched what you do at dances and concerts. It's like you're. . . Dionysus at an ancient Greek fertility festival or something."

"Gosh, I don't. . ."

"No, seriously. He's the god of wine, and ecstasy, and madness. He communicated between the living and the dead. It's like you're the leader of the maenads."

"Who were they?"

"The raving ones," Mark said with a leer. "They feed the dead with blood-offerings. Dionysus is like Jesus. He dies and is resurrected, only time and again."

"But you guys . . . don't even drink—do you?"

"I like a little sip of wine," Linda said with a giggle.

"Too much wine isn't good for you, but a little is good to get you started. I prefer pot and fruit. It's better fuel for your journey."

Rachel inhaled, then let her breath out as if she were doing yoga. Mark watched her closely as she did so. "There's no rush," he said. "We realize that in the great chain of being, we are really subservient to you."

Rachel tried to smile, but the expression that covered her lips had more the air of queasiness. "I'm not sure I'm ready. Sounds like a pretty heavy experience."

"But you're already there," Linda said. "You could pull us up to where you are."

"That's the other thing," Rachel said. "Not sure I'm ready for the, uh, responsibility. I haven't been in charge of anything since I was fifth-grade class president."

The two smiled at her. "Okay, well, think about it," Mark said, "and we hope that when it's finally time for us to blast out of this godforsaken state of being, you'll lead the way."

They were all quiet after this explanation, and Rachel looked down into her mug. "Sure," she said. "I'll think about it. And I'll talk to my boyfriend about it. I'd want him to—to come along."

Mark's face lost its glow when she said this. "The drummer? The tall guy with the leather jacket?"

"Right."

"I'm not sure he's qualified to move on to the next level of consciousness," Mark said.

"He's kind of a breeder, isn't he?" Linda asked.

"Breeder?"

"You know, his end in life is to produce lots of offspring, to sow his seed among the fields of the earth," Linda explained.

"I don't know. We always make sure we use birth control."

"He seems, you know, very macho," Mark said. "I think he's probably one of the earth-bound ones."

They were silent again, and Rachel decided she would feel better—freer, easier—if she stood up. Maybe that would help bring the tone of their talk down out of whatever layer of the atmosphere it had risen to.

"So, we'll wait to hear from you," Mark said, taking her change of position as a sign that the evening was over.

"We really want to follow you to the next level," Linda said, her face aglow with pure joy.

"Sure. I'll think about it," Rachel said, moving towards the door that opened into the hall.

"That's great," Mark said. "We really appreciate it."

"Goodnight, pretty lady," Linda said. "We love you so much!" Linda hugged her gently, so lightly it was as if there were nobody there. Mark stood behind her and beamed at the two of them.

"Goodnight—lots of love to you guys," Rachel replied.

Rachel closed the door behind them, then walked down the hall to her room. She lay down on her mattress and looked out the window to the building across the alley, with the moon hanging above it. She didn't know whether she believed in the things that Mark and Linda had described to her. She decided to try the routine Mark had described to her. She lay down on her back, closed her eyes, and folded her hands on her chest, level with her heart. She focused her consciousness on her feet, then her ankles, and proceeded slowly up her body with a mental spotlight on each separate body part until it relaxed, then tingled, then began to vibrate with the hum of the city around her. It was as if she could feel the power lines and the telephones and the radio and television signals flying through the air, through her body, which felt as porous as a colander by the time she reached her neck. There she let her thoughts rest for a minute before pushing them up the last step to her head–which seemed aglow with the energy she'd collected from the world around her by simply tuning out.

She tried to imagine the place where her drummer was playing that night. After a few moments, she seemed to be sitting in a club—for some reason, she knew it was Los Angeles–at a table by herself, looking at the bandstand, while her drummer played along with the band.

The lead guitarist was playing an extended solo as her drummer looked out into the audience. She smiled at him, but he didn't seem to notice. He seemed to be looking at a point slightly behind her and smiling—but not at her.

She turned in her vision and saw a young woman, younger than her, and slimmer. She had blonde hair and was batting eyelashes at her drummer, smiling, trying as hard to get him into the sack as she had when she'd first seen him. She sensed they were progressing from flirtation to consummation at a speed that defied the laws of both love and physics.

She decided to leave the club, quietly, so as not to make a scene. She saw herself scooting between tables, excusing herself from rapt fans nodding their heads in time with the music.

When she reached the door of the club, a bouncer directed her down a spiral staircase. With each step, her legs grew heavier, her breath shorter. She was aware that she wasn't dreaming, but she didn't think of herself as awake, either. She was following a force that drew her onward into an unseen field of resistance, like a wind that made no sound.

At the bottom of the stairs, there was a black door with a red and white EXIT sign above it. She pushed it open and saw— an empty bed. She exhaled–she could breathe freely again.

Rachel opened her eyes, back in her physical body, and stared up at the ceiling. She sensed someone . . . or something . . . in the darkened room with her. She propped herself up on one elbow and looked around.

She stepped out into the hall and saw two people—a man and a woman–peeking around the corner that led into the kitchen.

The man wasn't Phil, the anthropology major; he had a

beard, and the man down the hall was clean-shaven, head and face, almost mummy-like in appearance. She couldn't see the woman, who had ducked back out of sight.

"Hello," she said tentatively. "Who is that?"

She heard the two mumble in a sort of pidgin tongue. Some words seemed familiar to her, but she could derive no sense from the whole of what they said.

"Hello?" she said again. "Who are you?"

The mumbling grew louder, and then the two flew at her in a formless roar, like a tornado funnel bearing down on her. She felt them blow into her and through her like Mark had said, and screamed weakly, unable to give full voice to her fear.

She made it back into her room, shut the door, and turned on the lights, dispelling the sense of the uncanny that had pervaded the apartment moments before.

Then a knock.

"Rachel?" her roommate asked through the door.

"Is that you, Phil?" she asked, her voice quavering a bit.

"Yeah. You okay?"

"Yes, I . . . just had a nightmare is all."

"Were you sleepwalking?"

"I guess you could say so. I'm all right now."

"I'm making some coffee—do you want some?"

"No, I think I'd rather go back to sleep. But thanks."

"Okay. Good night."

She turned off the overhead light, turned on her desk lamp, and got under her covers, fully-clothed. She needed the glow from the low-watt bulb to feel safe.

She rolled over and buried her head in her pillow.

She wished she could undo the evening, hadn't sat next to Mark and Linda, never spoken to them—that she could be alone with her drummer now, far away, and not where she was. ◉

Ah, the crisis of explaining **Patrick Borosky's** story of his emergence into the world of writing. His first career in the world involves working with the latest high-tech equipment to ensure that the denizens of this world can sleep at night. Honestly, he loves his job, yet on one fateful project where he had nothing to do and boredom threatened to consume him, he thought to himself: "I guess I'll try writing a book then." He recently self-published an eBook titled "The World of Ato." As for other short story publications, there is "Barely Human" published by The Flying Ketchup Press and "Dancing Colors" published by Curating Alexandria in May 2019. He may even have a secret love story that he's working on. Reach out to him on all social media sites, and enjoy getting lost in his worlds!

Barely Human

Patrick Borosky's

*I*t was cold. However, it wasn't the same type of cold that one normally encounters. It was a cold that started from the left side of his body. As time passed, it slowly crept from his side until it reached what would normally be his kidney, and then by midday, it had edged its way slightly past his belly button. He lay there silently – unable to stop the inevitable fate of when the chill would consume him.

He could hear the clattering footsteps of people walking by and ignoring his existence. He felt their lifeless shadows robbing him of the little warmth that remained. At first, he had hope that one person would spare a second of their time to help him. One by one, person by person, he eventually discovered how dreadfully naïve that dream was. Of course, he tried to move himself, but with the relentless cold, his limbs became heavy, and any means to help himself simply disappeared. The feeling had become his existence. This was his life, one he had grown accustomed to.

"Hello, there. Are you all alone too?"

He didn't know where the voice came from, not to mention that it took him a while to realize that it was even addressing him, as no one had ever bothered to say a single word to him before. This newcomer's shadow covered him like the rest, but unlike the others, it dawdled and continued to blanket him. He attempted to turn his head to discover its source but found that he couldn't.

Luckily, the darkness shifted, and soon, the shadow had an owner. A small girl who couldn't have been older than eight stared at him with a shockingly deep-brown eye that bordered on black. It almost didn't seem human. It was more akin to the eye of a doll that a girl her age would normally be playing with at this time of the day. The other eye was cloaked by unkempt dirty-blonde hair–"dirty" or simply covered in filth.

She continued to stare at him as if she were expecting an answer from him, but when she didn't get one, she continued talking as though he had. "Me too. If you can believe it, I've been alone most of my life."

I've always been alone.

She gave him a small smile that was slightly shy but, at the same time, bright. "Don't worry. Now that I've found you, you won't have to be alone anymore. I promise that I'll take good care of you."

A promise is a heavy thing. Don't regret it later.

With little effort, she grabbed him by his arm and lifted him out of the icy puddle where she had found him. The water fled from his body and flowed freely into the puddle that he had finally escaped. The shyness in her smile disappeared, and now it widened as she brought him closer to get a better look at him.

"What's your name, little guy?" she asked.

It is... Honestly, I can't remember. He scrambled his brain, trying to remember his name.

She turned him upside down and then backward, twisting him all about to see every nook and cranny that his being offered. It was almost as if she were expecting to find his name written somewhere on his body. Eventually, she returned him upright so that he faced her, and she contorted her face as if she were thinking of something dreadfully important.

"Let's see... some people would call a fine bear like yourself 'Teddy,' but you're mine now, so I couldn't possibly give you a boring name like that."

She bit her lip and twisted her face even more until it began to turn a deep red as she continued to ponder. All at once, the shade vanished, and her mouth shifted easily back to her smile, which fit her face ever so perfectly.

"I've got it!" she proclaimed so loudly that some of the people around her turned to see what all the fuss was about. "Your name is Stitch on account of your missing left eye and because someone stitched you right back up."

It's not like I want to be missing an eye. I don't even remember how I lost it. I had completely forgotten about it until you had to dredge it back up.

"Don't worry about it. I know it isn't your fault," she said. She then leaned her face a bit closer to his and whispered, "Besides, if anything, it gives you a little more character, like it does mine."

Before he could even wonder what she meant by that, the young girl took one of her hands and moved the hair that covered her left eye to reveal a deep scar that ran vertically across it. Although the eye itself wasn't damaged, instead of the near-black color of her right, it was a cloudy white – completely lifeless.

She let go of her hair, and it effortlessly hid the eye so that no one else could see it. "Oh, come on, now. Don't give me that look."

I'm sorry. This is the face I was born with. It wasn't like a teddy bear could change his face on demand.

"I told you, didn't I? I'm fine with it," she said with an uncomfortable grin that told him otherwise. She paused for a second before saying another word and then shot up with excitement. "I never gave you my name! I'm Rory! It's nice to

meet you, Stitch!"

He stared at her without blinking, which was the only thing that he could do because he couldn't blink to begin with. Now that I think about it, I think Stitch is a rather nice name. It's not like I had a name before I met you, anyway.

After that, he became Stitch, and for the first time that he could remember, he felt the cold slowly receding from his belly button and down his paws as Rory carried him away from his puddle. After thinking about it a bit more, though, he decided that it was most likely because he had lost most of the water that had built up within his body over time.

"Let's see, what should we do now?" said Rory as she wandered down a crowded street. She kept on glancing nervously behind her as if she were expecting someone to be there. But every time, she would only see faceless onlookers who walked by her while paying her no mind.

She held Stitch gingerly against her chest as if she were afraid that he would suddenly jump from her arms. After a while, the crowd dispersed, and Stitch noticed that she had a rather disgruntled look on her face. She lifted him up, bringing his stomach inches away from her nose, and gave him a hearty sniff.

"Oh my gosh, Stitch! What was in that alleyway? You smell like you were dragged through a pile of cow pies, found a skunk, got sprayed for kicks just to see what it was like, and then nestled under a nice pile of hot garbage for an afternoon nap!"

She tore him away from her nose and made a gagging motion. "This can't do... I like you, Stitch, but if we're going to be friends, you'll have to start taking better care of yourself."

I think you should look at yourself in the mirror. You don't look that much better yourself. You're lucky that I can't smell you, because I'm guessing you don't smell like a freshly picked rose yourself.

"There's no way around it, then," she said, nodding her head. "We'll just have to give you a bath and wash off some of this grime that you've become so fond of."

Rory picked up her feet and began jogging down the street, artfully and effortlessly dipping and dodging past the people around her. The crowd grew thinner and thinner until she cut a hard right turn down an alley that led her to a flight of steep steps. As she neared the bottom, she jumped the last two and landed on a poorly paved path with a loud thud. Stitch now faced an area flush with green and a small creek that he could hear cascading against rocks as they approached.

Rory bent over the creek and gave him a mournful expression. "I'm sorry, Stitch, but you're going to have to bear with it for a moment."

Ah, I see what you did there.

Then, without any warning, Rory dipped Stitch right into the creek's water. The brief feeling of finally being dry escaped him, and his entire body felt about three times heavier as water flooded into him. However, as the water poured through him, he could see the dirt and grime that he'd accumulated over time wash away. Rory gripped a portion of her shirt sleeve and began scrubbing him with all her might. Stitch was quite lucky that he was a teddy bear; otherwise, he was sure that he'd be rather uncomfortable, if not in a good deal of pain, as Rory's face was quickly turning beet red from all the effort she was putting into cleaning him.

She's also lucky that I don't have to breathe, thought Stitch, who'd been underwater for at least five minutes now.

After Rory was satisfied that Stitch had become somewhat clean, she lifted him out of the water and gave him a hard, appraising look. She gave him a cute grin, which was rather misleading as she suddenly started twisting his entire body to get him dry again. He was pretty sure that a bear's back wasn't supposed to bend that way – let alone his neck.

"There we go," said Rory breathlessly. It seemed like she had tired herself out after all the work. She put him next to her nose again, gave him one good sniff, and said triumphantly, "You don't smell good, but at least I can stand being near you now!"

I'm pretty sure that wasn't a compliment. Stitch couldn't stay angry at Rory for long. Even though the entire ordeal had been rather hectic, she had done it with the best of intentions, and he couldn't fault her for that. Plus, with the way she was smiling at him and how proud she looked, he couldn't hate her even if he tried.

Sadly, their moment of happiness didn't last long as, from the corner of his eye, Stitch saw an object fly out of nowhere and hit Rory right in the side of the head. The shock of it made her let go of Stitch, and as he fell, he saw the object that had hit her, a rather large rock, falling to the ground with him.

Stitch was facing the sky, and he could see Rory clasping the side of her face where the rock had hit her. A small trickle of blood slowly dripped down the side of her face as another rock flew past her – barely missing her.

"Come on, now! You can do better than that!" yelled a boy. "She wasn't moving or nothing!"

Rory didn't say anything, but her expression, which had once been so bright, had become almost lifeless. She took her hands from where the rock had struck her, revealing a nasty gash on the side of her face, and picked up Stitch. She held him tightly to her chest, as if doing so would protect her, and faced her attackers.

Stitch could now see a group of three children. They were at least a couple of years older than Rory and had nasty smirks on their face.

With each step the three took

toward Rory, she took a step back into the creek and fell with a loud splash.

It was now the third time in one day that Stitch had become drenched in water, and once the water settled, he could hear the loud, maniacal laughter of the three children. They made their way to the side of the creek and pointed their nasty fingers at Rory as they continued to laugh.

"You better watch where you step! We don't want you to hurt yourself. That's our job!" said one of the boys, the tallest of the bunch.

"Yeah, that's right," chimed in the girl, who had bent over to get a better look at Rory. "We don't want your face to be marked up more than it already is, do we?"

Stitch felt a flame burning in the pit of his gut. He had experienced so much in one day that he had never experienced before. He'd felt his normal bit of despair as he'd lain in his puddle, powerless to even move; however, he had also felt pure bliss from this small girl who had expanded his world. But now... now he felt nothing but hatred for these three children who stood over him. Honestly, he couldn't even call them children. To Stitch, they were nothing but little monsters who enjoyed the suffering of others.

He wanted to stop them–give them the same torment that they had given Rory and to see their frightened faces as they got their just desserts.

The rude girl flung her arm forward, grabbed the hair that covered Rory's scarred eye, and then yanked it hard so they could all gawk at it. She scrunched up her face, acting sick, and said, "I don't know how you can live with something like this. I wouldn't be able to stand looking in the mirror if I had a face like yours."

The three roared with laughter. Rory lifted her arm and smacked the girl's hand from her hair. Then she stumbled back onto her feet and put some distance between them once again. The rude girl cradled her hand and looked at it as if something dirty had just touched her.

"Oi, what do you think you're doing?" said the last boy, who had remained rather quiet aside from joining in the laughter with his friends. He was rather bulkier than the other two, and when he decided to speak, the other two immediately stopped their laughter. In fact, they looked like they'd have preferred to run away from him. "Don't you remember the last time when you tried to fight back?"

The boy jumped into the water with a loud splash. Stitch felt his body shake. At first, he thought it was from his anger, but soon he realized that it was because Rory had begun trembling uncontrollably at the emergence of the new child. He towered over her, motioned toward the girl of the group, and demanded, "Apologize to her...now."

Rory faced the ground and turned her head from him. She said in an awkward, frightful voice, "I' m... I'm ...sorry."

The other girl didn't say anything in response but only watched with bated breath, wondering what her friend would do next.

The boy scoffed and pushed Rory back into the creek. The other two laughed, but he just looked at her with disgust. He seemed like he'd be more than satisfied if he never saw her face again. "Next time, you take what you deserve. You're lucky that we have to be somewhere, or you'd be getting a lot worse right now. You stay there where you belong, and don't let me see you getting back to your feet until we're gone." The boy raised his hand, and Rory instinctively flinched. He let out a single hearty bellow and made his way out of the creek. His friends did not laugh at this, but as the bulky boy walked down the path leading back to the city, they followed him without a single word. He took one last look at Rory to make sure that she stayed sitting in the creek.

Rory stayed there without saying a word, still trembling. She remained there a good minute even after the three terrors had disappeared. Eventually, she stood up and made her way out of the stream. She wrung Stitch dry once again and placed him softly on the ground. Then she started doing the same to her own clothes in an attempt to make herself dry, but she couldn't stop the tears that had formed in her one good eye, and she started to cry without making a sound.

This hurts so much. I want to say something – anything to make her feel better. I wish I could've done something to stop that, but I could only sit and stare while it all happened. Am I even better than those people who just walked by while I lay in the street? It's obvious I'm not. I did nothing. I can do nothing.

The flames remained in his

stomach. His hatred couldn't be quelled after what he'd just witnessed.

Rory sniffed loudly and then bent over and picked Stitch back up from the ground. She wore a forced smile that was still riddled with tears and a bit of snot that hung from her nose. "Get ready, Stitch, because I'm about to show you something out of this world."

Before they went on their way, Rory had dug something out of her pocket: a decent-sized pink ribbon that she had squirreled away. She looped it around Stitch's stomach and fastened it to the worn belt that held up her skirt. She looked back down at Stitch and said merrily, "There, I think you'll be able to see just fine from there. Plus, I don't want to go losing you, now, do I?"

Rory started off in a sprint as if she wanted to put the painful memory of what had just happened far behind her. The sun had begun to set, and it hid behind some of the taller buildings. For such a large city, it seemed like Rory knew every inch and crevasse. She ran with nearly a skip, darted blindly over walls where she barely missed falling into thorn bushes and showed amazing balance while traversing from one fence post to the next. As expected, the higher the distance from the creek, the larger the smile on her face became. Eventually, she became the same girl who had picked Stitch up from his puddle.

She made her way to an abandoned warehouse that looked like it had at one time been a successful business. The fence that she was balancing on led directly to a wall that gave her just enough height so she could hop over the wall without any problems. Once on the other side, she scrambled over to an old wooden ladder, which she wasted no effort in climbing. The ladder took her to a window of the highest floor, which she barreled through. Stitch now saw why she had decided to tie him to her side. It would have been a tall feat for her to clutch onto a teddy bear while traversing a building in this manner.

To Rory's right was a doorway that exposed a stairwell that obviously led to the roof. She took a moment to catch her breath and continued her journey up the stairs. As she made her way to the top, the sun's dying orange light illuminated the last of the steps. A light touch of wind met them as they exited the staircase, welcoming them to their destination.

Rory sprinted to the center of the building and did a sort of odd twirl, showing Stitch the entire world around them – and he was glad that she had done so.

He saw the painfully tall buildings that surrounded them casting shadows to the streets below, which now had a handful of lit street lamps. They looked like tiny stars flickering beneath their feet. This was an odd contrast to the quiet moon that had just peeked over the coastline, signaling the end of day and accompanied by the few stars brave enough to fight off the sun's light. Speaking of the coastline, it had been set ablaze in the sun's final moments, the final act before the curtain was drawn for the prologue of the night that would soon consume the day.

This was obviously Rory's favorite spot in the entire city and one she visited often. She made her way to the edge of the building and sat facing the coast. Its wind scattered her hair, which uncovered her scar that she tried so desperately to hide. At this moment, though, and only this moment, it seemed like she could have cared less about it.

"Isn't it beautiful, Stitch?" she said with a hearty smile.

Yes, it's the most beautiful thing I've seen in my entire life, he thought, wishing that he could speak aloud.

"I'm the only one who knows about this spot," she said, a strict look in her eye. "Make sure you don't spill the beans to anyone else, alright?"

I promise. It's not like I could blab about it to anyone anyway given that I'm a teddy bear – but I still promise.

"Today has been fun, do you know that?" she said as the sun's light had become so dim that she could now stare directly into it. "It's been so long since I've had a friend that I could take here. It's embarrassing to say something like that, but it's true, and we'll be able to come here as many times as you want."

I'd like that. I bet it's even better during the night.

Sure enough, once the sun had finally gone to sleep and the full expanse of the night's sky appeared above them, the stars glittered magnificently against the water.

The two sat staring at the night sky for what seemed like hours, but as time passed, Stitch noticed

Rory becoming more timid by the minute. He wondered if she were getting cold.

She took in a deep sigh and muttered so softly that he could barely hear her, "He has to be asleep by now."

Stitch wanted to ask Rory what she meant by that, but before he could even ponder it, she jumped to her feet with a short hop and dusted off the back of her skirt. She then made her way back down the building, taking her time while doing so. She didn't even walk down the street with her usual energy. In fact, she watched her feet with every step, carefully deliberating the distance of each one.

Stitch wondered if she were purposely making sure that this someone, whoever it might be, was indeed asleep. It must have been at least two hours before she finally stopped in front of a small cabin surrounded by buildings at least five times its size. The house was so completely unimpressive compared to the grandeur of those around it that if it hadn't been for the flickering street lamps that allowed a glimpse of it, or the almost dead candles in the window sills, a normal person would have been oblivious to its existence.

Rory slowly walked up the small set of stairs leading to the front door of the cabin. She opened the door to reveal a room littered with trash that was mainly composed of empty ale bottles. She looked to the right and surveyed the man currently passed out on a small dining table. The ale bottle that he had been drinking was tightly grasped in his hand, but sadly, it had still tipped over. What contents had remained had spilled across the table, coating the man's sleeping face.

He snored loudly like a bear stuck in a trap and struggling to get free.

Rory closed the door behind her as quietly as she could and proceeded to walk across the living room, taking care with each step she took. She had no desire to kick an empty bottle that could possibly wake up this man. She eyed the room across the hall, which was clearly her own. However, fate wasn't on Rory's side that night. Even though she took every precaution to make no noise while making her way to her room, she couldn't have prepared for the sloppiness and clumsiness of an old drunk.

He turned over as if he were in his bed and fell hard to the ground. He let loose a grunt that was half pain and half anger and then opened his eyes to see the small girl, who was still standing on her tiptoes.

Rory stood horror-struck for a moment. Then, with all the determination she could muster, she said shakily, "Hello, Father. How was your day?"

The man belched loudly and sat up while scratching his head. Stitch would have never guessed that this man was Rory's father from the way that he was looking at her.

Stitch couldn't exactly call it hatred. If anything, it was the look of a man staring at an insect whose existence was nothing but an inconvenience to him.

Shockingly, the man smiled at her and staggered to his feet. "Aurora, I've been waiting for you all night. Don't you know how worried I was?"

"I'm sorry. I lost track of time," said Rory, watching her father cautiously.

Rory's father made his way to her side and placed the back of his hand gently across her cheek. "We've been over this before. You can't stay out that late. There's dangerous people about."

I'm pretty sure there aren't that many people that are that much more dangerous than you, thought Stitch.

Her father continued to slide his hand up and down the side of her cheek while looking her over. He stopped his hand when he saw Stitch sitting tightly against her hip. He gestured at him with an oddly disturbing grabbing motion. "Oh? And what do we have here?"

"It's nothing!" Rory exclaimed as she moved her hands to shield Stitch, but she let out a yelp as her father smacked her hands aside and grabbed the teddy bear. He yanked against the ribbon with such force that he tugged Rory to the ground while ripping the ribbon.

He brought Stitch closer to his face and gave him a good looking over. Stitch noticed that his eyes went in and out of focus as he stared and that they had an odd glaze about them that could only belong to a man who'd had one drink too many.

"Why, this thing is broken," chortled her father while looking at Stitch's stitched eye. "Why'd you bother to pick up something useless like this?"

I'm not the only thing that's broken here.

Rory had sprung back to her feet, and she moved to grab Stitch from her father. "Give him back!"

"Him?" her father said with amusement as he placed his other hand over Rory's face to keep her at bay. His hand was so big that it covered her face entirely. "When are you going to grow up and learn you don't need things like this?"

Rory's hands continued to reach for Stitch. They flailed about wildly against her father's arm, and he looked at her with a disturbingly satisfied grin on his face. "C'mon, you almost have it. You're almost there...ouch!"

Rory, in her desperation to get Stitch back from her father, had accidentally scratched her father's arm. Any joy he was having while toying with his daughter disappeared from his face, and he released Stitch from his grasp.

As the bear fell, he watched the drunk's hand fly across and smack Rory across the cheek, forcing her to the ground without any effort.

"You dare! You dare raise your hand against me!" roared Rory's father. "You're nothing but a rat who lives in my house and eats my food, and you still have the gall to say something against me?"

Stitch lay on the ground, facing Rory. Her entire body was trembling again, and she was making awful gagging noises as if she were trying to gather the courage to apologize to her father.

Run!

Rory's eyes darted over to him just for a moment.

Run far away from this monster and never look back! Forget about me! Run!

Rory's father began tumbling toward her, each step more staggered than the next. To Stitch's great surprise, she leaped toward the bear, shoveled him in her arms, and darted to the back exit of the house. She swung the door open with all her might; before she could run down the stairs that led her to the freedom, her father closed the distance between them. He grabbed a handful of hair, yanking her back to him.

Stitch once again found himself falling to the ground, and he watched helplessly as Rory started to claw at her father's hands to get free. Her father's face was cold and uncaring as his daughter struggled to get away from him. Much to her and Stitch's surprise, he let go of her and, in one quick movement, pushed her hard down the cement stairs. Rory twisted and contorted as she crashed down them, and she landed on the ground face to face with Stitch.

In the dark night, her eyes were closed. A small trickle of blood started to come out of her nose. And she wasn't moving a single muscle.

No. Please don't be dead. Anything but that.

He watched as Rory's chest contracted slightly, and she let out a small, weakened cough telling him that she was still alive. However, she still wasn't moving, and her father began making his way down the stairs, clearly not finished with his daughter, Stitch lost all sense of reason. That same flame that had appeared when those children had tortured Rory began to grow and expand uncontrollably within him.

I must do something. I can't just sit here and watch her get hurt again. Why won't my legs move? Why won't you move? Move, dammit!

"What is this?" said Rory's father as he stopped his stride. He raised his hands and then

rubbed his eyes furiously. Once he was done, he looked down at the small teddy bear that his daughter had brought home with her.

"I must have had one too many," he chortled as he watched the once lifeless body of Stitch stand and look him squarely in the eye.

"I think that's an understatement," said Stitch loudly. His voice was much deeper than he imagined. It grated slightly as if he had a cold.

"I'm dreaming," said her father. His eyes trailed from the bear to his daughter, who still lay motionless on the ground. "Good. I was worried I'd killed her for a second. I'd go straight to jail, I would. She'd be an inconvenience even after she died, the useless little brat."

The fire burned brighter in Stitch's stomach, and it spread throughout his entire being. "Unforgivable."

"What was that?" said her father as he stared at the bear. "Did you just say something?"

"I said, unforgivable," repeated Stitch. "Your entire existence is foul. You don't deserve a daughter like Rory. Does it feel good to raise your hand against someone who can't even raise one back to you?"

The man frowned and shrugged. "I've never seen her as a daughter from the start. She was just an accident. Forced upon me, she was. Taking up space. Eating my food. Now that I think about it, she'd be better off dead. Since this is a dream and all, there's nothing wrong in trying, is there?"

The man looked at Rory and then, with a grimace, reached his hand toward her.

"Don't you touch her!" yelled Stitch. The fire in Stitch had grown too strong, and he could no longer keep it under control.

Rory's father watched in utter bewilderment as Stitch began to convulse. The light-brown dyed cotton that had once been his fur molted as long strands of hair took their place. He heard loud, horrible cracking as his limbs extended and contorted into proper place. Stitch grew to such a height; now, on his hind legs, he easily towered over Rory's father who watched in horror as the small stitches that had once been the bear's mouth ripped horribly apart to display dangerously jagged teeth. The black bead was now only an eye, and Stitch stared at the man who was more than a beast than

himself with a hatred that he had never felt in all his life.

"It's a dream," said the man as he stumbled backward. "It's alright. I'll wake up any moment now."

"It's not," said Stitch coldly. He reached his claw forward. He took his time, tracing it along the man's flesh, starting from the shoulder and leading it down to his hand. He put just enough pressure to convince the man that this was now reality, and he would have to face the consequences. The man's face became paler the farther the claw traveled. Stitch could tell he wanted to scream, but he couldn't even manage the courage to do so. He was so pathetic now. How paper-thin his strength was when facing something stronger than himself. Stitch's mouth warped into a smile that showed the full arrangement of his teeth. "I have to say I'm feeling awfully hungry. I was hoping that my first meal would be a delicacy, but I guess you'll do just fine for now." He surveyed the man, who was trying to crawl away from him. "What's the matter? I thought you said this was only a dream? Then why do you seem so scared now?"

"Forgive me," the man begged.

Stitch snorted. He stomped over to the man, hovering right over his face, and the man started to cry. "I thought I told you. What you've done can't be forgiven." He opened his mouth and inched his teeth closer to the man's throat.

"Stop! I swear it! I'll never raise my hand against her again," the man pleaded.

Stitch's tongue was now close enough to where he could taste the man's skin. It tasted putrid.

"I'll stop drinking! I'll throw it all out!" the man screamed as his eyes darted about, waiting for anyone to save him. A small bead of blood streamed out of his neck where Stitch's fang had pierced the skin.

"Save me, someone! Anyone!" pleaded the man. "I'm not ready to die! I'll do anything!"

"You said it," said Stitch, his voice muffled, and then he released his jaw from the man's neck. "You said you'll do anything?"

"What?" said the man, who was just barely managing to breathe in between his sobs.

Stitch growled at him. "I asked if you meant that. If you are really willing to do anything."

"Wha... No, I mean, yes! I'll do anything!" the man said, a look of renewed hope dawning on his face.

Stitch grunted. He sat down in front of the man and observed him just in case he tried to run for it. "Trust me, I'd like nothing better than to end your life right now, but I have to be realistic here. This isn't a town where Rory would be safe without a parent or someplace to call home."

Stitch sighed and shook his head. "Although I can hardly call you a parent, you are her father. You give her a roof to sleep under, and though I haven't seen it, I imagine that you give her food on occasion. So, here's the deal. You'll do what you said before I was about to bite your head off. You will never touch her again. You will never put your hand on an ale bottle again. And finally, you will take care of her until she's old enough to take care of herself. Understand?"

"I understand. I swear it. I'll do all of it." The man nodded feverishly.

"Fine," said Stitch, and as he muttered those words, his body shook and then contorted back to its normal teddy bear size. His hair molted, and new brown cotton sprouted all over his body.

"I'll be here to keep an eye on you. If I ever see you raise a hand against her, it'll be the end of your life. When she comes of age...if I feel like you did a decent job of it, there's a possibility that I won't kill you."

"You mean you might still kill me?"

"I'll say this one last time. What you did was unforgivable. I will never forget it, and if I decide to kill you at the end of all this, you will still deserve it. Now, tend to Rory and put her to bed, and pray to whatever god you believe in that I don't change my mind."

The man opened his mouth to try to rebuke Stitch, but after one glare from the bear, he stumbled back to his feet, picked up Rory, and carefully, as if she were the most fragile thing in existence, brought her back into the house.

* * *

I woke up the next day with my head throbbing. My hand reflexively went to my head to discover bandages wrapped around it tightly. My vision blurred slightly, but I could still see the small teddy bear sitting next to me as if he were on guard.

"Stitch!" I said, beaming. I grabbed him and hugged him tightly against my chest. "I thought I'd never see you again! What happened last night? I can't seem to remember anything after I fell."

The bear didn't answer back – he never did – but if he had, it would have been in his usual stoic voice I imagined a bear to speak with. He'd stare up at me with that beady black eye and say, "Nothing much. Nothing you have to worry about, at least."

I grinned and nodded as my head ached horribly. "That old bugger must have given up halfway and decided to pass out somewhere. Maybe it'd be better for me to leave my window open and stop using the front door. Sorry you had to see that. He gets like that sometimes."

Sometimes? Stitch stared at me with his regular blank expression.

"Okay, it happens a lot," I admitted. My nose twitched. "What's that smell? It smells wonderful."

It was at that moment that my father opened the door and carefully peered inside. He glanced at me, and then his eyes flickered to the bear at my side. "Hello, darling. I'm glad to see that you're up. Are you hungry? I've made bacon and eggs. Come down and get some when you're ready."

My expression went to one of utter bewilderment. "You made breakfast?"

"Sure enough," he answered.

I tried to get up but winced with the effort. My father frowned and stretched out his arm, palm up, telling me to stop. "Don't hurt yourself now. I'll tell you what, I'll bring it up to you. Take it easy today, alright? You had a nasty fall, after all."

He started to make his way out, but then he stopped and gave me a sympathetic look. "I'm sorry... You know how I get sometimes. I didn't mean it, though. I promise it won't happen again. I'll do better."

With that, he closed the door, and I could hear the clanking of plates from the dining room as he readied my breakfast.

"I think he's gone mental," I said in a hushed tone. Then I remembered the dream from last night – the image of Stitch rising to protect me. It was such a great dream. No one had ever stood up for me like that. I wish he'd do the same to those three bullies that tormented me daily.

The smell of delicious bacon distracted me, and my stomach growled demandingly. "Might as well take advantage of it before he gets back to normal."

I flopped back onto the pillow and held up Stitch to get a better look at him. I couldn't help getting my hopes up. "You must be some kind of good luck, charm, Stitch." I paused and traced my fingers along the stitching of his mouth. His teeth looked so real last night. I wished it were true; I needed it to be true. "Do you think he'll stay like this?"

I doubt it, but he better if he knows what's good for him.

Stitch still didn't answer. I felt my one good eye well up with tears. (My other eye hadn't been the same since the last time my father had had one too many.) I brought Stitch close to my chest again and held him tightly. The lingering rancid scent of the alleyway still seeped heavily within his fur. I needed to give him another bath.

"I don't believe it either," I replied with a nod while squeezing Stitch tighter. "Promise me that you won't leave me, Stitch."

I promise that I'll stay with you as long as you need me. Don't worry about your father... He'll only be here until you don't need him anymore. Then you'll never see him again. Count on that.

I grinned as I thought about that moment, which seemed so far away. At least now, I had a new friend who gave me the courage to face another day. ◉

Barely Human

Alice G. Waldert, holds an M.A. in Canadian Studies and
is currently a candidate for an MFA in creative writing at
Manhattanville College. In the true spirit of Carl Jung, she loves
dream studies, dream analysis, dream journaling and most of
all when her dreams have multiple layers of meaning and are
precognitive. Most days, following meditation, she spends 3-6
hours at her desk, writing for as long as possible with books and
art collected while working for the United Nations in Africa, Italy
and New York. She is a poet, short story writer, and memoirist.
She is currently completing her memoir about her early childhood
in a foster home, where she first became aware of having
prophetic dreams and insights beyond her age and everyday
consciousness.

Dream Connections

Alice G. Waldert

This is a work of nonfiction. Names have been changed to protect people's identities.

*D*reams, those nightly passageways we follow to penetrate the membranes of material time, have frequently provided an avenue of insight into my present and future. One night, however, when I was nineteen, a freshman in residence at university, I had the first of two visceral dreams. Their meanings were a mystery until I met a man named Paul.

First dream:

My tiny, white, ribbon-bound feet bob about in front of my eyes and are pressed into little black shoes. Pain prevents me from stepping down from the wooden bench where I sit. Outside the window to my left, villagers engrossed in their daily activity of carrying and carting wood, water, and other goods pass me by. I search for my mother's form. An anxious tension hangs in the air. This is a day, unlike all others.

In the distance, I see her, stooped under a heavy burden of wood on her back. She wears a frayed brown chemise and a wrinkled, dirty skirt. I can see only the top of her head as her eyes focus on the ground before her.

When she enters the hut, she sits her tired body next to mine and pulls some golden strands of straw from her torn skirt pocket. With swollen, brown, scarred fingers, she diligently crafts a doll's head, body, arms, and legs. Pulling some frayed material from the bottom of her skirt, she dresses the doll in it, and with tears in her slit eyes, she hands it to me. I know somehow that it is a parting gift.

I am in a moving carriage with the straw doll on my lap. I feel weighed down, immobilized by sadness, holding the toy to my chest. Suddenly, the carriage lurches to a halt, and a shadowy, dark figure, like a bandit, pierces the curtained window of the carriage. With one glance, he spots the straw doll. He snatches it from me and disappears with it. I open my mouth to yell, but it is useless, no one will come to my aid. The carriage pulls forward.

As we arrive at a house, we drive through open iron gates to a building's side door. The driver assists me to step out of the carriage, and a servant woman, clearly superior to the carriage driver, walks toward me. She holds a critical expression on her face and pulls at my long black hair and shakes her head.

"Take her to the bath," she orders.

In the bathhouse, servants remove my clothes, which disappear. I am bathed by a woman who does not speak to me, but dresses me in new clothes and brushes my long black hair into a ponytail. A lit, black, square candle-lantern appears, held by a short servant. She stands next to a tall woman with black, braided hair. They are standing in front of a closed door.

Next, I am in a bedroom lavishly furnished with red and gold fabrics. The door opens. The tall woman with the black, braided hair is standing in the doorway with her servant. She steps aside, and her husband steps forward dressed in a long, shiny, red robe that drapes over his shoulders and arms to the ground. He is a wealthy merchant and the owner of all that I see. I realize, also, my owner. The wife closes the door behind him, leaving me helpless, alone, with him. Seated, my heart pounds, and I watch wide-eyed as he disrobes. I feel dizzy with fear. I can't believe this is happening to me. He turns his back to me, and the last thing I see, before I awake, is a dragon tattooed on his back, rising-up over his left shoulder.

* * *

After the dream, fear, loss, and betrayal accompany me into my waking life. And for the first few minutes after waking, although my eyes were wide open, I was still in the Chinese girl's room. My college residence room is arranged the same way as the room in my dream. I sit up. The dream held themes of separation and the betrayal of innocence. Were there parallels in my waking life? I was away from home for the first time, separated from family, and still a virgin. Was my innocence about to be betrayed? Why was the dream so real to me?

Later, I realized my dream was a reflection of authentic Chinese customs. It was a common tradition for centuries for wealthy men to take young girls, from lower social ranking families, for their concubines.

Three months after the dream, I entered, for the first time, into a relationship with a young man my age. It lasted for two years. However, when it ended suddenly by betrayal, I remembered what I called my "Chinese dream." To me, the dream served as a warning against betrayal by someone who took away my innocence. That would have been the end of it; soon after, on a hot day in July, I had a second dream which appeared to be a sequel to the first.

The second dream

I am the Chinese girl again, only a little older, and am alone in a small house, seated on a cushion. My stomach is heavy with pregnancy. The merchant wife's personal servant enters. She says something to me, which I won't recall and bows to me before she

exits, drawing the door closed behind her. There is something upsetting about her final bow.

Tension is in the air. My breathing tightens as if constricted. Something is wrong. I know the merchant's wife is jealous of me for being able to bear the merchant a child. I hear what sounds like mice pawing at an outside corner of the house. Seconds pass and a flame appears. It engulfs the corner from where the pawing sounds emerged. Falling to the ground, I crawl, coughing and choking toward the sliding doors. Reaching them, I grip the door handle and strain to tug at it, but it will not budge. I realize in panicked horror the door is either locked or jammed from the outside. I yell and scream pounding my fist against the door, but slowly the smoke suffocates me.

* * *

I awake with the clear sensation of what it is like to have my flesh melt in hot flames, My pajamas drenched in sweat, the morning sun beaming through my open window.

Seven months after the second dream, I worked at the university library's audio-visual desk. A male friend approached me, accompanied by someone whom I had never met.

"Hey Alice, I want you to meet my friend Paul. You two have a lot in common. I think you'd have plenty to say to each other."

I grimaced, and my eyes flitted over Paul sizing him up: medium height, stocky build, brown hair, and a mustache. "Hello," I nodded. The event felt awkward because I was dating someone else. Later, I learned, Paul had a girlfriend at that point too.

I remember so well because the second our eyes met, there was something familiar about him. Not knowing what to make of it, I looked down at the top of the desk. There, I noticed an unused elastic band had formed itself into the shape of a musical treble clef.

"Oh, hey, look at that, the treble sign," I said out loud.

"Yeah, that's interesting." Paul stared at it with electric blue eyes.

Our mutual friend was right. Paul and I had plenty to say to one another. Every time our paths crossed on campus, we stopped to talk, as if we held endless yarns of information we wanted to share.

It was only after each of us had stopped seeing other people (and two days before Paul was scheduled to leave Ottawa) that we made a date. We met up at a café on campus. As it was a warm June night, we took a long walk along the Rideau Canal and Dow's Lake, where the sides of the footpaths had apple blossom trees and vibrant blue, yellow and red flower beds.

"It's like seeing a person's aura." We were talking about overexposed photographs in which people have bright lights around them.

"Well, isn't that something you sense more than see?" I asked, suddenly aware we were now broaching a subject we had never discussed.

"Some people sense, some people can see them." He chuckled, picking up a bright yellow dandelion by its stem and twirling it between his thumb and index finger.

I stopped. "Paul," I asked, "do you see auras?"

"Yeah, but I don't let it get around. Now that I'm leaving, it doesn't really matter," he said, plucking the yellow petals off the dandelion.

"Do you get strong hunches about what is about to happen before it happens?" I hedged, uncertain whether to be open and talk about my precognitive dreams.

"You mean extrasensory perception, also known as ESP?" His blue eyes twinkled with the light from the street lamp shining down on us. "I've had my hunches if you want to call them that."

"Well, I've had lots of hunches. Like knowing when a person…"

"Is about to call. Or being able to finish someone else's sentences or jokes." Paul said, smiling.

"Yeah." I laughed. "So, you've had some ESP experiences?"

"Countless," he said, rolling his eyes.

"Well, do share. I am open to hearing them."

Our conversation had no end that night. As numerous as my intuitive, precognitive, and déjâ vu experiences were, Paul either matched them or had more to tell. We sat on a picnic bench and talked until three o'clock in the morning. When we later reached my apartment door, he reached toward me with his head tilted, but something inside me made me dodge his kiss and instead I hugged him quickly and withdrew.

A smile crossed his face, but before he could say a word, I looked into his eyes and said, "This has been a great night. I hope we'll stay in touch." He nodded and watched as I unlocked my apartment door and slipped inside, and shut it.

We called each other from time to time, and months later, on Paul's return to Ottawa for a weekend visit, we decided to go out for lunch. In the car, we were trying to decide where to eat.

"Who do you see me with in the future?"

"I see you married…" I said. Part of me thought he wanted to hear me say me, but my heart told me to tell the truth. "I see you married…to a Chinese woman," I told him.

"Are you sure?"

"Yes," I reassured him.

He sat for a moment and stared out the windshield in front of him. The frown lines on his face and the fact that there was nothing but an empty car in front of him told me he was weighing something in his mind, debating whether to tell me. We sat quietly for a few minutes.

"Well, I think I might have been Chinese in another life."

The words landed like a

dropped bowling ball at my feet. This was an unexpected revelation. Paul had never shared this with me before. It was my turn to sit quiet. Do I dare tell him? My belief in reincarnation was something I held buried inside of me out of fear of ridicule. The visceral memory of my "Chinese dreams" were so strong, I couldn't help but say, "Yeah, I know what you mean. I think I might have been Chinese too."

"You think you were Chinese too?" Paul said, his frown line disappeared, and he looked visibly surprised and relieved.

"Yeah, I think it's possible," I said, nodding. We smiled at each other, amazed that with each of our conversations, there seemed deeper connections between us.

To honor our dreams, we decided to go eat Chinese food for lunch that day. As we walked up to the glass doors of the restaurant, Paul explained to me that one of the reasons he felt he was Chinese had to do with painful nerve endings on his back. "My doctor is baffled because the nerve endings are not connected, but to me, it feels like an image was tattooed on my back." The minute he said this, everything around me changed as if I had just been pushed into some surreal, aquatic world.

"What was the tattoo of?" I blurted with a quiver in my voice.

"A dragon," he said.

Dragon? My mind rushed to connect his words with the final image I had of the merchant disrobing in my first Chinese dream, four years earlier.

"Paul!" I said, almost shouting his name. "I think I know exactly where you feel the dragon tattoo."

"Where?" He asked, his puzzled eyes squinting at me.

"It was coming over your left shoulder, wasn't it?" I said, my right hand patting the top of my left shoulder.

"Yeah! But how? That's exactly where I feel it." Paul said. We stood in front of each other speechless, trying to absorb the significance of what was happening. Paul's eyes widened and then narrowed. "Do you remember the square black lantern my wife's servant held when she brought me to your room?"

Unable to say a word, I nodded a yes. And we continued to stare at each other until a stranger, a man, interrupted us. "Excuse me. I'd like to get into the restaurant."

We allowed him to pass, then followed him in. The hostess led us to a cave-dark table with only a weak candle as a centerpiece. When we were alone, I leaned across the table to stammer, "Do... do you remember anything else?"

Paul stared at the white tablecloth, then looked up at me with piercing eyes and said, "My wife, her hair was in braids, and your hair was in a ponytail."

I wanted to stand up and walk out of the restaurant. My world was upside down. I breathed deeply several times before asking through clenched teeth, "Paul, how do you know the details of my dream? I had this dream four years ago."

He sat back in his seat, disarmed. "I had the same dream, only I was the man in the dream," I heard him say, but my mind refused to compute its significance. I didn't know him four years ago! With my hands pressed over my eyes, I tried to calm myself. This is real, I'm awake, and he's telling me he had the same dream as me.

"You were the man in my dream? And you dreamed the same thing," I said slowly.

My mind poured over so many questions. Was this a dream we shared? A coincidence? Or was our dream evidence of reincarnation? Could I be having lunch with the man who made me his concubine? Is this the reason I didn't trust him to kiss me? I looked at Paul, who found it easier to read the menu than say anything more. I couldn't decide what to think and felt unprepared to accept these new revelations. What if it's just a coincidence? But then, he had told me he plans to do Asian Studies.

Hours after our lunch, Paul and I were back at my apartment to eat dinner. While I washed the dishes, Paul dried. I told Paul about an annoying person in the psychology class I had taken.

"There was just something about this guy that irritated me, he kept making a point of trying to sit next to me all the time."

"Maybe he's the bandit from your dream," I heard Paul say from behind me.

I spun around and peered at Paul. "What did you just say?"

"You remember," he said. "Your mother made a doll for you out of straw, and you had it with you when your carriage was stopped by bandits. One of them took your doll from you. Maybe this guy is the bandit."

"You know more details about my dream...our dream." I stared at him in disbelief, wishing I could live in the comfort of coincidence, but there were too many shared details to deny them. "How do you know these facts?"

"I had more than one dream of being Chinese. I remember lots of small details from them."

"Then, is this reincarnation or just a shared dream?" I asked.

"Considering that I still have nerve ending pains in my back, I would say it's reincarnation," he answered, tossing the dishcloth on the kitchen counter. He shook his head and looked just as confused as I felt. "I just don't have any other explanation for it."

That evening, Paul and I went to see the movie "Aliens." The theatre was crowded with excited moviegoers chattering all around us. Paul and I probably appeared to be the least excited. We chose to sit silently, waiting for the movie to begin. It was then that a thought occurred to me. Although Paul was three years younger than me, he projected the confidence of someone older.

"Paul," I said. "I was younger than you in that other life?"

"Yeah, you were," he said and looked away.

"Paul, I died before you did in that other life." It was more like a statement of knowledge than a question.

"Yeah, you died in a fire," he said in a low voice.

My jaw dropped. He knew about my second dream. Before I could say another word, the lights in the theatre dimmed, the dark red stage curtains parted, and the opening music exploded around us, obliterating the space to speak.

Paul and I had a relationship. But after a few months, the six-hour drive made it unsustainable.

A year after our dream connection, he phoned me.

"Hey, I'm in town, and we're all going to hang out and have dinner at a steakburger restaurant, why don't you join us."

"Yeah, sure," I said, excited to see Paul again and assuming "us" to be our mutual friends from school.

"Great, I brought Lee with me. You can meet her."

My heart fell, "Lee?" I knew who he was talking about. I visited

Paul once during the two months we were involved. We had gone to a Chinese restaurant one night, and while we ate, he whispered to me, "Do you sense anything about the Chinese hostess? Her name is Lee."

I recalled the small, slender Chinese woman standing behind the glass counter at the cashier, and how she had returned my glance with sharp, spiteful eyes.

"Are you a couple now?" I said, trying hard not to let my disappointment sound in my voice.

"Yeah, we've been seeing each other since the last time you visited me," he said.

"Good, then the answer is no. I can't meet up with you and Lee. In fact, I don't think I want to talk to you again." I hung up on him and refused to pick up the receiver when he tried to call me back.

* * *

Two years later, I dreamed that Paul came to visit me in my apartment. The only part of the dream I remember is that he said to me, "Lee and I are getting married."

A week or so after the dream, I visited a bookstore where the same young man, who introduced me to Paul so many years earlier, worked. We hugged hello and talked briefly, and as I was about to go search for a book, he said, "By the way, I have news about Paul."

I turned around, and before he could say another word, I said, "He's getting married."

"Oh, you know?" he said, shaking his head. "Paul told me he hadn't told anyone else. How did you know that?"

I simply smiled. 👁

Dream
Connections

Sandra Gould Ford is an author, educator, and former steelworker who presents arts experiences to encourage, refresh, enrich creative thinking, and inspire. She is an active member of the Author's Guild and Science Fiction Writers of America. Sandra established a writing program at a mega-jail, co-produced two major writers conferences, and published an international literary journal. Sandra perseveres with her creative writing: to make suffering endurable, evil intelligible, justice desirable, and love possible (Roger Rosenblatt's four reasons for writing). Follow Sandra's work and activities at SandraGouldFord.com. Work on "Wishes" was supported by a grant from Advancing Black Pittsburgh, a partnership of The Heinz Endowments and The Pittsburgh Foundation.

Wishes

Sandra Gould Ford

On October 31, 1958, moonbeams lit the stardust that sprinkled the Crescent Avenue's sycamore and hawthorn trees. On that clear, bright evening, candles dimmed inside jack-o-lanterns as Estelle Ringgold Pearson said, "We shouldn't see any more spooky movies."

Parnell held her hand as they strolled from the Roland Theater.

"Did *The Queen of Outer Space* really scare you?" he chuckled.

"When that mask came off, her face was horrifying," Estelle answered. Estelle was an earthy brown, and at twenty-two, she was plump and short. She pursed her lips and added, "So is a planet of nothing but women. And I'm done with outer space stuff."

Parnell was tall, mahogany, and twenty-four. He asked, "What did you think of *Attack of the 50 Foot Woman*?"

"Didn't that have a flying saucer?" Estelle asked with a frown.

"Don't worry. The previews showed *South Pacific* and *The Inn of The Sixth Happiness* playing next week. You'll like those better." Parnell said squeezing Estelle's hand. "They're in color."

"Good. I'll be glad when all movies are in color."

"Is that a wish?"

"My wish is that we always be together. And no fooling around like that fifty-foot woman's husband."

"You don't have to wish for that," Parnell replied. He held her at arm's length and crooned,

Embrace me, my sweet embraceable you

Embrace me, you irreplaceable you

Just one look at you

My heart grows tipsy in me

You and you alone

Bring out the Gypsy in me

"You're such a romantic, Parnell."

"Just for you, baby. Whatever makes you happy."

When they reached the next streetlight, Parnell peaked under hedges and reached for something.

Estelle thumped her forehead and groaned, "Not another one. Leave that dirty coin where it is. You're better than Nat King Cole. Keep singing."

"In a minute, sweetheart. You never know." Parnell grinned as he held it up to the street light. "And some say, stray-coins come from folks who love us."

"Do you mean dead people?" She shuddered. "More of your nonsense. When we're dead, we're done."

"You never know. Life can be right mystifying."

"That story about a magic coin is just a tall tale."

"Estelle, all kinds of things are possible, especially around here."

"No," she insisted. "That talk of shapeshifters and magic makers out in wild places is foolishness."

"You'll say that 'til you meet one."

Estelle scowled. "Have you?"

"Not that I know of," Parnell said with a shrug, putting the coin in his pocket. "It's just a buffalo nickel."

"And you'll never stop believing in magic coins, will you?"

"Looking doesn't cost anything. I'll add it to the jug. Extra change always comes in handy." He wiped the coin, straightened his shoulders and sang,

I love all the many charms about you

Above all, I want my arms about you.

Don't be a naughty baby

Come to papa, come to papa do

My sweet embraceable you

Clang! Clang!

Estelle turned and watched their rumbling trolley approach. "Come on, Parnell. We can't miss this one."

* * *

Thirty-five years later, silver clouds covered a gray morning.

jack-o-lanterns again grinned on doorsteps. Troll and ghoul, gargoyle and skeleton banners fluttered. The Roland Movie Theater advertised the *Attack of the 50 Foot Woman*– a remake.

Some kids were out early dressed like ghosts and fairies, wind walkers, and harpies. When they frolicked past her, Estelle recalled how Parnell enjoyed handing out foil chocolates that looked like coins. He liked telling them about the magic one that granted wishes.

"Parnell, we were always supposed to be together." Estelle looked up at the morning sky and sighed.

Thunk!

Estelle walked right into a dark bronze, muscular man. His right hand steadied her. The other held a shepherd's crook

"Goodness! Pardon me," she gasped.

"You seemed lost in thought. Are you all right?" His costume included bull's horns and a curly wig.

"I was thinking of my husband. This week is the seventh anniversary of losing him."

"And you still miss him?" The man's eyes were fawn brown, his expression sympathetic.

Estelle placed a hand over her heart. "Very much. After all this time, I should move on. I wish..." She sighed.

"What were you going to wish? Seven is a special number," the costumed man asked.

"Wishing does no good. And I must be going. My trolley is due."

"Have a good day, ma'am," he said with a twinkle in his eye. "And a good journey."

As more costumed children rustled past them, Estelle distinctly heard the *plink* of metal dropping onto the pavement.

She waited until the little goblins and dragons, griffins, and mermaids passed. There it was: a dull copper disk spun then flopped on the sidewalk along with the first raindrops of short fall drizzle.

Estelle stared at the rusty slug the size of a fifty-cent piece then at the children scampering away. The costumed man was nowhere to be seen.

"I'm not collecting another stray coin," she grumbled. "Anyway, this rain is making my knees ache. My back hurts too much to be bending. "

Estelle stepped away, but she looked back and glared at the disk. "All right. This is the absolute last one. For Parnell. For his sake." Estelle rubbed her aching knees then reached to pick up the coin.

"Are you okay, Miss?"

Heaving herself up, Estelle turned to face a thin teenager. She wiped rain from her face and said, "I'm fine, thank you. Just wish I had me an umbrella."

"Take mine. "He offered a black fold-up.

"I couldn't. You'll get wet."

"My ride's here." He pointed to an idling sedan. "And my English class has to perform random acts of kindness for homework. Let this be my first today. Please." He popped open the umbrella.

"Well, if you insist," Estelle said.

"I do." The young man grinned, bowed, and slipped into the car as it pulled away.

* * *

Later that morning at Capitol Department Store, Estelle punched her time card. On the way to the employee lounge, Estelle passed a new display of giant Gingersnap Dolls. They wore buttercup satin, lace, and crinoline.

"My baby grandchild would love this," she said with a glow.

But when she checked the price, she marched back out the front door into the bracing wind, fuming, "What are those dolls made of? Platinum?"

Estelle stuffed her hands in her pockets, fisted the contents, and grumbled, "Even though that pretty doll is overpriced, I do wish I could buy it. I can't be waiting on 'After Christmas' sales. And I better get upstairs before *Old Icy Eyes* writes a reprimand for lateness. She sighed, "And I *do* wish I could–"

Suddenly, a roll of dollar bills bumped her shoe. Surprised, Estelle studied bystanders then said, "No one's looking for anything. If they were, I'd surely return it...I'd..."

* * *

The lounge for Capitol Department Store's female housekeepers was pale green with a calendar, bulletins, and sales flyers on a wall that faced metal lockers. A big bronze clock tick-ticked above the door to the head housekeeper's office. Cast iron radiators gurgled as they pushed heat into the cologne and soap-scented air where a tall, lean woman glanced at the clock then stared at Estelle with frost-gray eyes.

"You're late."

"I stopped to get this doll, Miss Tate. I'll make up the time."

The pinched, pale brown woman squinted at the doll and sniffed. "I know what they cost. Where did you get the money?"

"A blessing."

The head housekeeper crossed her arms. "I've received complaints about your bathrooms not being cleaned on schedule. One department thinks you're taking toilet paper home. And the offices on the tenth-floor claim money is missing." Icicles hung from her words.

"They made a mistake," Estelle's said as her heart galloped. "None of us maids steal."

"I'll get the proof. Meanwhile, you need to be cleaning the seventh floor." Belva Tate again eyed the doll. "Otherwise, I'll add tardiness to my report."

Estelle shoved her umbrella, purse, and the new doll into her locker. Before unbuttoning her coat, Estelle paused then marched to the back stairs raced up. On Capitol Department Store's wide, flat roof, Estelle could have a moment to herself.

"Belva's being hateful again. She can't stand joy in anyone;

anywhere. How many discipline reports has she written because someone didn't kowtow low enough?" Estelle paced, hunching her shoulders against the gusting winds. She rubbed her hands then stuffed them into her pockets, grasping tissues and coins. As she watched the Wepawet River meander peacefully toward Lake Enkaki, Estelle's anger flared.

"Shame on me, but I wish that cold-hearted woman would jump in that lake. Those waters might warm her."

* * *

Late that night at home, after working all day and giving away bags of chocolate coins and admiring hundreds of costumes, Estelle turned on the television and sank into Parnell's easy chair. Instead of the new show, "Living Single," a reporter filled the screen, "Police just pulled a woman from Lake Enkaki. She is rambling and disoriented. If you know who she is, call the numbers on your screen."

When bright lights blasted the shivering woman into focus, Estelle gasped, "That can't be Belva."

"Again, viewers, if you recognize this woman, please

call," the reporter repeated.

Trembling, Estelle tapped the numbers and heard, "Mental Health Services. How can we help you?"

"The woman from the lake, her name is Belva Tate," Estelle blurted.

"How do you know the woman? Could you identify yourself?" the voice asked.

"Her name is Belva Tate. She works for Capitol Department Store," Estelle shouted and slammed down the house phone.

After several, stunned moments, she peeked over at the Gingerbread Doll on the table and asked her a question, "Did I wish for that money after...? Did I wish for an umbrella after I found that coin? And who was that man in that stupid, bull costume, talking to me about wishes? Was he a man?... Did I wish Belva would jump in the lake?"

Estelle dug around in her pockets until she found the metal disk. Her hands shook so that she dropped it twice. Staring at the grungy coin, she said, "This beat-up thing can't be what Parnell was looking for all those years ago. It can't."

Estelle grabbed her coat and bustled outside. Out on the porch, she said loudly in the direction of the street, "We really could use a working street light. And for my neighbors to quit arguing... And it would be nice to have a fur coat... red fox."

Nothing happened. She watched tree shadows waver across the coin and listened to distant traffic. Far off, a trolley's bell rang. Across the street, more kids in costume: a giggling ghost, a robot, and a gossamer-winged fairy checked their treats.

"Then again, maybe it should be less dramatic. Let's get this decided. Magic coin, make a red bird fly by clear as day and sing."

Walking down the street, Estelle listened to the wind and rustling leaves then sighed. Nothing. Her shoulders drooped. As she turned to trudge inside, a car passed and the radio playing Nat King Cole singing,

I love all the many charms about you

Above all, I want my arms around you.

"Parnell sang it better," she muttered. "And I need to get this wishing coin nonsense out of the way." Estelle gathered herself, held the coin tight, and repeated, "I WISH a red bird would fly right past here and sing, soon ...

before I get any colder. That's my wish."

After a minute, wrens, sparrows, cawing crows, even honking geese flew overhead.

"Whew! That was strange, but my wish didn't happen. This piece of scrap is nothing but a –"

"Swee-swee-sweet! Swee-swee-sweet!" Shining red wings fluttered past. The bird hovered like a hummingbird then flew over the roof, chirping,

"Well, if that doesn't just burn my biscuits!" Estelle spluttered. She planted both fists on her hips and stared at the roofline in amazement.

When Estelle reached her apartment, she clamped the coin into Parnell's jug and fussed, "What if a friend riles me? I might wish she were never born. What if I want some particular person to win an election? What if...? How's a person supposed to handle something like this?"

Estelle sank into Parnell's chair, *What about Mattie? That girl could use a raise¬ although the flirt should have been fired a long time ago, always late and always breaking things.*

* * *

The next time Mattie moaned

about bills and tuition expenses, Estelle said, "Try and impress the big boss and don't break any more crystal. And don't peeve me when you become head housekeeper."

When Estelle hosted a make-up party for a heartbroken and lonely friend, she made the guest of honor promise to maintain her facials and use her gym membership. But she wasn't surprised when that same friend confessed two weeks later that a handsome new man called on her.

Next, Estelle bought two *big-money* lottery tickets. The fourth Wednesday in November, while she waited in from the TV for the winning numbers to be drawn, Estelle reflected. She thought about Parnell and the family trips, the college funds, the nicer home they could have had *if* he had found *her* coin.

If only. Estelle sniffled, dabbed her eyes and wept.

The next night, after Thanksgiving leftovers were packed, dishes done and furniture replaced, Estelle handed both her son and daughter sealed envelopes.

"What's in here, Mom?" Joan, her oldest asking, shaking the envelope.

"If I tell you, it won't be a surprise. Open them tomorrow, darlings. And I don't want no foolishness."

"Are you okay, Mom? Are you taking your medicine?" Valiant asked.

"I'm fine, but I'm missing your Daddy."

"When do you want to visit the cemetery? We can go tomorrow."

Estelle sighed. "No. Not tomorrow. Now you two take your families home before the storm comes."

When her rooms were quiet, Estelle tugged on her boots and coat and pulled the coin from Parnell's jug. Outside, the falling snow made Estelle's world feel like an elevator rising. Stars glittered. She looked up to the sky and told the night, "I've been trying to make a wish for myself but can't think of a thing." She sighed, "I've asked for everything that could make me happy, and I don't want my mind filled up with wishings and worryings about wishing."

"Even though Parnell would surely laugh at my situation, he'd know what to do. I sure miss him. I sure wish..." Estelle tapped the metal slug against her chin.

Far off, a trolley clanged. Trees swayed. A breeze kissed Estelle's face as snowflakes twinkled. Each time plump snowflakes touched, they seemed to chime, their amethyst light filling the night with sparkles that wriggled like funhouse mirrors. Rainbows rose from the sidewalk.

"I didn't mean to wish anything. And I didn't finish my–!" Estelle cried out dizzy and frightened.

The smell of Parnell's special barbecue sauce silenced her. It was followed by the scent of the roses and peppermint he used to grow in their first back yard. A hundred other memories surfaced, leaving Estelle feeling gossamer and shimmery.

Don't be a naughty baby

Come to poppa, come to poppa, do

My sweet embraceable you.

"Ess, baby, I'll be doggone," Parnell chuckled.

"Parnell? What's happening?" Estelle whispered.

"Your wish. And you didn't believe they could come true." He hugged her.

When a trolley as bright as dawn arrived, Estelle squawked, "Where'd that come from? There's no tracks."

"Never rode anything like this before. Let's see where it's going." Parnell said taking her hand.

When they climbed aboard, the dark bronze man with tall, Brahman bull horns grinned.

"Fare, please. I'll take my coin now." His long, petal-shaped ears flopped back and forth. He winked. "Got to keep it in circulation." ◉

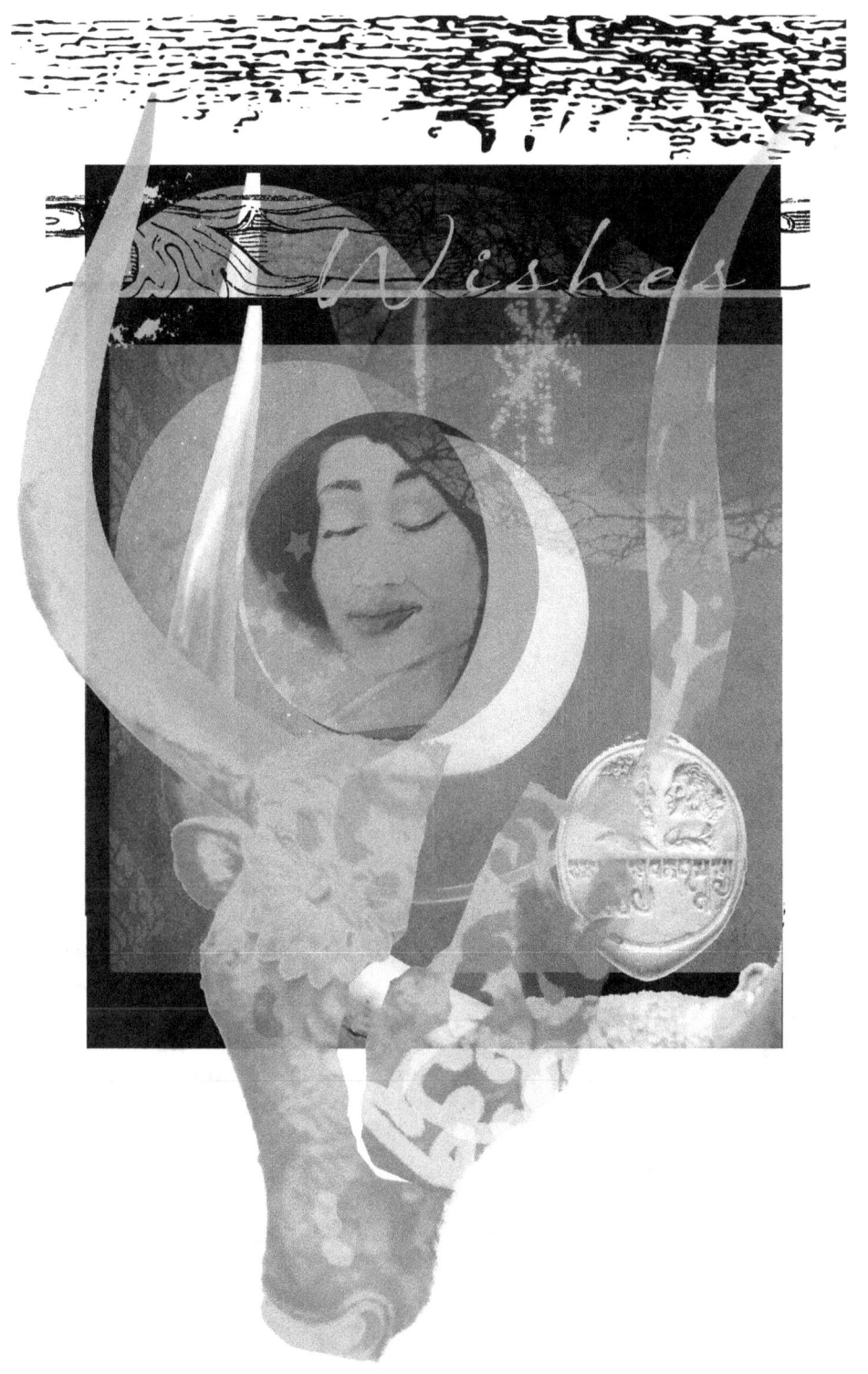

Wishes

Kēvin Callahan has a BFA from Drake University, post-grad work at San Francisco Art Institute, Larry Abramson, The Ox-Bow School, Art Institute Chicago, and Phil Hanson/Michelle Grabner. His award-winning artwork hangs in collections throughout the United States, and in Canada, Europe, and Israel. After a career in graphic design, he has published a novel and two short story collections, plus numerous poems often in conjunction with his art. His distinctive modern portraits and figures are shown worldwide including a line of handcrafted wood items at Prairie Primitive.com. He maintains a studio and gallery, *The Elegant Line*, in Parkville, MO. Find his new book of poems, *Road Map* on Amazon, published by Flying Ketchup Press.

Tangled Tale of a Walk in the Woods
Kevin Callahan

*I*went for a walk in the woods.

My name is John Morgan, and do I have a story for you! First, a bit about me. I'm a youngish thirty-seven, single, with a growing tech business. Orphaned, my parents both died in a tragic accident when I was a young boy, and I was raised in a succession of foster homes. Reading and learning were what took me away from my loneliness and longing for family. That's when I discovered my affinity for language and the world of technology.

With few friends, I've been called an old soul, and my word choice often is akin to an earlier time. I chalk it up to voracious reading. With no current love interest, I live alone in a large Midwest city and often travel. I want to see the places I have read about, so I visit large cities and hike through deserts and jungles on my mini-vacations.

Many people consider modern electronics to be a sort of magic, well, I suppose it is in its way. Although, technically, I can explain how it all works.

Recently, and inexplicably, I decided a mid-week trip to Portland, Oregon would be on my agenda. I don't usually take unplanned vacations, but I'd been running myself pretty hard lately. I'd always heard it was a great place. It was the first Monday in May after a particularly rainy April, and I woke up and just decided to go. It was as if something was pulling me there. I phoned my executive assistant and requested that my schedule be pushed into next week and opened the Expedia site.

Flight & car booked and off to Portland. Sitting in my rental car, I Googled downtown hotels, picked one, and drove off the lot. But, leaving the airport, instead of downtown, GoogleMaps directed me south and east on Highway 26. Weird, I thought, but there must be a reason I'm here, so I kept driving. The map was taking me to Sandy, a town in the shadow of the Cascade mountains. When I saw a cozy-looking motel along the highway, I veered into the parking spot open by the door. Checked in, planning to stay a couple of days. In the morning, the motel owner mentioned Sandy River Trails, a vast expanse of woods nearby complete with walking trails. A grand adventure. Just what I needed, a new place to explore, I had never walked the woods in Oregon. Luckily, I had packed shorts and walking shoes in my ever-present backpack. I set off on my lone journey.

I found the trails, no problem, and parked my rental car at a small café for breakfast before my hike. The path into the woods was broad and well-trodden. At the entrance to the park, I stopped and studied a large poster that maps the trails. A box attached to the post held smaller printed versions for hikers–like me. I smiled, thinking I was going Old School using a printed map. After a few minutes reviewing the map to determine a good way in and out, I set off at a nice pace. My pack held a breakfast bar, a bag of peanuts, two bottles of water, and my fully charged iPhone. The ideal May weather made it a glorious day for a stroll.

As I walked, I eagerly took in flora and fauna, keeping an eye out for the unusual, animal, or mineral, having never been to this part of the country I expected to see different types of plants and maybe animals too. A short way into my journey, I spied an old tree limb lying perpendicular to the trail. "Oh ho, what's this?" I asked myself. I stooped to retrieve the branch– a perfect length for a walking stick, knobby on one end when I picked it up I could see it resembled a sorcerer's staff. Curiously, it seemed very primal, well worn, out of place. I liked the heft of the stick. I always found walking with a stick made me feel like I was with a friend. My new companion and I set off together, down the path.

Making my way deeper into the forest, I passed several branching trails. Soon the path began to narrow to a track, but I decided to keep on. I'm not sure at what point it happened, but gradually it seemed as if the stick was taking me, not the other way around. I began to feel a weird energy pulling me along.

Coming abreast of a brushy, nearly indiscernible path, and not wanting to get lost in an unfamiliar place off the map, I made to continue, but the stick had other ideas. Oddly, it pulled me forward. As I turned back, the staff became heavier. What is this? I tried to drop it, throw it, anything, but I couldn't let go. The rod stuck to my hand.

What happened next shouldn't have been surprising to me, but it was. I turned to walk back the way I had come. That is, my body twisted, the sick remained in my hand with my arm extended down the lesser path. I turned back. As if that ended our argument, my new rustic friend settled lightly and more cooperatively into my hand.

Within a short distance, the path again became well-worn and visible. Most curious. I stopped for a water break and a consult with my map. Hmmm, no reference point, so I don't know where I am. Turning back, I discover that the path is no longer discernible, just leaves stretching back among trees as far as I can see. What? Out comes my iPhone, but when I hit the button, the screen is blank. I don't understand? I charged the phone all night, and I checked at the park entrance. Turning,

again, I resumed trekking forward, the only path open to me.

Rounding a slight curve on a hill, I stopped for a rest. The day had grown warmer; the sun overhead meant it was already a bit past noon. Hmmm, I didn't think I had been walking that long.

Sitting down on a log, I unwrapped the energy bar and ate it. I washed it down with my last swig of water.

That's when I spied the cottage. "Wait. What? It was not there a minute ago." But there it was, blocking the path, though not much broader, an ancient-looking tiny house. Oddly out of place, the dwelling is like a drawing in a Medieval storybook come to life, complete with a thatched roof, round windows, and wooden door covered in strange carvings.

Having no other recourse, I step up and rap soundly on the door with my now friendly staff. The door swung open.

"Come in, friend, I've been expecting you," came a disembodied voice from within.

Expecting me? Not sure how that could be possible.

Gingerly I stepped across the

threshold, pausing just inside for a minute so my eyes can adjust to the darker room.

"Oh, please, step on in, don't be frightened," the voice spoke again.

My eyes begin to regulate, so I continue with several more tentative steps, then stopped, amazed.

The tiny cottage is larger on the inside. It is a vast great room, many sizes more expansive than it appeared outwardly. Filled with Old-World furniture, each surface covered in taxidermy animals of all descriptions, vessels, and objects too numerous to name. Some strewn with papers, filled with writing in languages I couldn't read. Several boxes of pens and Chinese brushes near jars of inks of many colors lay upon the desk.

Standing next to one table is a little man, his shoulders are barely above the tabletop. I knew he was old to be sure– leathery skin, bald with a fringe of snowy white hair and a full white beard, his eyebrows looking like two caterpillars. The man wore what looked like those white Kurta pajamas from India, covered in strange symbols.

For a long moment, I just stood there, mouth slightly open, staring around, trying to take it all in. Both room and man looked like something out of the Arabian Nights or King Arthur and the Round Table. To say I was dumbstruck is putting it mildly.

"Welcome. My name is Marvin, Marvin T. MacLaine. You can call me Marv if you prefer. Tell me about yourself?" his voice cheerful and high pitched.

"I, I–I'm John, John Morgan. I'm just here in the area visiting. I like to travel; I have an active business that affords me the resources and time to, uh, visit locations such as this state park. Ah– and I'm an only child. Both my parents are deceased. So there's just me– I'm young, but eventually, I hope to see the world or as much of it as possible..." I paused, unsure why so much information had come tumbling out. Then...

"May I ask a question? Where am I?"

"Well, John, you are in MY forest."

"But, but," I stammer, "your forest? This is a public walking trail, isn't it?"

"Well, it is, and then again, it isn't. I don't get many visitors here. I see to that."

I said nothing.

Marvin smiled, and I swear his eyes twinkled as if they were star shine.

"You brought my friend back," he said, clapping his hands in a child-like manner. "Put him over there." He indicated a rack along a wall, which held several other odd-looking sticks.

I did as instructed. When I placed the staff in the rack, the stick seemed to sigh with contentment. Reaching out, I softly ran my hand over the line of sticks, which all elicited soft sighs. Was I merely imagining?

"Uh Marv, if you don't mind me asking, well, you seem to expect me, so, how and why did you get me here? And where the heck is here? Am I still on the Sandy River Trail?"

Marvin doesn't seem to have heard me for a moment. Then he beams a mischievous smile. "My stick friends are known to go out on their own and return with someone they feel might like a visit with me. It seems you are one of those people. Before you arrived, I was preparing a meal. Why don't you sit, and we'll eat while we talk?"

Having no other recourse and realizing that my stomach is

growling, I take a seat at the table. How long ago did I eat that energy bar? Marvin hustles around his cooking area, filling two wooden bowls with some form of stew from a large cauldron hung near a fire. He places a bowl and a wooden spoon before me.

I filled my spoon full of broth, blew on it, and then took a tentative slurp. Then an odd thing happened. I began to feel comfortable as if I had known this strange man in another life. He seemed somehow like an old uncle. Again, I gazed around the room.

"Your cottage appears so small from the outside but is huge inside. An optical illusion? Do you live alone? How long have you been here?" A torrent of questions aimed at my host.

Marvin pauses, his spoon hanging in midair, stew dripping back into the bowl. He looks skyward as if calculating a number. Finally, "Oh, a very long time."

"But, but," I stammer, "How is that possible? I was walking down a trail when your stick seemed to pick me up. It was like magic..." John's voice trailed off.

Marv smiled an enigmatic smile, sipping some dark liquid from a horn cup.

"Your spoons are fascinating," I said, reaching for a warty one and then stopped remembering the walking staff. I pointed to a large, elegantly curved one. "Are they decorative, or do you eat with them? I mean, are they like the walking staff? Are they… alive? I mean, would it hurt them to be used? Would they… dislike it?"

"Oh, most of my items are just what they seem, spoons, bowls, plates, cups. But, the walking sticks and my special mixing spoons are another thing altogether. You've already met my sticks; they like you, John."

Like me? How does a wooden stick like someone?

My gaze fell on an extensive collection of wooden spoons, which are myriad. There are short warty looking ones, large elegantly curved ones, long thin spoons with various sized bowls, like measuring instruments.

"Those spoons are fascinating. You said they are special, do you make them or merely collect them? Are they for use or decorative?"

"Ah, my tools? No, each of those spoons has a purpose, used for measuring the exact amount needed for my potions. Each of these spoons was carved from woods obtained in an ancient forest that vanished long ago. These utensils are old beyond measure, created by craftsmen, each who have since faded into another world. My father and his father and many others before have used these spoons."

"Um, uh," I continued, "Used, you say? For cooking?"

"In a way," Marv mused, "Used in making potions. You see John; I am a wizard of the old order."

"Ha! No way! A wizard?" escapes my lips. "Oh, come on, a wizard? Seriously? Don't you mean magician, of the new order?"

Stunned, I pause to collect my thoughts. "So, are you a magician who can do wizard-like tricks?

"Magician, wizard, I prefer wizard. And yes, I am a real wizard, of the old order," Marv smiled and gave a little bow.

"An actual wizard? Spells and incantations? That sort of thing?"

"Exactly that sort of thing. You see, my grandfather was Merlin in the court of King Arthur. Merlin's knowledge has passed down to my father, and he passed it down to me."

"Oh, come on! Everyone knows

about the legend of Merlin; he wasn't real, only a children's story." I stutter. "You're telling me he was a real living wizard-person?"

"Oh, indeed, Merlin was real, John, whether you believe or not."

"Marv, you seem rather kindly, but, really, aren't these practices you speak often called the Black Arts?"

This time, Marvin laughed out loud.

"Well, what I mean to say is that many stories about wizards that passed down through the ages have some wizards using their magic for nefarious purposes? Isn't that so?" John paused.

"Well... of course that is true with a few wizards, but virtually every story told about my grandfather Merlin, is wrong. We magicians have powers, yes, but we try not to interfere with the world as such.

I have lived through many generations, my boy. While my memories and practices are most certainly from the long-ago, I must live in the present, taking on aspects of speech and dress of current times. At any rate, I suspect you think I am just a crazy old crank you stumbled

upon during your walk. Isn't that accurate, John?"

"Well, to tell the truth, Marv. I don't know what to think about you, or any of, of... this." Throwing my arm up, I gesture around the great room turning in a complete circle.

"My problem is I am lost and need to find my way back. You seem to have pulled me here, for what reason, I'm not sure, but all of this confuses and scares me some. Am I being held a prisoner here?" I gesture around me again.

Marvin once again gave me that grandfatherly look, "Oh, pish posh. A prisoner? I should say not! You'll be back on your path in no time. I do have my reason for wanting to meet you, though. But first, won't you join me in a nice cup of my special tea? Then I'll send you on your way."

"Well, I really should be... You aren't going to cast some kind of spell on me are you? John laughed nervously.

"John, I already have." Marvin's eyes once again twinkled at me from under his bushy eyebrows.

Marvin smiled a knowing smile. "You know John, as I explained, you are not here by accident. Once I found you, I knew I had to meet you to introduce you to your family."

"My family? What do you mean my…"

"Morgan, that's not your original family name." It was not a question but a statement.

"What? Wait. Why no, our original name was Morgana, I believe." I stopped talking, realizing what that name might mean in the world of wizards and tales of Merlin.

Marvin pressed on, "Yes, you see John, Morgan le Fay, Morgana was my grandmother. Yes, that Morgana, but she was no evil witch, that is just something people invented to spice up their stories. Morgana was a great wizard though. When grandma Morgana and grandfather Merlin married, they produced my father. Morgana had a brother, my uncle. He was not involved in the Dark Arts, as you called them. My uncle is your grandfather, many times removed. You see John, you and I are cousins.

"Let me fix that cup of tea." Marvin started to turn away.

"Wait, so you are saying that YOU and I are cousins?" My voice cracked on the word cousin.

"You are telling me I have a family? That YOU are my family? Marv, Marvin, I'm finding this entire conversation to be incredulous. Your story is just too outlandish. I'd like to get back, please."

"Just one cup and it will be done," Marvin promised.

"You're not lying? Just a cup of tea? Okay, one cup, then please send me back on the path."

"Yes, John, believe me, or don't, we are cousins, and that is exactly my plan. Listen, my boy; I've spent years looking for you. To put you on a good path, I've brought you here to help you, you'll see… Well, then!"

Clapping his hands, Marvin bustled over to his stove and placed a large kettle on the fire. He selected a container stenciled with the word TEA in block letters, then looking thoughtfully at his spoons, he paused as if in deep consideration.

"Now let me see…" he mused aloud. Nodding, then shaking his head, then finally, "ah, I have just the right one."

Marvin selected a tiny thin spoon and scooped a portion of tea into the teapot. The kettle seemed to go on the boil unusually fast. Soon, I am sipping a cup of strong black tea. Brew, unlike any I have ever tasted, robust and dark, but not bitter. Most soothing.

Stunned by this seeming revelation of family, I don't have words. This morning I had no family and now...? That is if I can believe what I am being told. I have my doubts. I sit quietly, sipping the soothing tea, thoughts running through my brain, I haven't actually seen this "wizard" do anything wizardly. But, then again, a magic stick brought me to a cottage that no one can seem to see hidden in a heavily traveled forest.

When I began to ask Marvin more questions, I found my mouth would not work properly. It seemed to me to be getting dimmer inside the cottage; the light was fading. That cup of tea is the last I remember of cousin Marvin T MacLaine, also known as, Marvin, the magician.

"Sir? SIR! Do you want another cup of coffee? Or shall I bring the check?"

Suddenly, I awaken from a fog of confusion. Was this merely a daydream?

"Wha, what? Oh, no, no more coffee, thanks." I peer around at my surroundings and find myself sitting at the lunch counter in the same diner where I ate my breakfast. Oddly the time is late afternoon. The entrance to the forested park is visible across the parking lot. Late afternoon sun illuminated the gates like a beacon, but the dark shadows of the forest make it appear impenetrable.

"Are you okay, sir?" The waitress handed me my check.

"Why yes, yes, I am. I was lost in a dream; that's all." I reached into my pocket for money and grasp something that felt like a pencil. I withdrew a small, ancient carved spoon. With it a piece of parchment with this written on it:

John, when you lose your way off the path, prepare a cup of tea, using this spoon. It will bring you peace and help smooth your path in life. I'll be seeing you again. – Cousin Marvin

This tangled tale is the story of my walk in the woods. I understand it's a wondrous yarn to believe, but if you are ever in my neck of the woods, stop in. I'll fix you a nice cup of tea. Trust me; you'll feel better. ◉

A Tangled

Tale of a Walk in the Woods

Jeremy Schnee lives in Portland, Oregon. Aside from writing, he likes to garden, practice martial arts, and spend time with his family. He strives to write most days of the week, and finds that following a schedule, even if sometimes begrudgingly, helps lull him into progress more often than not. He also strives to write topics that enrich some part of his own interests, whether that requires research on mythical creatures, or digging out a Nintendo Entertainment System from the attic to smell it. To find out where to read more of his published work, and to read articles in his monthly series, 'My Yesteryear Opinionated and Probably Irrelevant Analysis,' check out www.jeremyschnee.com.

Tethered: An Escape in the Clouds

Jeremy Schnee

Part 1

While Sally Freewheel had the misfortune of not sleeping for a single second in nearly six years, her son Adam had the most extraordinary fortune. When he slept: he floated in the air. First his eyes fluttered. Uncoiling springs moaned as he lifted from the mattress. Blankets drooped, dropped. Then his small body bounced on the ceiling like a feather in the breeze. On occasion, he would flicker out of dreams and crash to the floor. She used to catch him when he was a baby. At three, he fell like a sack of potatoes into her arms. At five, he was too big. Though he coasted down most mornings to awake in bed, tonight she would not wait for morning. Tonight, she and her son were leaving this house, leaving the man sleeping in the next room over.

Little Adam shared a room with old electronics and growing stacks of newspapers. His floor space was limited to a mattress and milk crate dresser. The ceiling was at least all his. Sally pulled the mattress around the room, ready to catch him. His shadow, limbs, and hair— overdue for a cut—dangled and danced. When he got floated into the corner, she pushed the mattress under him.

"Adam," she whispered.

He hovered for a second. Blinked. His arms flapped. Then he plopped down.

"We're leaving," Sally said. "Leaving this house forever."

"Really?" he whispered and stood. "Okay!" He hopped from the mattress.

She had a backpack full of food, clothes, and three hundred

twelve dollars. She lifted it unto her shoulders as they tiptoed through the creaking house.

"What time is it?"

"Four in the morning," she whispered.

"I've never once been up at four in the morning."

She pulled the heavy paint-chipped door open. Adam ran outside.

Thick clouds blotted out the moon, and even just steps ahead, he practically disappeared into the dark. For a moment, Sally considered calling him back in. Dare she think she could care for her son alone? They had no friends, no family. An echo boomed through the house, a snore that sounded like a bear in a cave. Jim would come looking for them today. Of this, she was certain. Adam came back to take her hand; she stepped outside with him.

"So where are we going anyway, Mom?"

She wasn't sure. Not having slept in six years, her thoughts were always blurry. Of all her planning to leave the house, she'd only thought up to this moment.

"Somewhere better," she shrugged.

Adam had been at this house since he was born. Jim wasn't his father. In agreement for a place to live, a place to raise her son, Sally became his servant. She cooked, cleaned, and when pushed enough, went to bed with Jim. Despite wanting to leave many times, Jim often spoke of money owed him for bills when Adam was born.

If she tried to go, he said, he'd hunt her down and drag her home by the hair.

Until recently, Jim had never been a threat to Adam. He never held Adam as a baby, never played with him, and rarely even talked to him. He certainly never cared about Adam's sleeping habits. With kindergarten planned to start tomorrow, Adam had been excited lately. He thumped the ceiling and walls extra hard when asleep. Jim asked about the noises. She caught him in the room yesterday, standing on a stool and staring at a scuff mark. She wasn't sure what Jim would do if he knew about Adam, but some semblance of instinct told her it was time to get Adam far away.

Grass brushed their ankles, and an occasional dandelion head arced in the air from their steps. Jim's one-story house looked like nothing more than a black triangle behind.

"You know, people use highways to go places," Sally said. "We could go there."

"Sounds like a plan," Adam said.

"Yeah, we'll go to the highway and walk far away."

They crossed the barren fields surrounding Jim's house and into the sleeping town of Wispville where the homes grew larger in size. As they neared the sidewalks of Main Street, Adam began to pull in excitement.

"Look!" he said. He was pointing at the streetlights ahead. Walking on uneven sidewalk, the white orbs seemed to move up and down.

"They look like bouncing stars, don't they?"

She tried to explain they were just simple light poles.

"It's okay if you don't see it, Mom," Adam said.

He stood close, protective as a five-year-old could be. He didn't have many toys or even enough time to play, but in all his short life, he never complained. Day to day, Adam mostly saw the same backyards and insides of people's houses as she brought him along with cleaning. If

their mothers didn't mind, she pushed him to play with children at these houses. Often, he even helped her clean. Once a day, she took him to the library or sat on benches as he ran in the park. His favorite pastime was to lead them both on random walks around town.

"You know, in a few minutes," Sally said. "You'll be further from that home than you've ever been."

He didn't look back. They passed the ketchup plant where Jim worked, were dwarfed by buildings of downtown— three stories considered tall for Wispville—and at the end of town, over the flat Ohio landscape, they saw the first slivers of rising sun.

"So Mom, did you maybe sleep last night?" Adam said.

He asked every morning. It was always the same. Not since months before he was born had Sally fallen into that world of limp limbs and jumbled thoughts. Her eyes were black underneath. She used makeup to keep from looking like a raccoon. She ate enough, just, her limbs and ribs were skeleton thin. At least she still had long black hair like shining silk, and her lips were naturally dark as the skin of an apple. Although at twenty-two, she looked much older.

"No sleep," Sally said, "Not last night." She still closed her eyes tight as knots and lay on the couch across from Adam's room. Just like Jim didn't know about Adam, she didn't want him to know about her.

"I just wish you could tell me about a dream," Adam said.

"I'm sorry," she said, "Will you tell me yours?"

"Last night I climbed a tree big as a mountain," he said, "Or maybe as big. I've never seen a mountain." In these past two years, he'd told her of many dreams. Dreams where they lived on a giant turtle in the ocean, dreams where they were small as dust, a dream dinner where he tasted time, or visited talking animals with accents.

Soon, the mundane gray highway came into view. Adam slowed his steps as he saw the broad road. Two lanes in each direction, flat and parallel to the sky.

"It's big," Adam said.

"It runs all the way across the country," Sally replied.

"From ocean to ocean!" Adam screamed.

He touched the edge of asphalt with the kind of care she'd taught him to give a stove. He gazed in both directions and asked if he might see ocean water soon.

"The country is much bigger than that," Sally said.

"How big?"

She pinched her chin and stuttered each time she tried to think of a way to explain.

"Is the road like this in the country?" He pulled a hair from his head and laid the thin brown thread across his palm.

"I suppose that's about right," she said. "Yeah, that's about right."

"Then we shouldn't have trouble finding a place to hide."

Adam insisted on taking a turn with the backpack and said they were like snails, carrying their home. Sally kept him to the outside edge of the road and held his hand as he watched trucks and cars. They saw occasional houses or run-down barns off the road. Never once did Adam ask about Jim. He did ask about school. Her first priority, once they got on their feet, would be getting him into kindergarten somewhere.

After morning rush hour, traffic slowed. Sometimes a whole minute went by without a car whooshing past. In these breaks, the silence felt peaceful. Sally even began to think they might be safe. Maybe they'd gone far enough Jim would never find them. Just as such a thought formed, she heard something. Very faint, easily mistaken for whistling wind, or a far off birdcall, the noise squealed louder. When Sally turned, she saw a sparkle of red in the distance.

"It's him!"

The brakes on Jim's truck were so rusted they screamed even when the truck wasn't stopping.

"Run!" She grabbed Adam's hand and pulled him off the highway. There were no trees to stand behind, no ditches to jump in. There was nothing but fields of grass.

"He'll see us!"

"Go for the tall grass," Adam yelled.

They ran until grass reached their knees, and then following his lead, Sally dropped and hugged the ground tight. Grass tickled her face. Brakes screeched louder. When the sound was like a wailing banshee, she closed her eyes. But, the truck passed without even slowing.

"You're a brilliant little boy."

She kissed Adam's forehead.

"At least we'll hear him coming," he said.

So they kept their ears open. Sally watched for abandoned sheds, fields of corn, and underpasses where they might hide if needed. For lunch, they picnicked behind a billboard. Walking and walking, Sally began to notice an unpleasant tingling in her legs. Her muscles felt tight as bowstrings. Her feet seemed ready to swell out of her shoes. Pain and exhaustion were something she long ago learned to ignore, but her body tingled with a new sort of pain.

While walking, the years stacked behind her, days where memories were difficult to see. She had forgotten so much. When had even her name became forgettable? She was technically still a kid when Adam was born. She fumbled with diapers, feedings, even holding him. At the same time, she had to keep Jim happy, and she had no one else to talk to, nowhere else to go. Quiet, obedient, she became like a table in the corner: serving a simple purpose and rarely noticed. Sally could see it clearly now: when she began to forget which day was which, even the meaning of some words. Especially, she forgot the world outside Jim's house.

At first, she wasn't even aware of what happened to Adam when he slept. He was light in her arms like she held an empty blanket rather than a sleeping baby. When scooped from the bed, her fingers slid so easily under him. Not until months after he was born did she understand what was happening.

When had things changed? She guessed it was when Adam began to talk and tell her his dreams. That's when she began to remember more of the world. Short trips out helped her find cleaning jobs. Work provided excuses to Jim for leaving the house. Yet, there was something so vitally important that Sally forgot to do back in those murkiest years.

"Like bouncing stars!" Sally blurted.

"Huh?" Adam said.

"Nothing, nothing." Even miles later, taking step after step, watching the landscape bob ahead, she understood what Adam had been talking about this morning with the streetlights. And she understood what she'd been forgetting then. She lost her imagination; hadn't played with him enough.

When she accidentally bumped Adam with her hips, he bumped back and giggled. She bumped him again. His laughter was loud, and Sally stood straighter. She looked up from the dull gray cement. Her eyes watered from the bright sun, but she didn't dare close them. Turning to the glimmering fields, unending sky, and her son, she looked hungrily around them.

"Come here, Adam." She knelt and told him to climb on her shoulders.

"Are you kidding?" he said, "But why?"

"You'll be able to see better."

He examined both sides of her face for a moment. Then he shrugged and climbed on. When she stood, he gasped and laughed, and pointed at a field of cows.

"Do you think cows can talk, Mom? They seem to move their mouths a lot."

"They can at least say moo," Sally said. "Maybe it means hello."

"Yeah," Adam said. "I bet you're right."

"If I could only say one thing for the rest of my life, I'd want it to be hello."

"Me too," he said.

She carried him nearly half a mile. The day went on. They had to hide from Jim twice more. At other times, Sally heard a radio or distant dog, and such sounds caused her to reach across Adam and hold her hand in front of his chest. By evening, he was so conditioned to this action, when she placed her hand out at the apex of an overpass, he held his hands to his ears to listen.

"I don't hear anything," he said.

She didn't either, but she stopped all the same. In the distance, the chimney of a small cobblestone farmhouse puffed. Trees in the backyard were dotted with red and yellow fruit. Upfront, an open meadow stretched around a tiny pond that glimmered like a mirror. Next to the water, an old wooden windmill spun its sails with the calmness of a clock.

"You know, Adam. I think I can remember dreams?" Sally pointed, "At least, don't they sort of look like this? The good ones I mean."

"Yeah, Mom. That's sometimes what dreams look like."

"I want us to live somewhere like that."

Their pace slowed as dusk neared. Sally began to watch for safe places to stop. Then Adam saw a strange blue light off the highway. At first, a twinkle. He tried to guess what such an odd light might be. Deep in her blur of memories, Sally recalled something from before Jim's house. The light grew brighter, came into an obvious view.

"I think I used to work off this exit," she said.

"At that place?" Adam asked. He tugged on her arm.

"Years ago."

It was called the Lighthouse Diner, just a little truck stop. The diner had chipped peach walls and a little plastic lighthouse on top with a blue light that worked as a bug zapper during summer. Yes, this was where she first met Jim.

"I like the light," Adam said.

"Do you want to eat here?" Sally asked.

"At a real restaurant?"

The three hundred twelve dollars was all she could scrimp and save for them. She supposed they could spare a little. Seeing the diner, knowing they'd come this far, she wanted to celebrate.

"Want to race to the doors?" she asked.

"You and me?" he asked, "Okay!"

The backpack bounced on her shoulders, and she let him take a slight lead. He pumped his arms and legs faster. She faked breathing hard, and as laughter overtook her until she lost her breath. Before reaching the entrance, she let him pull ahead. He cheered on the step outside the doors. He stopped and looked at her face, as though all this time, she'd been half-hidden from him.

Sally opened the diner doors. The plume of cool air conditioning brought a rush of familiarity: old red stools, plastic gray tables that easily wiped clean, bacon smoke with a hint of vanilla, and behind plastic, pies that looked like they were made of plastic too.

"What do you think?" she asked.

"I thought there'd be more boats at a lighthouse restaurant," Adam said.

"I hear they don't drive so well on land," she said.

"On land!" He squeezed his stomach and giggled.

The few older couples dining smiled at Adam as he and Sally found a booth. Of course, the staff had changed in years since she left. Their waitress looked of high school age. Adam wanted spaghetti burgers, a special request he often made at home. Before the waitress said no, Sally blurted out that she used to work here, even asked if the steam from the fryer still smelled like cabbage on Tuesdays. It seemed to help. The waitress obliged and agreed to get Adam's order, and Sally asked for the same.

"You know this isn't the first time in my life," Sally said, "When I've walked a great distance to get to this diner."

"Really?"

"When I was fifteen, I left home after my mom died."

Sally remembered how she had watched her mother wilt. After she died, Sally's dad turned rabid—part helplessness, and part angry at Sally, the mirage of her mother, the woman he had loved. Life varied from weeks of invisibility to weeks of verbal abuse. Of course, she didn't tell Adam the full details of the story.

"I traveled across three and a half states in a year's time."

A skipping stone on the landscape, she went from town to town, job to job. She made friends to stay with at times; at other times, she endured hunger and cold. Admittedly, some men were willing to help her find food and shelter, but only in exchange for a bit of her. These same kinds of men were often the reason she saw a need to leave for new places.

Remembering this, Sally partly felt sorry she could never tell Adam about his father. Adam had asked about him. She told him his dad wasn't around and wasn't ever going to be. The truth, some of those men were worse than others. She didn't want to think about it, to pinpoint who exactly. If those memories remained ever blurry, that'd be fine for her. Adam was wonderful; he was her son; that was all that mattered.

"Are you sad?" Adam asked.

"I've never been happier."

They ate and talked of places they might live, jobs she could get, the type of town they wanted. Adam would start at a good school, and maybe someday they'd get their own house.

"Tomorrow, we'll get closer to all that," Sally said.

Adam's eyes were baggy. She recalled a cheap motel about a mile away. She had stayed there a few times years before. One night when she didn't get enough tip money, she had decided to huddle up behind the diner. It was a cold night, with the grass like spikes beneath her. A customer found her—one who'd taken to coming in every day since her first morning on the job. He'd taken to only wanting her to wait on him, one she knew she ought not to encourage—Jim. She had only intended to stay with him until the cold passed.

After paying the bill, Adam watched her carefully fold the money into the backpack.

"Can I carry the bag again?" he asked. "Please."

"Sure."

She rarely had the chance to offer him responsibility. When they both needed to use the restroom, she sent him in alone after ensuring he locked the men's room door behind.

"Meet me out here," she called.

Her bathroom floor had dark tile. Walls had no windows, and pipes ran across the ceiling. She had bathed in here a few times years back. Maybe for the familiarity, she found the room relaxing. She dropped her head in her hands, her hair like lead curtains, toenails like tiny anvils, and her muscles a rag soaked in bleach. One problem with regaining more sensation—true exhaustion. She took deep breaths and let her body crumple for but a second. So, when the first faint whispers of whistling started, she dismissed it as water in rusty pipes. The more the noise grew, the more she figured it an echo creaking off the tile. Only as the sound mixed with the gravel crunching under tires, did she finally recognize the screech of Jim's truck.

She flung the door open and pounded on the men's room door. The door wasn't locked, and she opened it to an empty toilet and sink. People in the diner stopped chewing as they watched her.

"Adam!" she yelled.

The waitress pointed outside. He'd gone out to the parking lot to wait. A car door shut. In the faint blue light outside the diner doors, Sally saw her son's small shadow huddled between cars. Too late to join him, she wasn't going to dare hide and lose sight of Adam either. With only one option left, she stood at the diner's entrance and waited.

Heavy feet scraped. A silhouette like a lion on two legs came into view. Jim had a thick mane of beard and a hunched posture. He pushed the door open. When he saw Sally, he laughed. Maybe he laughed because she was here at the same diner where he first met her. Maybe he laughed out of exhaustion from searching all day, or because she tried to do something for her and Adam. Jim knew Sally better than that.

"You and Adam are coming home," Jim ordered with his hands on his hips.

"My debt is more than repaid," Sally said. "I'm leaving."

"Now, don't be stupid," he said. "I know you can't support Adam and yourself on your own. And don't you need a roof over your head, or how about his?" Jim smiled, showing his broad and crooked teeth.

"We're leaving," her words bellowed.

People in the diner tried to ignore the commotion; only a few conversations still mumbled.

"No!" Jim roared, "You can't go!"

Customers clanged silverware on plates as everyone stopped eating.

Sally didn't dare move. Outside, the tiny shadow bobbed between cars and came closer to the door. Adam pulled a flashlight out of the backpack. He held it like a club and moved like a bouncing balloon toward Jim. She shook her head 'no.'

"I woke up this morning," Jim said, "And the house was quiet. I walked into the kitchen, and you weren't there. It was just so quiet, I couldn't stand it."

Adam was almost right behind Jim.

"You can't just leave," Jim said.

Anger, desperation, loneliness, muddled somewhere in there, Jim might care about them.

Sally mouthed, 'no' to Adam. Just then, the bug zapper in the little lighthouse caught something big and clapped with a thunder strike. Sally jumped. Jim turned to see Adam behind.

For a five-year-old, he swung the flashlight with might. Jim simply swatted the blow aside. Jim chased Adam into the parking lot, and Sally plowed through the door. Adam staggered with the backpack, and Jim pounced. He lifted the pack, and Adam, wiggling him like a puppet on strings.

"Leave him alone," she yelled.

"If you won't come home, then I'll take the boy," Jim said. "But I have a feeling you'll follow real soon."

Adam kicked and punched. Jim walked him toward the truck. When her shouting did nothing, she swung at the trunk of Jim's arm. Twice her weight, he shoved her and she fell to the gravel. He tossed Adam in his truck and pushed her off once more as he got in the driver's seat.

"Maybe walking all the way home will teach you a lesson," Jim said. He started his car and pinned Adam to the seat.

She kicked at the truck and tried to open the door. Jim backed it up. Her fingers grazed the handle as the truck peeled away. Stones swarmed through the air and stung her legs. Sally didn't stop or slow. She stayed in the red of tail lights even as Jim accelerated on the road. When he slowed for the on-ramp, Sally was ready to dive in the truck bed if she could just get close enough. Adam had fought free of Jim. His hands pressed against the rear window, and his mouth moved as he yelled out to her, but she could not hear it over the screeching brakes. The truck again picked up speed and pulled out of her reach, pulled far ahead on the highway. The air began to chill. The sun had set.

Sally gasped for breath. Her legs shook and teetered below her. She stood upright. Soon, she couldn't even see the lights of Jim's truck. But she knew what she had to do. As far as she and Adam had walked today, she'd have to go back and even faster than before. Yes, Jim may well discover what happened when Adam slept, but now it changed nothing. Out of all the things Sally saw today, she saw nothing clearer than her need to get Adam out of that house. That was still the plan. One step at a time, she began the long walk back.

Part 2

As night pressed on and cars dwindled in number, the only sounds on the highway were occasional cricket chirps and the stomping of heavy steps. Sally's feet felt like clay. This didn't slow her. She knew Adam would try to stay awake until the house rumbled with Jim's snoring. The day had tired him, though. And if not at night, Jim was likely to look in on Adam when he woke for work. She had to be home by then. So one swift step at a time, she walked. Just before dawn, she reached the edge of the road where a day before, Adam had marveled at the size of the

highway, 'like a hair across the palm.'

When they left Wispville, she thought she, for the last time smelled burning tomato from the ketchup factory. She thought she took her last look at the big houses she cleaned near the park. The crooked sidewalk on Main Street jarred her sore feet, but proximity to Jim's home invigorated her. Jim's house was once blue, but time had turned it gray. In back, a shed roof peeled. Scattered tufts of weeds stood taller than the rest of the grass in his big open yard. The truck sat in the driveway, and lights were off inside.

Thank goodness! Maybe she wasn't too late. The cage of her ribs constricted on her lungs. Her tired body wanted nothing more than to collapse, but she stifled her breath and stood up straight at the back door. She removed her shoes and tiptoed into the kitchen.

The house always smelled like stale bread. The floor creaked in warming from night to day. Quite familiar with the sounds of the house at night, she immediately noticed something off. She heard silence. No grumble, no sound of snoring. She listened for stirring sheets or water running in the bathroom. Only then, in the very kitchen she stood, did she hear the breathing.

"Hello, Sally," Jim said. His voice cracked like dynamite from the table. "Well, I see you walked all the way home like a lost dog or something."

"Jim!" Her back hit the counter. "You're awake." Morning light hadn't yet reached the window above the sink. Jim's thick shadow arched over the table.

"I'm glad you're home," he said, "Real glad. And I hope we won't be having anymore nonsense like yesterday."

"A shame you were worried," Sally said.

In an odd way, Sally cared about Jim. That care had become something she'd prefer to do from a distance. Something like selling an old dress, a thing she'd never see again but would hope was holding up well enough over time.

"So Sally, aren't you going to ask the obvious?" He rubbed his beard and set his hands on the table. "Don't you want to know why I'm sitting here in the dark?"

Cool morning air blew in the window and licked her damp clothes. From the few times Jim had really lost his temper with her, Sally knew he was most dangerous when angry and calm. She looked right at him, never down the hall towards Adam's room.

"I got up to see if you were home," he said, "Thought I'd check my lotto tickets too." An avid player, he bought tickets every day, griped when he lost. He had the newspaper in hand.

"And I'm sitting in the dark," he said, "Because the way light creeps under a door like a snake, I just hate that and didn't want to wake Adam." (In five years, Jim had never cared about how many lights he turned on in the morning.) "Wouldn't that be something," Jim said, "To win the lottery." He flipped the light switch on and started tearing losing tickets in half.

"Since you're up," she said. "I should get breakfast going."

Sally pulled a skillet out of a cupboard while banging it against pots and pans. She slammed the refrigerator, shook the utensil drawer. She hoped to hear a thump on the floor, but her son didn't wake.

"You know what I'd do if I won," Jim said. "I'd share, share with you, and Adam."

Sally turned as he tore his last

ticket in half. If there had ever been hope they could become a family, it ended when Adam first learned to talk. He'd call to Jim, carry toys to him, even follow him sometimes. Jim never once acknowledged him.

"Yeah, if I won, I wouldn't do anything like hide it," Jim said.

"A shame you didn't win then."

"Didn't I?" He stretched. He looked as he had last night, his beard and hair grungy, his strong but heavy body lurching. From working at the ketchup factory, bending over conveyor belts, Jim no longer stood straight.

"What do you mean?" Sally asked.

"I really hope we won't have any more nonsense with you trying to leave."

She stood at the stove and threw butter on the frying pan.

"I've been thinking about something else this morning," Jim said. "I think I ought to adopt Adam. Make him my son too."

The butter sizzled. Sally gripped the pan's handle.

"I've given him a home all these years," Jim said. "I suppose a court might see me having rights to him. Especially considering the state his mother was in when she came here."

She lifted the pan from the burner. Her knuckles turned white. The chunk of butter stopped melting. She took a deep breath and wanted to swing the pan with all her might. For more than five years, exhaustion had made her docile. With a heavy stomach, tears in the corners of her eyes, she knew it was fear that stopped her now.

Jim moved quiet as a shadow across the kitchen. His hands snatched her shoulders; his black fingernails dug into skin. She was no match for him physically, even with a frying pan.

"Me and the boy are going to become friends," Jim whispered, "Partners too." His breath tickled her ear.

"If I would have won the lotto Sally, I would've shared, not you, though." He let go of her shoulders and backed away.

She set the frying pan on the burner, and butter began to sizzle again. Sally knew she had one advantage. Jim didn't know she was a different woman than the one who had left the house yesterday.

"Don't try to take the boy away!" Jim shouted. Walls shook. Then the floor did too. There had been a thud in Adam's room.

"By the way," Jim said. "Isn't the kid supposed to start school today?"

Yes. If they were here anyhow, she supposed he would start school. The door to Adam's room opened, and he zigzagged out as he rubbed his eyes.

"Mom!" he yelled.

She knelt and spread her arms to brace herself. Worn to the bone, she expected Adam's hug to feel like a charging bull. A cloud puffed into the air when he hit. Specks of white covered his hair like he'd been in a snowstorm.

"What the hell is on you?" Jim asked.

Adam seemed just as surprised as he checked his clothes and coughed from the dust. Jim walked towards Adam's room, and before Sally could follow, her son leaned closer.

"Mom, did you dream last night?"

"I was too busy walking."

"I just hoped you might," Adam said, "After how you started acting yesterday."

"No dreams," she said.

"I did," he whispered. "I dreamt big."

Before she could ask, Jim cheered and clapped. He flipped the light on in Adam's room, and Sally joined him inside. A donut of the white dust covered the floor, piles of boxes, newspapers. There was a crater in Adam's ceiling. Drywall bubbled toward the attic in the center of the room.

Adam tried to apologize. She shushed him. Then they followed a normal routine, with Adam helping to make the bed on the floor. Sally next hurried to pick out some clothes from the milk crates. Adam caught her eye and didn't say anything more about his room or sleeping last night. Jim followed them into the kitchen when they went to eat.

"Don't you have to get ready for work?" Sally asked.

"Today's a special occasion," Jim said. "Adam's first day of school, after all."

"Is it really," Adam said, "Do I get to go?"

"You do," she said.

"Don't get too excited," Jim said. "I hated school."

Adam set his cereal spoon down and asked if it was scary. When Sally tried to tell him otherwise, Jim laid his hand on Adam's shoulder.

"School is the end of childhood," Jim said, and he went on about yelling teachers, grades, the principal's office. Adam stopped eating entirely. "Don't worry," Jim said. "Starting tomorrow, you can stay home, and your Mom can teach you." Jim sounded almost rehearsed. For whatever reason, he seemed to want Adam out of the house just for today.

As the sun rose and the house grew brighter, Jim's shadow got bigger. He was there while they cleaned after breakfast, packed a lunch, and readied her old backpack. Jim insisted he drive them, and she knew if she said otherwise, he would be more than happy to leave her home on her son's first day of school.

With the truck brakes screeching, talking was impossible. But once the big brick school came into view, Adam inched forward in his seat. School bells rang. Adam stretched his seatbelt and stood to see windows decorated with construction paper art and more kids than he'd ever seen together as they played in the schoolyard. Jim reached out and pushed Adam back down in the seat. He parked the truck. Then as Jim got out on the other side, not distracted, but the furthest from them he'd been all morning, Sally grabbed the backpack and pointed to the doors of the school.

"Hey Adam," she said. "Race you."

"Like yesterday?"

Jim was bulky and strong, but not fast. They left him behind and weaved around children and parents. Just as they reached the front doors, another bell rang and kids filtered to the door like sand into an hourglass. Sally grabbed Adam's hand and rushed them toward the kindergarten classroom.

"Adam." She bent below the waves of shuffling students. "You're going to have a great time at school. Just look around you." The schoolhouse was old, with wooden staircases and floors. Teachers welcomed students into the many classrooms.

"Listen to everyone," Sally said. Laughter and voices bounced off the walls. Floors rumbled under excited steps.

"Do you smell that?"

He sniffed the air. "It's like we walked into a box of crayons," he said. He finally faced the kindergarten classroom. Alphabet blow-ups figures lined shelves, and cardboard numbers hung from the ceiling.

"Don't be afraid," Sally stood.

"Wait!" Adam yelled. "I still have to tell you about my dream last night."

Sally saw Jim push through the school doors. He shuffled through hip-high children and called for her.

"What in the world happened in your little room?"

"Because of yesterday," Adam said, "Because I was excited about all the things we saw. Know what happened when I dreamt," he pulled her down and whispered, "I flew."

"You always do that."

"No, in my dream, I could fly. I saw the whole town. I saw the road we walked yesterday, and the places we hid from Jim. I could see all of it."

Even amongst running and laughing children, she heard heavy steps. She pushed Adam into the classroom and winked. From behind, a vice seemed to grab her arm. On thin muscle, the bruise spread like ink on paper. Sally watched Adam walk into the classroom and stop cold. He didn't run for the toys or talk to other kids. He just stood, and she was afraid nerves had seized him. Maybe he wasn't ready for

school yet.

"Don't you give me any more trouble," Jim said.

Sally noticed something across the room then. Adam wasn't nervous; he was awestruck. A globe sat on the teacher's desk. That was his first time seeing a globe, seeing the world scaled down thus. She smiled and followed the tug of Jim's hand.

Outside the school, fatigue caught her. Her toes and fingers curled in. Even her vertebrae each individually seemed to ache.

"I hope you behave, Sally. If not, I'm coming straight back here for Adam."

"I won't be any trouble."

"Don't you forget, Sally," Jim said, "You need me."

She had needed him. Barely sixteen and near a year into drifting, he was an alternative to sleeping out in the cold. Like other men she had met since leaving home, he was awkward and possessive. After a few days at his place, she collected her one and only paycheck from the diner and set off to find a new place in the world. Enduring hunger and thirst, extreme cold and heat, it was normal sometimes to get queasy, to have abnormal bodily cycles. As she left Jim's that day, something was different. Lightheaded and hungry, she collapsed aside a country road fifteen miles from Wispville.

She woke in a hospital. Doctors asked what she'd been doing, about where she lived and worked. She explained enough of it, supposed they guessed at the rest. She was already planning a getaway from the hospital. Then the doctors told her something surprising. They said if she kept up with her current lifestyle, she would lose her baby. Sally wasn't into any sort of substance abuse. Her addiction was movement, drifting. Except, then she did need help. So she called the one person in the area she knew: Jim.

For more than five years, she tried to repay him for living in his place. For more than five years, she was bound by servitude. The arrangement was quite unbalanced, but as Sally left Adam in the kindergarten classroom, she had seen her son look happy. Maybe, just maybe, she could endure such an arrangement a bit longer. They got in the truck, and before Jim started driving, she spoke.

"We both know what Adam does when he sleeps."

Jim turned toward her. One corner of his lip twitched.

"If you can leave him alone," she said, "Let him just go to school, I promise I won't leave."

"I have bigger plans," Jim said.

He drove to the ketchup factory. Sally thought she'd have to wait through his entire shift. Bigger plans indeed, he went in only to come back a minute later, practically skipping through the parking lot.

"I quit," Jim said.

They next drove out of Wispville, until the road grew wide and tall buildings offered consistent shade. Jim went to the local newspaper and came back saying he dumped half his savings into buying ads for the next weeks. At the next stop, Jim hired an attorney. Someone to help with the adoption, someone to keep meddlers from interfering, he told her.

For Sally, trying to save energy was like collecting water in a cracked bucket; she sat docile during all this. They next stopped at a hardware store. Jim came out pushing a cart loaded with cement, ropes, a huge wooden sign, and new locks for the doors that'd need a key even from the inside.

"What do you think?" he said. "Everything I need to start my business." Sally finally understood. All those times Jim played the lottery, he was looking for his escape too. She asked what he had planned, and he tried his best to close his lips. Then he hummed, Jim actually hummed as he loaded the truck. "I'll charge five bucks a head," he said. "Once word gets out, people will flock to our house. I even got the sign painted so it can dry on the way home." He held it up, and in bright red letters, it read: ADAM FREEWHEEL: THE BOY WHO FLIES WHEN HE SLEEPS.

"You can't do that," Sally said.

"You'll keep him awake at night. By morning, crowds will gather to watch Adam strung up out back." Jim explained his plan. Adam would float tethered to the ground. At night, he'd have them locked in, and she could teach him, eat with him, play games, or whatever she did now, but he insisted Adam wasn't leaving the property. "Once I get more money, I'll invest in better advertising, and I'll put a giant fence around my yard to keep away freeloaders."

"He won't be able to see beyond the yard," she said.

Jim didn't answer. She looked out the window. She saw blue sky and brown fields. The beauty in the flatness of this area was the spot where land met sky, where colors mixed and blurred at the horizon.

"I suppose I better get some sleep," Sally said, "If I'm to start tonight."

"That's the spirit," he said.

With her eyes closed, Jim paid her no more mind. He left her in the truck when they reached his house. He carried everything to the backyard, dug a hole, and screwed an iron hook in the ground. He mixed cement that'd soon solidify. Sally still didn't have a plan, but even just crossing town and fleeing with Adam seemed better than doing nothing.

Just as she opened the truck door to sneak away, the phone rang inside the house. Jim rarely got calls; she got fewer. He continued working, not even turning her direction, but the phone continued to ring and ring.

"That damn thing," Jim yelled. He stomped the ground, and when he turned to face the house, he saw Sally standing outside the truck.

"Want me to answer that?" she

asked.

"Sure Sally, and after you do," he grabbed the broomstick he was using for mixing cement, "You come right back here and sit." He tapped the ground. "Just sit."

She had needed Jim years ago. That was true. Over those first years of drifting, no one from her family, aunts, uncles, or cousins ever came looking for her. She did call her father once, left a message with a number, but he didn't bother to get back to her. She drifted so far from home that there was no going back.

The phone continued to ring. It seemed odd, seemed almost desperate as Sally walked into the creaking house. Before she picked up the receiver, she held her breath and feared this call might have something to do with Adam.

The principal of the school sounded out of breath on the other line. He'd been trying to reach her for many minutes, he said.

"Your son," he said, "He's, uh, on the ceiling of his classroom."

"Have you," she swallowed, "Have you tried to wake him?"

"Miss Freewheel, he is awake."

Sally dropped the phone.

She ran outside. When Jim saw her, he pointed at the ground again with the stick. She walked straight to his pile of supplies. Jim had enough rope to tie down an elephant. Sally threw a bundle over her shoulder.

"Where the hell do you think you're going?" Jim said.

"I'm going to get Adam. He's in trouble." The rope bundle tipped her frame forward like a wet flower as she walked.

"What do you mean, trouble?" Jim held his arms out to block her path.

"He's on the ceiling of his classroom," Sally said.

"People are seeing him for free?"

"He's probably so afraid."

"How could he be afraid?"

"Because he's up there, and he's awake." She stepped around him.

"Well, damn!" Jim said. "I'm going to have to change my sign."

She walked to the truck.

"Stop," Jim yelled.

The twenty-some steps she took felt good, felt free. Then from behind, she heard huffing breath and a trample of grass. What Sally didn't hear was Jim's fist. It hit like a brick; she fell like one. The yard spun, and if she was able to pass out, she would have, but passing out was too similar to sleeping.

As Jim yanked the ropes from her, got in his truck and drove off, she lie face down in the lawn and didn't move an inch.

Sally remembered after she found out she was pregnant, she called Jim for help, but not right away. Aside from a bag of clothes and a few dollars, she owned nothing. The hospital doctors had an option for someone like Sally, someone who wouldn't even be able to care for herself during pregnancy, let alone a child. The option seemed logical. She asked for some time to think about it and sat in the hospital waiting room. Her hands on her stomach, she wondered as well, what could she ever hope to give her child?

Only when she heard the squealing brakes return from the school did Sally attempt to stand. The ground rocked back and forth. She saw the red truck, saw the hunched shadow of Jim getting out, but no sign of Adam. Then Jim tugged on the rope, and Adam bounced from the roof of the cab, and the rope pulled taut as he shot up in the air.

"Are you okay?" Sally called.

"I'm fine, Mom." He flapped his arms.

Jim had the ropes around Adam's chest in an X.

"How did this happen?" she asked.

Adam explained he'd been looking at the whole world, the globe, and he couldn't stop thinking about how big it all was. He felt funny like he had a bubble in his stomach.

"I started to tell the other kids about yesterday, about our walk and the things we saw. And I started to lift from the floor, and I couldn't stop."

Sally took a step and stumbled.

"Mom, are you okay?"

Pain washed down her body with each step. When she finally neared Adam, she raised an arm. He flipped upside down, reached toward her. Jim let ten feet of rope slither through his hands, and Adam sailed out of her reach. Breeze ruffled his hair, and he laughed at the sudden jolt. Sally couldn't help in watching, stand on her tiptoes.

"I can see the roof of the house," Adam said. "There's my baseball."

Jim tugged on the rope and

pulled Adam along. Laughter sifted over the yard. Then Adam saw the iron anchor in the wet, but hardening cement.

"What's that for?" he asked. He shook the line and flopped at the end.

"We can make a bundle tonight," Jim said. "Little incident at school stirred free publicity."

Adam pulled on the ropes around his chest. Jim had tied the knots at his back.

"So Sally, what's it going to be?" Jim said. "Are you going to be a problem?" His blue eyes glimmered like the edge of a knife.

"Tell me what to do," Sally said without looking up. "Tell me how to help."

"There's the woman I know," Jim grabbed her arm. "But don't try anything funny."

"What could I possibly do now?"

The sky was a mixture of blue smears that seemed almost painted on. Clouds were the fluffy kind with sharp edges, and bountiful enough to seem like islands. There was no gray to be seen, and certainly no rain.

Still, Sally felt a drop fall on her arm, then her neck. These fell from Adam.

"What happened to you, Mom?" Adam said. "Are you lost again?"

She didn't answer. Jim told her to clean the yard, and she threw tools in the wheelbarrow and pushed it to the shed. He ran with the sign down the driveway and came back hooting.

"They're coming," he said. "They're coming!"

Dust rose on the road behind the first car. Humming engines echoed from the edge of town. Sally stood at the door of the shed and watched Adam rub his eyes, slap his face, and pinch his arm as he tried it seemed to wake up.

All those years ago, maybe some doctors had thought Sally unfit to become a mother. When she went to the hospital waiting room to make a decision about the pregnancy, she intended to spend only a few minutes thinking. As she laid her hands on her stomach, time faded. Lost in thought, she sat for whole days, for nights. She didn't talk, eat, and especially, didn't sleep. True, she had no possessions, no money, and not much to offer a baby in ways of wealth, but as hours passed and one sleepless night followed another, she began to believe there was something she could offer her baby. Maybe she could give the baby dreams: its own and hers as well.

As the first car pulled in the driveway, Jim clapped his hands waiting in front of the rope to greet his customers.

"Bring me a bucket," he yelled to Sally, "To put my money in."

"Please Jim," Adam yelled. "Can I go in the house? I don't want to be stared at."

"Quiet."

Sally searched the shed. Jim knew she couldn't make a run for it with Adam like this, and he no longer scrutinized her as she searched the shed then crossed the yard. He held his hand out, expecting the bucket. When she neared within a few feet of him, Sally stopped under Adam's rope. Jim was right. There was no obvious method of escape.

The rusted creak of metal silenced the air. Both Jim and Adam looked to see Sally, not with a bucket, but with arms flexed as she squeezed handles of sword-length hedge clippers.

"What do you think you're doing?" Jim said, taking a step toward her; rusted blades slid around the rope.

"Stay back!" she said.

"Mom?" Adam's voice cracked.

"You let him go," Jim said, "And he'll float so high you'll never see him again."

"Adam," Sally yelled. "Do you remember your dream from last night?" She didn't take her eyes off Jim, but she could see Adam's shadow over the lawn nodding yes.

"I think you had that dream for a reason," she said. "Imagine a leaf floating down on the wind, Adam, or a ship sailing up into the sky. Imagine it, and I think you can control this."

The rope began to twang. It moved despite the fact that Adam wasn't swinging his arms or kicking his legs. Another car pulled in the driveway. Doors opened, and people pointed.

"Adam," Sally said. "Do you remember yesterday, seeing a place that seemed like a dream to both of us?" They agreed that it was the kind of place they wanted to live someday: the little cobblestone farmhouse with a spinning windmill the pond that glimmered like a mirror.

"I remember it."

"All right, Sally," Jim said. "If you put those clippers away, I'll get rid of these customers. I'll take Adam down and put him inside." He took a step closer.

She tightened the sheers. One thread snapped from the spine of the rope.

Jim stopped.

"Adam," Sally said, "Do you think you can be really brave? Braver than you've ever been in your whole life?"

"I can be brave."

"I need you to go to that place from yesterday. I need you to go all by yourself and wait for me."

"I can do it," Adam yelled. His voice cracked. The rope shivered. Jim tightened his fists.

"And one more thing, Adam. You're going to have to hide as you go. You're going to have to hide from Jim."

"But where?" Adam asked.

"Hide in the clouds."

She snipped the blades with all her might. The rope didn't just cut; it shattered like a guitar string. Jim charged. Sally dropped the clippers and dove in front of the dangling rope. Jim tossed her aside. Once again, she crashed hard. This time as she fell, she looked up. Adam thrashed like a fish. He whimpered, and she feared she made a mistake. But then Adam looked her in the eye and hovered in place. Jim leapt for the rope, and it ticked back and forth after his fingers slapped it.

"Go," Sally said. "Go."

Adam began to glide across the air with the silence of a paper airplane. Jim jumped for the rope and cursed. It swayed just outside his grasp and rose higher as Adam reached the street and floated towards Wispville. Past town, he could follow the highway until he reached that little farm.

When Jim realized he couldn't catch Adam on foot, he turned back to the yard.

"Damn you, Sally!"

She no longer lay on the ground. Nowhere to be seen, her getaway wasn't near as grand as Adam's. With Jim chasing her son, spectators yelling and pointing, she'd simply hidden against the wall of the house.

"Where are you?" Jim yelled.

She snuck a peek around the corner.

Jim's lower lip trembled. He growled and dug his heel down. More cars pulled up, and even with other people around, she knew what Jim would do if he got a hold of her. He'd hurt her, but worse, he'd force her to lead him to Adam. She didn't move, didn't breathe. Her heart even seemed to stop. Jim searched only a moment longer before he jumped in his truck and sprayed dirt as he sped through the yard after Adam. Over the sound of his screeching brakes, Sally sat and gasped.

In the hours to come, she'd follow back roads, cut through fields and woods. If she moved without a moment of rest, she'd reach the farm before nightfall. From there, they'd keep moving in secrecy, and someday, she knew they would find their place in the world.

For the moment, however, she took one last look at her son. He rose above the small houses of the town. Like a lost balloon, he soared into the sky. Even from the edge of the puffy white clouds, she swore she heard the echo of laugher. Leaning against the house and before starting the long journey ahead, for just one second, Sally closed her eyes. She closed them tight, and against the dark of her eyelids, Sally was able to picture all the wonderful things that Adam was about to see. 👁

Leah Kuntz is a senior creative writing student at Miami University, graduating in May 2019. During her time at Miami, she has received the Montaine Writing Award and the Greer-Hepburn Prize in Fiction for her work. She finds time to write both inside and outside the classroom, but ultimately would like to finish her novel. Her short fiction can also be found/is upcoming in Happy Captive Magazine and Garfield Lake Review. Leah is interested in classical ballet, fiction with strong female leads, and finding the world's best French toast.

The Dream Keeper

Leah Kuntz

Diana's body was an empty shell, and if she didn't get back soon, she knew the monster would beat her to it. He would invade the husk she called home.

"You shouldn't be here," Jae said. He slunk further into the chair. "This is my hell, not yours."

"Please, we have to hurry, he's coming," Diana insisted. She tugged on Jae's arm as hard as she could, but he simply would not budge from his seat. "He's going to get us."

"You can't keep saving me forever," he hissed. His eyes had lost their gleam. "What kind of life is that? Just leave me be."

"We need to go home," Diana said. "We need to wake up."

Jae leveled his gaze at her. "I need to do this myself."

Diana could feel the darkness like cold breath on her neck, sliding an icy wet finger along the miniscule hairs on her back. The ground trembled with his approach. "Don't do this, please don't do this."

"What could he possibly do to me if I don't make it out? I'll be fine, Di."

"You'll never escape, Diana cried. She knew, but she didn't know how. Why would you want to live in a nightmare?"

"I was going to ask you the same thing."

She looked at Jae in horror as the shadows coalesced into a hooded figure. Diana didn't see the monster's face, but she did see teeth as his jaw unhinged, ready to swallow them both whole.

Diana woke up screaming.

***

Dreaming. Most dreams occur in the REM, or rapid-eye movement, stage of sleep where your brain is whirring and spitting, alight with activity, and in that sense it's very resemblant to the state it's in while you're awake. For many, dreams can be incredibly real, where the unfeasible things happening around them are as tangible as their own bodies; however, some dreamers slip into the tiny cracks between this world and another, reaching out to touch the impossibility of another realm. Unknowingly, they go tumbling down the rabbit hole into a space beyond their comprehension.

There are also those who will themselves there, into this in-between space. Through meditation and a great force of will, they send out their souls into the body of the other.

This is what she told people when she found them, those lost in the pitch of their own minds, floating out into the universe without knowing they are drifting beyond reach of their bodies. She told them they needed to come back before they were trapped out there in the ether forever.

It is where she found all of them, and where she eventually found him.

***

With a swift and quiet exhale, Diana entered The Dark Place. The separation of body and mind was like the stretch of a rubber band; she was tethered, and extending outwards. She was hopping through what felt like walls of water, ones trying to slow her progression, and then she was there.

The last time it had been a locked room filled with sweets. The walls had been made of cake, the floor of Snickers bricks, and all the doorknobs were wafer cookies that snapped under her hands. Hansel and Gretel warped. The boy sat in the middle of all the junk, sobbing like a starving baby. Chocolate was melted around his mouth and had dried under his fingernails. It was smothered on his jacket, the soles of his shoes. There were traces of melted marshmallow in his hair.

Diana had taken him carefully by the hand and said, "It's all a dream."

He'd cried harder as ice cream had begun to melt down from the ceiling, raining vanilla drips and rainbow sprinkles onto them both. She dodged a popcorn ball comet hurtling down.

"It's real in here," she said, tapping his forehead. "You just have to pull yourself out of here. And fast."

Diana hadn't wanted to scare him, but she could see the dreams multiplying more and more rapidly upon one another, increasing in terror, and that could only mean one thing: the Dream Keeper was coming.

"Take a deep breath and get out," Diana said. "Eat your way out if you have to. But you need to wake up."

The boy had pushed up onto his knees, avoiding the vat of cream cheese icing forming near his head, and wiped away his sugary tears. He crawled, and with pudgy fists began to punch at the chocolate prison. They'd both burst through a hole in the door just as a single, dark figure entered from the opposite side.

The one before that, there'd been a swimming pool, one of the Olympic sized ones. Out in the middle of the water was a woman. Her arms flailed futilely in an attempt to tread, but it was not working; she was going to drown.

"Hey it's going to be alright," Diana called out. She stood at the edge with outstretched arms. "Swim to me."

The woman spun to face her, lips blue and trembling. Her hair fanned out around her in seaweed strands. "I... I can't."

"This is a dream," Diana said. "Your subconscious put you here, and now you need to get yourself out."

"I'm so tired," she coughed. "I don't think I can."

The woman's legs kicked and kicked, but her head was beginning to sink lower. Waves from an impossible tidal pull began to slap at the woman's sides. She coughed and gagged on the encroaching surf. At the very bottom of the pool, a black stain began to spread. Not mold, much worse. She knew who was coming.

"Imagine you have a kickboard," Diana said. She kept her voice as even as possible. No panic, not yet. "Use it to swim to me."

The girl huffed in frustration, and began to inch her way to Diana. One doggy-paddle at a time, splish sploosh, the woman grew closer. The stain grew larger, the waves taller.

Diana had wrenched her up and out of the water just as the inky darkness had begun to pollute the water, turning it as black as tar.

She tried not to think of the people she didn't save, but that was all she ever thought about.

This time, there was no candy, no chlorine. There was only corn, unending rows upon rows, too tall to see over. Normally, the Dark Place was buzzing with activity, humming with an inhuman life Diana could not put into words; this felt cold, empty.

She took two steps forwards, looked over her shoulder, and took two steps back again. Up above, the sky was devoid of stars; only the fat bubble of the moon hung overhead, and even that seemed off. After squinting at it, Diana realized it didn't have any dark spots. It was just a great white circle, a cheap imitation.

"Hello?" she called out. Her voice was squashed by the night, devoured whole by the silence. The only sound was the occasional rustle of the corn in the nonexistent wind. "Is anyone there?"

But then the stalks beside her split wide. She jumped, and the intruder jumped too.

"Come on," he said. "Hurry."

Without hesitation, he took hold of Diana's arm and began sprinting. He nearly tore her arm from the socket in the process, but as he yanked her along, she watched the row collapse behind them. She struggled to keep up, and kicked it into a third gear when she saw the chaos being wrought behind her. The stalks bent in as if being crushed by giants' feet, slapping the ground with sickening thuds. Plant by plant they were smashed to bits right before her eyes.

She ran faster.

They whipped around the corner. A right. Where had her shoes gone? A left. Her bicep burned under his iron grip. Another right. He didn't once look back.

And then there was a dead end.

It stopped him only for a second, but even that was crucial time. She felt the whoosh of air at her back as the corn caved, and then he was dragging her directly into a wall of stalks.

The terrain morphed, the corn melting from vision. They bled yellow and orange and green and brown and dripped, dripped, dripped. The Van Gogh swirls toppled end upon end into one another.

Then stillness.

Diana put her hands on her knees, tried to breathe in through her nose and out through her mouth. She rose to meet him eye for eye as their surroundings came into hazy focus.

"Who are you?" Diana asked.

"Better yet, who the hell are you?"

They stood, facing off. Diana clenched her fists at her sides, ready to swing; the man stood with feet shoulder-width apart, and looked prepared to punt Diana across a football field. For several minutes, neither of them moved. She knew precious time was being wasted, but she couldn't pull her gaze away from him. Behind any one of the rows, the Dream Keeper could be waiting with his bloody grin, ready to seal them away in darkness forever, and yet Diana couldn't find it in her to move him along.

"How do I know you're real?" he asked.

Diana sighed. "You don't."

"How do you know if I'm real?"

"I suppose we'll have to trust each other."

He gave her a hard stare. His tongue darted out to wet his lips. "And why would I do that?"

She hesitated. That was an excellent question, but he had just saved her from being crushed into cornmeal. "Because maybe we can help each other."

For several long seconds, he didn't move. "My name is Akim."

"Diana," she said. "Pleasure to meet you."

He pushed his hair out of his eyes. It was black streaked with rich red. Like cherry wood, like bricks, like congealing blood. Diana wondered if it was like that in reality, or just another smear of color in his Dark Place.

Diana felt compelled to say something she'd never said before. She wanted proof.

"Where do you live?"

"What?"

"I asked where you live. In the real world."

He inclined his head. For a moment, his eyes looked yellow, the pupils long.

"What does it matter?"

"Well, I'm curious."

He sighed. A minute passed. "Cairo," he said.

"Egypt?" Diana asked. "I've never met someone from Egypt

before."

"Well you are not meeting me, per se."

"Of course I am," she said. "We're talking, looking at each other. You know, meeting."

Akim laughed. He shrugged and said, "You know what I mean. This is not really me."

Diana inhaled. She'd almost forgotten. "We need to get out of here. He won't rest for long, and we've probably made him real mad."

"He?" Akim asked.

"The Dream Keeper. He doesn't like people trespassing in someone else's Dark Place."

Akim's dark eyebrows shot upwards and disappeared into his mop of hair. "And we are trespassing?"

"You're not, but I am," she said. "I'm in your Dark Place with you, projecting myself into your nightmares. Trespassing."

His eyes narrowed. "You have done this before?"

Diana nodded. "It's harder for him to catch two people."

"Catch?"

"He'll trap you here, and you won't ever wake up. He feeds on the fear," she said. Her words felt heavy in her mouth.

Akim scoffed, crossing his arms across his chest. "And how do you know this?"

The lump in her throat thickened. She swallowed hard but it wouldn't go down. "I just do."

"How do I know you're not making this up?"

"Never mind that. The only way to save yourself is to wake up," Diana insisted. "Come back to your body. Can you do that Akim?"

For a brief second, his head inclined, like a dog listening carefully to something behind him. If his ears had been long enough to swivel, they would have.

"That's it?" Akim asked.

"Yes, that's it."

And then he was gone. Vanished into thin air like he'd never been there at all. Aghast, Diana stood alone in the hazy in-between world.

She woke up.

* * *

The cash register clanked open. Diana counted out twelve dollars, fifty-two cents with her sticky hands. The layers of ketchup had to be entering her bloodstream, it was laid on so thick. If she had to make another triple stack burger, she'd scream.

"Have a nice day."

The customer would; Diana most certainly would not.

Minutes tick-tocked by far too slowly. Diana's pot-bellied boss, Gordon, came out from the back, crunching on a Kit-Kat. He took one look around and smirked.

"Hey, Slug," he said. Another munch of the Kit-Kat. "Go clean the bathrooms."

Diana sighed. She tapped at her nametag; it had been cutely decorated with curling script and a heart sticker. Gordon took another huge bite. His mouth opened wide in between chews, displaying a brown goopy mash that clung to his tongue and teeth.

The men's bathroom was surprisingly clean. Someone had only clogged one of the urinals with pubic hair, so good day on that front. The women's bathroom, however, was particularly rank, where someone had conveniently taken a shit on the floor and then wiped all over the walls. Just your average day at YumYum Burger.

Every scrub of the rag, every flop of the mop, was just one more brick laid on her back. She couldn't wait to be asleep again, asleep so she could finally live.

***

Jae had locked himself in his room for 4 days when Diana first learned to navigate the Dark Place. She knew he was asleep, not eating, not taking his meds. He wouldn't answer the door, or her calls, or her texts. No matter how hard she pounded her fists into the wood and screamed, she was met with silence. He'd told her about the night terror realm he kept visiting in his sleep, his own personal slice of misery. Curled up on the floor outside his room, breath hitching in her chest, she found her way to him.

When she came upon him, he was slumped in a moldy recliner, massaging his temples.

"Jae?"

He'd jolted upright, clutching the armrests fiercely. Green goo squished from between his fingers and splattered the ground at his feet. "You aren't real, you aren't real, you aren't real…"

She inclined her head. "What do you mean?"

He shrank back when she stepped closer. "You can't be here."

"But I am. I found you."

"Why do you always poke your nose where you're not wanted?"

She winced. "You won't talk to me, then? Not even here? In this disgusting place?"

Jae tried to stand, but the green goo had attached itself to his back, his palms, his calves, his neck. It sucked him right back down into the chair. "This is my Dark Place, Di. My nightmare-scape. I don't want you to be stuck here too."

"Then let's leave."

She couldn't explain what she was feeling, not that first time. It was the age old sense of being hunted, the sense of being watched in the dark, the sense of the murderer hiding behind the shower curtain, the sense of the creature with claws under your bed. It was prickling along the surface of her skin as she crouched down to look Jae in his watery eyes.

His voice broke. "Don't you think if I could leave, I would? I don't know how."

"Isn't it easy?" Diana asked. "You just wake up."

Jae's face contorted in pain for the briefest of seconds, but when she blinked again, it was to the sound of his door unlocking.

In the midst of their run-down apartment, Jae clutched onto her through his sobs, begging her over and over not to leave him alone.

* * *

Plunging into The Dark Place was a welcome relief. The feeling of falling without any place to land was a respite from the endless drudgery of making fries, making a ton of burgers that weren't really meat, and making the restrooms look less like the 10th circle of Hell. When she did find herself blinking into the space, like a camera lens coming into focus, it was good to be anywhere but in her own life.

It was a house this time, one with far too many doors crowded into a singular hallway. They lined the walls on both sides around her, even above and below her on the ceilings and floors. A place where Alice Liddell might belong.

The nearest one was a pastel blue, silver knob. A long crack ran up its middle, almost like someone had kicked it long ago, hard enough to splinter it. She tested the handle. Locked.

The next one was black wood, black knob. She gave its handle a tentative jiggle. Locked.

Diana put her hands on her hips, blew air out through her nose. Just as she was about to reach for the next knob, the door behind her burst open.

"Akim!" Diana cried. "What are you doing here?"

"You're here," Akim said. "Again."

She stammered to find the right words to say, but she couldn't make her tongue move; it was leaden in her mouth.

"You are trespassing in the, how did you say? Dream Keeper's realm?" Akim said. "Again."

Diana shook her head. "Listen, the longer you stay here, the easier it will be for him to find you."

"Then I suppose you better get out of here," Akim sighed.

"No, no I came here to save you."

Akim's eyes rolled. Hard. "My mother always told me I could master the night and everyone who inhabits it, if I tried. I do not need a little white girl to save me."

Diana gaped. Again, she was speechless. She remembered another stubborn boy who didn't want her to save him. "You don't want my help?"

"I, as you said, woke myself up last time, did I not? I can do this myself."

She felt the fear like a spike plunged through her chest. Not again. "Well, you should still be careful. The Dream Keeper is dangerous…"

Akim began to walk away from Diana down the long hallway. She had to jog to keep up with his long legs.

"What do you think my fear is, Diana?"

She took another glance around. "I'd say you're looking for something."

Akim halted very quickly. He did not look at her, did not even so much as tilt his jaw in her direction. "Why do you say that?"

"The corn maze. The house with too many doors. You don't know which way to go."

He laughed sharply. "And what is it you are afraid of, Diana? How does your fear manifest?"

Diana shrugged. She felt like an asshole saying it aloud. "I've never been to my Dark Place."

Akim took up walking again. He tested several doorknobs, yanking at one after the other to no avail. "Are you not afraid of anything?"

"Oh I'm afraid of plenty," she said. "I just can't be there if I'm somewhere else. Like here."

"What are you running from?"

She took a quick look around. No mysterious dark splotches or hooded figures had materialized yet. "Mostly the Dream Keeper."

"Why are you so afraid of him?" Akim asked.

Diana didn't blink. "Because he's evil."

Akim tried the next door, muscles straining as he pulled. "How do you know?"

Diana thought of Jae, peacefully asleep in bed for the rest of his life. "My best friend got trapped here. I watched the Dream Keeper eat him up."

Akim stared at her, rooted to the spot. "What was his name?"

"Is. His name is Jae."

"I am sorry."

Diana wiped away the encroaching tears. "It doesn't matter now."

"What does he look like? The Dream Keeper."

"You ever seen Halloween? Michael Myers in that mask?" Diana said. She shivered involuntarily. "I hate that stuff."

"Oh come on, you are afraid of a little mask?"

"It's not the mask that scares me. You can't see what's underneath."

"Well he would not be as frightening if you knew what he looked like."

Diana opened her mouth, then snapped it shut. "I suppose you're right."

Akim flashed her a crescent moon grin right before the floor fell away beneath them.

As they went tumbling through the emptiness of space, Diana's hands flailed out for him involuntarily. She caught ahold of his ankle; he caught ahold of her wrist. They followed each other, looping end over end, down and down and down.

"Wake up," Diana screamed. "Wake up before you hit the bottom."

Another turn and he vanished with the flash of a smile. His skin disappeared beneath her grip and suddenly she was clutching her own fist, hurtling away into nothingness alone.

"Wake up, wake up, wake up, wake up, wake up…"

Diana sat up in bed, arms still outstretched to hold onto him.

Trembling and covered in

sweat, Diana rolled off the mattress and onto the floor. She crept as quietly as she could into Jae's room, not that it mattered, and sat, watching the rhythmic rise and fall of his chest.

* * *

Diana forced the spoon into his mouth and applesauce dribbled down his chin as he spluttered. Applesauce had never been his favorite, but the cheap store-brand was all Diana could afford to give him now.

"C'mon Jae, just a few more bites."

She had to hold his mouth shut and plug his nose to get him to swallow, but she had the process down to an art. She had been force-feeding his comatose body for 4 months now.

They'd once joked about how they would be taking care of each other's diapers when they were 90 years old; Diana never expected him to take her up on that offer so many decades early. She had to wash the bedpan in the kitchen sink; the bathroom sink wasn't deep enough to fully rinse out the urine. With the rubber gloves pulled up as far as they could go, she scrubbed at the grime until it was acceptably clean.

"Think you'll be alright while I go to work?" Diana asked. She pulled the sheets up around his neck, tucked it in at his sides, and made sure his feet were covered. He gave a soft snore.

"Thought so," Diana said. She flicked off the lights. "See you later, Jae. Don't do anything crazy while I'm gone."

* * *

When the ice cream machine broke and the new hire dumped piping hot coffee on her shoes and the woman with that haircut asked to speak to the manager, Diana held it together. Soon she'd be able to go to sleep and to what waited in the Dark Place, or perhaps more aptly, who waited in the Dark Place.

"Hey, Slug!" Gordon barked. "Take out the trash will you? Someone threw up in one of the cans."

Diana sighed, adjusted her nametag. "Yeah I'm on it."

The can smelled something awful and there were little mottled chunks of puke drying on the black plastic. Every thirty seconds, Diana told herself she needed the money. Money to eat, money to pay the rent, money to live, money to make sure Jae kept living. If her father had been around, he would have told her this was what she got for not finishing high school. Diana was just convinced that all reality, every version, was shit.

The bag ripped, spilling warm vomit all over her shoes.

"Unbe-fucking-lievable."

* * *

The third time she entered The Dark Place to find Akim, he was waiting for her. The colorful plastic tubes of a Chuck E. Cheese playset shouldn't have been big enough to fit the both of them, and yet she still found herself crawling on hands and knees, skin catchy on the sticky surface. The ping of arcade game machinery trickled in, muffled.

"Knew I'd find you here," Diana said. She crawled closer to him.

"I have been waiting for you. You know, since you were going to trespass anyways."

She went to sock his arm playfully, but ended up smashing her forehead against the top of the tube. He laughed at her, and it echoed along the network of tunnels. Smiling, she rubbed at the new-forming knot and crawled after him.

"I'm glad I could find you so easily," Diana said. "I really

needed the company."

Akim looked back over his shoulder. His face was cast in an orangey-red hue from the thick plastic of the tube. "Lonely?"

Diana nodded, careful not to whack her head again. "Yeah. Life kind of sucks."

"You would rather be here?" He took a sharp turn into a blue tunnel.

She did not hesitate. "Yes."

"What about the bad things here? The Dream Keeper and all."

"I'm scared sure, but not miserable. I feel good here, in your Dark Place. With you."

He froze. Diana had to come screeching to a halt to avoid getting a face full of his ass. "Yeah? You like it here?"

She tried to peer around his broad shoulders, but the tunnel seemed to have shrunk, and his body was taking up nearly the whole space. "I mean it'd be better if I knew we were safe."

"The ancient Egyptians had a very different concept of the soul, you know," Akim said.

"What? What are you talking about?" Diana asked.

"The soul was divided into parts. Some that stayed with the

body, some that could travel, he said. I was thinking about what part of the soul the Dream Keeper... keeps."

Diana exhaled a shaky breath. "He swallows the best part of you. Then there's only fear."

"What if he didn't?"

Diana hissed. "He does."

"Eh what does it matter? You are clearly pretty good at escaping," Akim said.

"But what if one day it's not enough? What if he gets me?"

His voice grew quiet. "What would you do? If you were caught."

"I don't know," Diana sighed. "I can't even imagine. What about you?"

"Oh I am not worried. I am not worried at all."

"Why not?"

Akim continued forward without answering. His palms slapped against the plastic as he began moving with fervor, leaving Diana hastening to follow. She caught hold of his pant leg for just a second, but it slid through her fingers like smoke.

"Akim! Akim wait!"

She followed the sound of him, the thwacking of skin meeting plastic, but eventually lost sight of him. He must have taken a different turn. The sound of him grew fainter and fainter, fading away off in a different channel of tubing.

She rocked back onto her knees and tried very hard to listen. "Akim?"

The tunnel opening on the right was viciously yellow. The tunnel on the left was a yawning green pit. The tunnel behind her seemed to be growing darker. The tunnel ahead of her looked as if it wasn't all quite there. Each of them was a mouth that looked ready to snap their jaws shut.

His voice was back, as close as if he were whispering directly into her ear. "I found something, Diana."

The dream morphed. She went sprawling down as the tubing evaporated in curls of color, leaving only the hard ground.

Diana rose on shaky legs. In front of her, Akim stood very tall, very straight. Over his shoulder, there was a dark figure. She choked on her breath.

Akim smirked. "Or better, I found someone."

He stepped aside.

"Jae?" Diana whispered. He

was there, eyes bright and open. He was awake. "Is that you?"

She pushed past Akim and broke into a run. It felt like her hands flew right through him because they were too intent to reach Jae. Diana knew exactly what the hug was going to feel like as her arms wrapped around him, warm and welcoming.

Except he was freezing cold. The solidness of him felt like a block of ice, but she couldn't stop squeezing him. "I'm sorry I left you, I was so afraid, I'm so sorry Jae, I'll never leave you, I promise."

He hugged back hard. Diana didn't think she would ever let go.

From over Jae's shoulders, she locked eyes with Akim. For a moment, she'd doubted him. "How is this possible?"

"Maybe there's more to this place than you know," Akim shrugged.

Diana released Jae just enough to look at his face.

Until she was falling through him too, and right back down. She felt the tile with her hands, smelled the place before she saw it.

YumYum Burger stitched together around her. There were the torn up leather booths and ramshackle chairs she wandered through every day. There was the cash register and the greasy credit card reader she wiped off with her shirtsleeves. There were the smashed French fries ingrained into the cracks in the floor and the spilled soda stains she cleaned. Last but not least, there was Gordon.

"Hey there, Slug," he said. "You're a bit late to your own party."

He pointed towards the back. All the way at the rear of the kitchen, through the finger-smudged glass of the freezer, she could see Jae's face, frosty and blue. His head was all that was left of him. The eyes were open, staring out at her in a frozen plea for help.

Diana turned to face Akim.

"Tell me. What does your Dark Place look like?" ◉

About the Editor

POLLY ALICE MCCANN founder and Managing at Editor Flying Ketchup Press "curates" galleries of talent inside small sharable packages. She says her favorite thing is to tell stories– other people's, her own– maybe yours. Polly graduated with an MFA from Hamline University. She credits much of her creative work in art and poetry to her research in the subconscious creative process which won her the 2014 Ernest Hartmann award from the International Association for the Study of Dreams from Berkeley, CA on self-awareness for writers through dreamwork. Her meditative symbolist art has been published in US newspapers and magazines and is showing internationally. Visit her at pollymccann.com.

Design

The Art Director on this book was Kēvin Callahan. Kēvin is the author of *A Tangled Tale of a Walk in the Woods* - in this story collection. His book *ROAD MAP- Poems, Paintings & Stuff* is available through Flying Ketchup Press in print and Ebook. Callahan earned a BFA from Drake University with fine art graduate studies at SFAI and SAIC–OxBow. He currently works and resides with his wife in Parkville, MO. For more info contact the designer at kevin@bsfgadv.com

About the Typeface

The typeface Kēvin choose for this book is the family Cheltenham. Cheltenham was designed in 1896 by architect Bertram Goodhue. Over the years Cheltenham's primary purpose as a text face morphed into one of the most popular "display" faces. As a publication designer, "Chelt" was Kēvin's go-to choice in magazine design for beauty, readability, and consistency.

if you liked these...Find More Short Story Collections BY FLYING KETCHUP PRESS

- *Tales from the Deep*– Our 2020 Short Story Winners illustrated by Alex Eickhoff, coming soon... 2020

- Write Over It: Short Stories for Teens by Teens, coming soon... 2020

- *The Right Accessory for Murder–Melody Shore Mysteries* by Carole Lynn Jones, coming soon... 2021

- Tales from the Goldilock Zone II, our 2020 Short Story Winners, coming soon...2021

- Time, Space & Robot Dogs, our 2020 Scifi Short Story Winners, coming soon...2021

- *Tales from the Wish Zone:* Stories for Kids by Kids, 2019

- *Tales from the Goldilocks Zone- Our 2018 Short Story Winners, released in 2019.*

Flying Ketchup Press A Kansas City Publisher. Our mission: to develop new and diverse voices in poetry and short story. Our dream is to salvage lost treasure troves of written and illustrated work- to create worlds of wonder and delight; to share stories. Maybe yours.

Thank You...

dreamers, readers, and thank you Flickr artists who loaned copyright free photographs and art for our collages to help illustrate these beautiful dreams.

Mark Turnauckas, Annie lion, Ashley Van Haiften,
Awayukin, Jared, Renee, Dave White, Emil Pakarklis,
Erich Ferdinand, Esin Ustun, Garry Knight,
Anders Sandberg, Holly Lay, Deborah, Jay Ray,
Joey Cannon, John, and Janet Beasley, Liz Jones,
Loid D-Goth, Mark Turnauckas, Malcolm Cerfonteyn,
Nevil Zaveri, Nicu Buculei, Paul K, Paul Townsend,
Roman Harak, Simpleinsomnia, Johan Bryggare, Nfi,
Tracy, STH, Bren Leimenstoll, Yuliya LIbkina.

www.ingramcontent.com/pod-product-compliance
Lightning Source LLC
Chambersburg PA
CBHW071901220626
47052CB00002B/159